What readers are saying about *Divine*

"I just finished reading *Divine* only minutes ago and am truly amazed. I have always loved the story of Mary. Thank you for pouring your heart out on the pages of your book. I see Jesus in you, and I am thankful for your ministry." ~*Kendra*

"I have read every novel you have written and I am continually amazed how you integrate God's complete involvement in our lives. *Divine* kept me up late reading to see what would happen next and to hear more of Mary's story. Wow! What an ending." ~*Jeanna*

"I just finished reading *Divine*. It was wonderful! The Lord touched my heart in ways that I do not understand as I was reading the book, but that is usually what happens when I read one of your books!" ~*Kimberly*

"I got your new book *Divine* and I could not put it down until I had finished it. I know so much of that is happening in our real world today, and your book just helped me to know how people are suffering with drug and abuse problems." ~*Barbara*

"This is one of your best works yet. It never ceases to amaze me just how real your characters are. I feel like I'm part of the story, living every moment with them. *Divine* has truly touched my heart in ways that no one can imagine." ~*Ashlee*

"I just finished reading your new book *Divine* and felt like Jesus was sitting right next to me. I was so overwhelmed and the tears flowed down my face, especially at the end. The scenes in the book were so vivid that I could almost feel what Mary went through." ~*Dorothy*

"One of my thoughts when reading [*Divine*] was how helpful it could be to women in abusive and abusing situations. I pray that I will find some opportunities to share the story—and with it the Good News—that you wrote about." ~*Pam*

"Your book *Divine* and how it describes God's love made the hair on my arms stand up and brought tears to my eyes. God is good, and it is so nice to know a Father like him that forgives and loves me still no matter what." ~*Linda*

KAREN KINGSBURY

Tyndale House Publishers, Inc., Carol Stream, Illinois

ivine

A NOVEL

NEW LIFE CENTER

Visit Tyndale's exciting Web site at www.tyndale.com

TYNDALE and Tyndale's quill logo are registered trademarks of Tyndale House Publishers, Inc.

Divine

Designed by Jennifer Ghionzoli

Edited by Lorie Popp

Scripture quotations are taken from the *Holy Bible*, New International Version®. NIV®. Copyright © 1973, 1978, 1984 by International Bible Society. Used by permission of Zondervan. All rights reserved.

Published in association with the literary agency of Alive Communications, Inc., 7680 Goddard Street, Suite 200, Colorado Springs, CO 80920.

This novel is a work of fiction. Names, characters, places, and incidents either are the product of the author's imagination or are used fictitiously. Any resemblance to actual events, locales, organizations, or persons, living or dead, is entirely coincidental and beyond the intent of either the author or publisher.

Library of Congress Cataloging-in-Publication Data
Kingsbury, Karen.
    Divine / Karen Kinsgbury.
        p. cm.
ISBN-13: 978-1-4143-0765-7 (hc)
ISBN-10: 1-4143-0765-9 (hc)
ISBN-13: 978-1-4143-0935-4 (sc)
ISBN-10: 1-4143-0935-X (sc)
1. Washington (D.C.)—Fiction. I. Title.
PS3561.I4873D58 2006
813'.54—dc22   2005036088

Printed in the United States of America
13   12   11   10   09   08   07
 7   6   5   4   3   2   1

Acknowledgments

I bring you the novel God placed on my heart. It couldn't have come together without much help. Therefore, thanks to my great friends at Tyndale House Publishers, especially Karen Watson, who stepped into a new role as fiction director and led me through what was a particularly intense project. Also a special thanks to my Tyndale friends in sales and marketing. It is an honor to work with you.

A big thank-you to my agent, Rick Christian, president of Alive Communications. I am amazed more as every day passes at your integrity, your talent, and your commitment to getting my Life-Changing Fiction out to all the world. You are a strong man of God, Rick. You care for my career as if you were personally responsible for the souls God touches through these books. Thank you for looking out for my personal time with my husband and kids. I couldn't do this without you.

As always, I couldn't have finished this book without the help of my husband and kids, who are so good about eating tuna sandwiches and quesadillas when I'm on deadline and who bring me plates of baked chicken and vegetables when I need the brainpower to write past midnight. Thanks for understanding the sometimes crazy life I lead and for always being my greatest support.

A great thanks to my only brother, Dave, who helped me research various aspects of Washington, DC, in the early goings of my work on this book. On October 1, 2005, as I was coming into the final stretch of editing this novel, Dave died unexpectedly in his sleep. He was 39, and he will be missed very much. He had just come to a place of much deeper faith in the weeks leading up to his death and had found a favorite song in MercyMe's "I Can Only Imagine." Well . . . you don't have to imagine anymore, Dave. You are missed, but we rejoice to know you are safe in His arms.

Also, thanks to my mother and assistant, Anne Kingsbury, for having a great sensitivity and love for my readers. And to Tricia Kingsbury, who runs a large part of my life. The personal touch you both bring to my ministry is precious to me, priceless to me . . . thank you with all my heart.

And thanks to my friends and family who continue to surround me with love and prayer and support—especially in this time of loss. Of course, the greatest thanks goes to God Almighty, the most wonderful author of all—the Author of Life. The gift is Yours. I pray I might have the incredible opportunity and responsibility to use it for You all the days of my life.

Dedicated to...

The memory of Mary Magdalene, a woman who understood and believed in the divinity of Jesus Christ . . .

The memory of my brother, David, who understood the importance of this project and helped make it possible . . .

Also dedicated to:
Donald, my prince charming
Kelsey, my precious daughter
Tyler, my beautiful song
Sean, my wonder boy
Josh, my tender tough guy
EJ, my chosen one
Austin, my miracle child.

And to God Almighty, the Author of Life, who has—for now—blessed me with these.

Author Note

History and Scripture combined have given us very few facts about the real Mary Magdalene, the woman who so fascinates our generation, our culture. In fact, though it is widely held that Mary Magdalene was a prostitute, there is no concrete evidence supporting this notion. The idea that Mary had more than a deep discipleship relationship with Jesus is absolutely unfounded. Worse is the popular thinking that Jesus may have been married to Mary Magdalene. This, of course, is absolutely false, heresy by the Bible's standards.

So who was Mary Magdalene?

Scripture tells us for certain that Jesus saved Mary from seven demons (Luke 8:2). What those demons were, we aren't told. But once she was free, we know that Mary and a few other women were so devoted to Christ that they helped support His ministry out of their own means (Luke 8:1-3). In other words, they were vital to His ministry and the furthering of His message.

We also know that Mary stayed with Jesus until the end and was one of the women at the foot of the cross, witnessing the horrifying death of their Savior (Matthew 27:56; Mark 15:40-41; John 19:25). In addition we are told that Mary Magdalene was one of the women who went to the tomb that brilliant Sunday morning to anoint Christ's body with oils (Mark 16:1-9).

But maybe most telling of all is the account we are given in John 20:1-18. On that resurrection Sunday, when Mary and a few women found the tomb of Jesus empty, the others returned to their homes.

Not Mary. Mary stayed outside the empty tomb by herself, weeping.

Because I write emotional fiction, this part of Mary's story touches me the most. At one time she belonged completely to the darkness. Jesus saved her, as only God can do, and she became devoted to Him for the rest of His days on earth. Devoted in time and financial resources, devoted with her whole heart. When Jesus was killed on a cross, when His body was—Mary assumed—stolen from the tomb, she felt as if her entire world had come undone.

She was devastated.

Jesus saw that, the way He sees us when we are crushed. He had compassion on her and sent two angels to comfort her. They asked her why she was crying. "Because," she said, "they have taken my Lord away. I don't know where they have put Him."

She must've heard something behind her, because she turned around and there stood Jesus. The sight was such a shock that at first she didn't recognize Him. But when she did, she must have run to Him and taken His hands, or maybe she tried to hug Him.

Even then—in what might've been their greatest act of friendship—Jesus was clear about who He is, what His purpose is. He said to Mary, "Do not hold on to me, for I have not yet returned to the Father. Go instead to my brothers and tell them, 'I am returning to my Father, and your Father, to my God and your God.'"

Basically He told her, "Don't hug me because this isn't about us. Instead, go tell the others that I'm doing what I said I would do." Don't get this wrong. Jesus wasn't angry with Mary. He cared enough for her to send the angels and to appear first to her, above all the powerful men He might've appeared to.

But still, He was clear about His role in her life. He was her Lord, not her lover. Her Father, not merely her friend.

This is where many struggle today—understanding the relationship between Mary and Christ.

Divine is a modern-day parable of Mary Magdalene. I have taken liberties—as a novelist must do—in finding seven demons or horrors that a person like Mary Magdalene might've been rescued from. In *Divine*, Mary Madison suffers all types of abuse, among other horrors. There are sections of this book that—though not graphic—will be difficult to read, sections that will put knots in your stomach for what this modern-day Mary suffers.

You may not relate to a story about abuse or faithlessness or promiscuity. But as long as the enemy of our souls exists, all of us will suffer abuse in some form:

fear, doubt, loneliness, addiction, lifestyle sin. We are all in need of rescue by the only one with the power to do so.

Jesus Christ, the divine one.

I bring you a story about a modern-day Mary Magdalene for one reason:

Mary's story is our story.

I see myself in Mary Magdalene, and I pray you see yourself there too. Floundering and falling prey to the demons and darkness of this world, trapped by our own frailty and futility—until we meet Jesus. Then, as He rescues us, we have the incredible chance of a lifetime: to follow Him for all our days, letting our life and our resources bring Him glory and honor.

The way Mary Magdalene did.

Chapter 1

The speaker leaned toward the microphone. "And now—" his tone took on a timbre of importance— "it is my privilege to introduce to you Mary Madison."

A hush fell over the storied room, and the packed crowd of senators and lawmakers turned their attention to her.

Mary stood and with a practiced grace made her way to the podium. She was thirty, though there were days she felt one hundred. She clutched her notes in her left hand and felt the familiar rush of otherworldly peace. How many times had she done this? The smell of centuries-old tomes and rich wood, the click of her heels on the marbled floor, the walk to the front of the grand place—all of it was familiar.

Polite applause echoed through the room. Washington, DC's most influential and powerful nodded their subtle greet-

ings as she passed. A few even smiled. After five years of testifying at Senate hearings, the sea of faces was as familiar to her
as she was to them. She was the voice of faith and reason,
a woman whose beliefs and position were clear-cut and one-
sided. But they asked her to come anyway. They sought after
her and listened to her for one reason.

They knew her story.

Her horrific past, her public humiliation—the details were
something they were all aware of. Every senator in the room
knew the pain she'd suffered. Each was aware of her determination and drive, the way she held her head high now and
had put herself through school, earning nothing less than a
doctorate in family counseling.

She was an icon in DC, a pillar. She could've had her own
talk show or made a fortune writing books and running a private practice. But Mary's days were spent in the heart of the
city at one of her five shelters for abused women. Social work,
they called it. She was a survivor, a fighter. The DC elite
knew that too, and they liked her for it. Liked her enough to
listen to her when an issue was on the floor and moral input
was needed.

The issue today was abstinence.

At the beginning of the current president's term, a bill had
been passed approving three years of federal funding for abstinence programs in public schools. Now time was up and
money was running out. Mary's goal was simple: convince the
senators to approve another three years.

"Good morning." Mary took hold of the sides of the
podium and made eye contact with a group of senators ten feet

from her. Her eyes shifted toward the back of the room. "More than two years ago I stood in this place and convinced you that it was time for change." She paused and found another group near the left set of doors. "You agreed, and you gave our children a program that has altered the picture of teenage pregnancy across the nation." Her voice rang with sincerity that flowed from deep within her soul. "Today I come because the battle has just begun, and we must—we *must*—continue to bring our kids the choice to say no."

Though the first two speakers had bashed the program as being thinly veiled religious training, the faces before her were alert, ready for whatever she'd brought them.

She glanced at her notes. The statistics were daunting. For the next five minutes she rattled them off. Teen pregnancy down 40 percent. Eight out of ten students presented with abstinence training were making the decision to wait until marriage. There were 28 percent fewer known cases of sexually transmitted diseases.

Next Mary told her listeners about three teenagers, two girls and a boy, from different parts of the country. All of them ran in circles where sexual activity was a given, and each of them had made a decision to wait. The final story ended with Mary reading a quote from Susan, one of the teenage girls: "'If someone hadn't taught me it was okay to say no, I never would've said it. Today I'd be pregnant or sick or used. Maybe all three.'"

Mary gripped the podium more tightly. "When a woman walks into one of my shelters looking for help, more than 90 percent of the time she was sexually active as a teenager.

Women who practice abstinence are healthy women in every sense of the word. The same is true for young men. When they make a choice to wait, they tell the world they are worthwhile, valuable, special. Every other action they take toward their future will fall in line with those feelings."

She paused and gave one more look at a few specific faces around the room. "Please understand, ladies and gentlemen of the Senate the power to help kids like Susan is entirely in your hands. We must—we absolutely must—continue funding this education." She leaned into the microphone. "Thank you."

A break was called, and for the next fifteen minutes Mary was surrounded by senators thanking her for coming and nodding their agreement. Even though a significant number in the room were clearly opposed to the program, seeing it as a violation of separation of church and state, Mary felt good about her talk.

She'd done her part. God would do the rest.

Members of the media converged around her next, and she told them all the same thing. "Abstinence is worth fighting for. It's the only way we can look our kids in the eyes and tell them they'll be safe. Safe in body, mind, and soul."

Ten minutes after the last interview she was in her four-door Toyota headed for the S Street shelter, the one closest to the Capitol, the one where her next appointment would take place in just half an hour. She pulled out of the parking lot, drove past the manicured lawns and carefully kept landscaping, and headed west past the impressive buildings and detailed architecture.

The transition happened in the next few blocks. Lush

green grass became cracked sidewalks and dirty gutters, rose gardens gave way to littered alleys, stunning buildings to old brick and graffiti. Mary felt herself unwind. She had a voice in that world, but she was more comfortable in this one. More fulfilled. Especially today. Her appointment was with a woman who wanted to end her life, a woman fleeing with her two young daughters, running from an abusive boyfriend and convinced at twenty-three that life held nothing more for her.

Mary gripped the steering wheel. *God, give me the words . . . the way You always have.*

My grace is sufficient for you, daughter. The words breezed across her heart, full and rich, assuring her.

A group of guys in their late teens was gathered at the next stoplight. They looked rough, with their tight white T-shirts, metal chains, and tattoos. They spotted Mary, and two of them grinned and waved. She knew them. They were regulars at the youth center—another project she'd won funding for.

"Mary . . . hey, Mary!" one of them shouted.

The light was red, so she rolled down her window. "Good morning, guys. Staying out of trouble?"

"Anything for you, Mary." One of the others saluted her, and she smiled. A week ago he'd told her the good news. He was coming to the youth center for regular Bible studies. Another life saved from the streets.

The light changed and she waved good-bye. "Come see me sometime."

"We will!"

She turned her attention back to the road. The women's shelter was three blocks up on the left, an old five-story brick building with apartments on all but the first two floors. A living room, library, and kitchen, along with a day-care facility and several private offices and meeting rooms, made up the first level, and the second held a workout room, classrooms, and an oversized meeting area for church services.

Mary found her regular parking place in the back lot and headed for the side door. She loved every inch of this place. This was her life's purpose, the reason Christ had rescued her. She squinted against the bright midmorning sun. *Use me in this woman's life, Lord. Give her a reason to stay, a reason to come back. A reason to live.*

Inside she stopped at the front desk.

Leah Hamilton was working at the computer. She looked up, curious. "How did it go?"

"Very well." Mary picked up a stack of mail with her name on it. "They don't take their vote for a while. I think they'll fund it again." She peered around the corner. "Is she here yet?"

"Signing her kids into day care." Leah was nineteen, a lovely girl, inside and out, from the wealthy enclaves across the river. Three days a week she took college courses in theater and music, but the other two she was here volunteering her time and energy to work alongside the team at the shelter. She had an uncanny way of connecting with the women, helping them feel safe and cared for from the moment they entered the building.

And that was always the hardest part—getting abused women to step out of a harmful situation into the safe haven of the shelter.

"What's her name?"

"Emma Johnson. She's twenty-three with two little girls." Leah frowned. "I'm worried about her."

"Me too." Mary took the file marked *Emma* from the corner of the desk. In their initial phone discussion, the shelter's staff counselor had written in the file that Emma had gotten into drugs as a teenager, and now she was bruised and battered because of her boyfriend.

In addition, the counselor had noted that Emma was suicidal. "I feel trapped, like I'm in a prison and I can't get out," Emma had told the counselor.

It was that part that had caught Mary's attention. *Trapped in a prison.* The words could've been her own once, a lifetime ago. Mary sighed. Dozens of abused women filed through the doors of the DC shelters every day. She couldn't meet with all of them, so for the most part she left counseling to her very able staff.

But this one . . .

Mary tucked the file under her arm and nodded at the door down the hallway. "I'll be waiting." She smiled at Leah. "Bring Emma to my office when she's ready."

Inside the small room, Mary shut the door and studied Emma's file again. Once in a while God brought someone who needed to hear her story. Her entire story. Her story of gut-wrenching heartache and sorrow and finally her story of victory.

Her love story.

Without ever meeting her, Mary was convinced that Emma was one of those women.

She stood and went to the window facing S Street. The

sun was passing behind a cloud, and an anxious feeling plagued her. Days like this it all came back, the horrors that had trapped her and threatened to consume her. Fear and deceit, pain and addiction. Faithlessness and promiscuity and a desire to end her own life.

In Bible times people would have called her possessed of those horrors. Demons, they would've said. People today were reluctant to use that word, but whatever the wording, the effect was the same. Bondage and helplessness, with no way out.

Until she met Jesus.

She was no longer a slave to her own seven demons but a willing servant, dedicated and indebted to the Master, determined to make every breath count for His purposes alone. Her devotion was that strong.

Mary looked up and found a place beyond the passing cloud. What horrors did Emma Johnson face? In what ways did she need to be rescued?

A long shaky breath left Mary's lips. Her job was easier when she stayed busy, stayed in the present day, making rounds between Senate committee hearings and ministry on the streets of DC. But sometimes when the situation warranted it, she allowed herself to go back to the sad, sorry beginning. Telling her story was one way of underlining the truth, one way of making sure that the pain she'd suffered hadn't been without reason.

She swallowed hard and leaned into the windowsill. What were people thinking these days? Jesus wasn't merely a good teacher, and He certainly wasn't only a man—the way the world saw men. There had been no marriage or family for

Jesus Christ. He'd come to set people free. Period. And that's just what He'd done in her life. People didn't understand the power of Jesus—not the real power.

It was her job to tell them. Her job to tell Emma Johnson.

Jesus had rescued her, saved her from horrors that otherwise would've killed her. That wasn't something a normal man could've done. Her rescue hadn't come at the hands of a mere mortal—no way. It had come through the working of a mighty God.

Mary felt her anxiety ease. She would tell Emma every piece of her story so the woman might understand the real Jesus, the one people often didn't know about. Her story alone was proof that Jesus was who He claimed to be. Not just a good teacher or a kind leader, but God in the flesh. Because it would've taken God to redeem someone like Mary. Someone like Emma Johnson. God Almighty, Lord and Savior. Wholly man, yes. But more than that.

Wholly divine.

Chapter 2

*E*mma Johnson's hand shook as she signed the names and ages of her two daughters on the day-care form—Kami, four; and Kaitlyn, two. Both had Emma's pretty brown skin and delicate features. She lowered herself to their level and kissed them each on the forehead.

"Be good for Mama." Emma stood just inside the day-care door and watched them stand shyly together a few feet away and eye a pile of dolls and building blocks. "It's okay. You can go play, girls. Go on."

But they only moved closer to each other. Emma wanted to cry. What had they ever done to deserve the life she'd given them? They shouldn't be here at the day care of a battered-women's shelter. It was a weekday morning. They should be watching *Barney* or *Sesame Street*, safe and secure at home while she thought about what to fix for lunch.

But life had never been that way for them—not a day of it.

"Mama—" Kami looked up at her—"is Daddy here?"

Emma's heart sank. "No, baby. Daddy's far away. You're safe now."

Relief eased her little girl's features. Kami took her sister's hand and made four tentative steps toward the toys. Emma could read her mind. If Daddy wasn't here, then maybe it was okay to relax long enough to pick up a dolly or build a tower with her sister. Emma felt tears in her eyes. How could she have let things get to this point? She shivered and crossed her arms in front of her. "It's all right, girls."

Kami gave her one more look, and for a moment their eyes held. Then with fearful little steps she led Kaitlyn the rest of the way to the toys. Slowly they dropped to their knees, and Kami picked up one of the dolls. She hugged and rocked it and patted its plastic head. "It's okay," she said to the doll, her voice a precious singsong. "You're safe here."

One tear spilled onto Emma's cheek. Her girls were in a safe place now. She looked over her shoulder at the hallway and beyond it to the front door. So what did her children need her for? She could walk out, couldn't she? What was stopping her? She could leave the girls with the day-care lady and disappear into the streets. She could buy enough crack to take her from the nightmare of living, and that would be that. Charlie would live the rest of his life knowing he had caused her death. And her daughters . . . well, someone would take them, give them a home.

"Emma?"

She jerked her head back around and raised her eyebrows.
"Yes?"

The woman behind the counter had gray hair and soft
wrinkled skin. Her eyes held a kindness Emma had forgotten
existed. "I need you to sign one more form."

Run, Emma . . . sign the form and run. She held out her hand.
Her fingers shook harder than before. "Okay."

Across the room, Kami passed the baby to Kaitlyn. As
Emma signed the form, the gray-haired lady walked over to
the girls and squatted so she was eye level with them. She
took another baby doll from the pile and handed it to Kami.
"There. Now you each have one." The woman's voice was
gentle. She motioned toward a box across the room and nodded for the girls to follow her. "Come on; come take a look at
the doll clothes over here."

The girls looked at Emma, their expressions as familiar as
they were fearful. "Mommy?" Kami pointed toward the box.
"Please?"

"Yes." Emma nodded and gave the girls a small wave. "Go
. . . Mama'll see you later."

She watched them take the hands of the older woman. Yes,
someone would see that they found a good home. She could
leave and never look back. It was the right thing to do. She
would return to Charlie one last time and tell him it was over.
At least he couldn't threaten the girls then. And if he beat her
up, so be it. If he didn't kill her she'd find the drugs to do it.
Or maybe she'd skip seeing Charlie, get the drugs, and be lost
to the world in an hour.

Emma took a step back. "Bye." The word was quiet, empty.

The gray-haired woman looked over her shoulder, and their eyes met. "They'll be just fine. Go ahead to your appointment."

Emma didn't want an appointment. She wanted a fix—and fast. Why was she here, anyway? She took another step back and nodded. "Thank you. I . . . I won't be long."

"Take your time. Leah phoned up from the front desk." The woman smiled. "Mary's waiting for you."

Mary Madison.

That was the reason she'd come, wasn't it? Several days ago when Charlie had exploded at her, she'd been desperate for help, desperate for something that would take her and the girls out of the apartment and away from his rage. When he was finished with her, Charlie did what he often did. He sped away and left her moaning on the floor, the girls screaming from their bedroom.

Then she'd taken the girls and gone to stay with a friend, but it was hardly a healthy atmosphere. Her friend sold crack, and Emma had spent most of the next four days as high as a kite. She knew that if she stayed there, she'd overdose for sure, and if she went back to Charlie he'd kill her. So this morning she'd grabbed the yellow pages. She found the heading *Abuse Shelter* and dialed the number before she had time to think.

After an initial discussion with a staff counselor, she had an appointment with Mary. *The* Mary Madison.

Emma turned and headed down the hallway. Mary was the reason she'd come. Everyone in the country knew Mary Madison's story—at least the public details. The woman was always in the news, gaining ground for the city's downtrodden. She was powerful and beautiful, a survivor. No question something had turned life around for Mary, and Emma was curious. But now . . . with her girls safe, the other possibility—getting enough drugs to end it all—loomed even more tempting than meeting Mary Madison.

The door was ten feet away. She had twenty bucks in her pocket. She could buy some cheap crack, take it in an alley somewhere, and be dead in an hour. Her breathing came quicker, shallower, and somewhere deep in her chest her heart skittered into a rhythm too fast to feel.

Do it, Emma . . . end it all. You're worthless. No one needs you.

She put her hands over her ears. The voices had left her alone all morning, but they were back. She gave a quick shake of her head. "Stop!" She hissed the word and waited.

Your girls are better off without you. . . . Leave and don't look back, Emma. Crack's as close as a cab ride away. . . .

Her hands were damp with sweat, and she wiped them across her jeans.

Don't waste time, Emma. Go! The voice was shouting at her, laughing at her.

Fine.

No one needed to tell her the obvious. She would go, and she would take three times the crack she'd ever taken before. No more terrifying nights, no more hiding in the closet with Kami and Kaitlyn, no more longing for a man who couldn't love her without hurting her. She could take the drugs, and an hour from now there would be no more missing her mother and Terrence and the life she'd left behind. No more

nightmares or drugs or voices in her head. No more danger
for her girls.

Never mind about Mary Madison. She walked to the door
and gripped the steel bar.

"Emma?"

She turned and tried to grab a full breath. It was a young
woman, a girl no older than twenty. "Yes?"

The girl smiled and held out her hand. "I'm Leah Hamilton.
I work at the front desk."

"Oh." Her throat was so dry she barely squeaked the word
out. What was the girl doing, stopping her? Emma ran her
tongue along the inside of her lips. "Okay."

"You aren't . . . leaving, are you?" Leah looked down at
Emma's hand still on the door. "Mary's expecting you." She
smiled. "She's looking forward to meeting you."

Air, that's what she needed. She pushed the door open a
crack and sucked in a partial breath. The whole time she kept
her eyes on Leah's. "I . . . I'm not feeling well." She could get
away from this girl. Slip out, grab a taxi, and be dead before
lunchtime, right? No one would know the difference.

*Go, Emma. Run and don't look back. You're worthless. . . . What good
are you doing anyone by staying alive? Better dead than living your
life. . . . Everyone you know will be better off without—*

The voices were incessant. Emma pushed the door farther,
but Leah stepped around her and opened it before she had a
chance. "Let's stand out here together." She patted Emma's
shoulder. "The first time's always the hardest."

"It is?"

"Yes." Leah was pretty, and something in her eyes spoke to

the dark places in Emma's soul. "It's easy to convince yourself you shouldn't be here. You're not worth the time." Leah looked intently at her. "Know what I mean?"

The voices were silent. "Y-y-yes. I think so." Emma hugged herself and tried to stop shivering. It was summer after all. Eighty degrees and sunny. Did Leah know what she'd been thinking? Were the voices in her head loud enough for even a stranger to hear? She watched an empty cab drive by, the cab that could've taken her to another part of the city, where the drugs would be a sure thing. But with Leah standing here . . . what would it hurt, meeting with Mary? Just this once. She could take a cab and get the drugs later.

"Emma?" Leah's voice was gentle. She leaned closer, searching her eyes, her heart. "Did you just leave the man who's been hurting you?"

"A little while ago. I . . . stayed at a friend's house until I came here."

Leah took a step in the direction of the door. "Emma, you ready?"

"Yes." Fear put its icy fingers around her throat.

You're nothing but trash, Emma.

"Come on." Leah held out her hand. "I'll take you to Mary."

Emma squeezed her eyes shut and shook her head. "I can't . . ."

"You can." Leah took her hand and led her back inside.

The fight left as quickly as it had come. Tears flooded Emma's eyes, and she felt her body go limp. What was she thinking? She couldn't kill herself, could she? What would happen to Kami and Kaitlyn?

When they were inside, Leah let go of her hand but stayed next to her. "Mary's office is just down the hall."

Emma blinked so she could see. Leah was taking small steps, hardly making progress, and still it took every bit of Emma's energy to move her feet. She looked up and met Leah's eyes. "Is it . . . always this hard?"

"Often." Leah stopped outside a plain door. "But I can tell you this: no matter how hard it feels, no matter what you've been through, Mary's been there." She offered the slightest sad smile. "You'll like her, Emma. Give this a chance, okay?"

Emma was shaking again, but at least the voices were quiet. She didn't have the strength to speak, not when fear was clamping its fingers on her throat, making words impossible. Instead she nodded and watched as Leah opened the door. It was too late now. She couldn't run even if she wanted to, couldn't think about getting a cab and driving a few blocks away, going to the nearest alley and—

"Mary?" Leah leaned inside. "Emma's here."

From the other side of the door came a voice that was as kind as it was strong. "Thank you, Leah. Send her in."

Emma managed to get inside, and suddenly she was hit by a force that shook her to the core. She dropped to the chair closest to her, and only then did she look into the eyes of the woman with the face America knew so well. "Hi," Emma said weakly.

"Emma." Mary stood from the sofa opposite Emma's chair and held out her hand. "I'm glad you came."

"Yes, ma'am." They were the only words she could manage. Even still, her next breath stopped in her throat. Mary was far more beautiful in person. As she sat back down Emma was struck by her appearance. The woman had delicate features framed by long golden curls and the most brilliant blue eyes she'd ever seen. But that wasn't what made it hard to catch her breath. It was something deeper that came from inside the woman and filled the room. Whatever it was, Emma didn't recognize it.

Mary sat on the edge of the sofa, and their eyes met. "I read your file, Emma." She reached for a folder, never breaking eye contact. "You need help. That's why I'm here. "

Emma produced a slight nod. Mary was dressed in a navy jacket and pants with a white blouse. Clothes that could've belonged to someone uppity. But the woman across from her was as welcoming as a summer breeze.

"I've asked God to lead us today." Mary set the folder on her lap. "You don't want to talk, do you?"

"No." Emma felt another chill. "How . . . did you know?"

Mary's voice grew softer. "I've sat in your seat, Emma. You think there's no way out of the nightmare." She put her hand on Emma's knee and gave it a gentle squeeze. "Every once in a while God asks me to give a battered woman space, time. So instead of telling me your story, why don't we start with mine?"

"Yours?" There it was, the strange rush of emotions, the feeling she couldn't identify. She had figured Mary would demand the details of her life the minute they got started. Details she wasn't ready to share. She had never thought for a moment that they would start with Mary's story. The muscles at the base of her neck relaxed some. "That . . . that would be good."

Mary leaned back on the sofa. "See, Emma, I was just like you not that many years ago. Life wasn't worth living. But then—" her eyes glowed from a place deep inside her—"I met the love of my life. And everything—absolutely everything—changed."

Emma sat very still. Thoughts of taxicabs and drug over-doses faded from her mind. She nodded. "Tell me about that."

"One condition." Mary searched Emma's eyes, her heart, and her soul. "It'll take several sessions to tell you the whole story." She hesitated. "You have to promise me that you and your girls will stay here at the shelter and you'll keep coming until I finish the story." She gave a sideways nod. "Along the way we might talk about you, but only as much as you're ready for."

Emma blinked. Could she do that? Could she stay here with strangers when Charlie must be desperate for her to come home? She looked out the window. And what about the voices? They were right, weren't they? Several sessions? Days and nights at the shelter? She wasn't worth the time. Mary must have a hundred more important things she needed to do. Why should she think she was worth anything when—?

"I want to make something clear to you." Mary's voice was pleasant, but it demanded her attention.

Emma lifted her eyes to the woman across from her once more.

Mary studied her. "Jesus saved me for one reason."

The shaking was back. "One reason?"

"Yes." Her tone softened. "To share my story with women like you."

The chill passed from Emma's shoulders straight down her spine. Had she known? Like Leah earlier, Mary seemed to sense the exact thoughts screaming at her. "You're . . . busy."

Mary folded her hands and smiled. Again the feeling that Emma couldn't identify filled the room. "I work for God, but this is what I live for. I mean that." Mary waited a few beats. "Do I have your promise?"

Emma gritted her teeth. She was curious, almost desperate to know about Mary, what she'd been freed from, what had led to her very public life now. If it meant keeping the voices at bay for a few days, so be it. And if sharing her story was what Mary lived for, well, then . . . "Okay. You have my word."

You're a liar, Emma. You don't mean it. You're worth nothing. Tomorrow you can find a dealer and buy what you need and—

"All right then, let's pray and then we can get started." Mary's voice fell a notch. "Every time I tell this story, God works a miracle. The same will be true for you, Emma." She placed her hand over her heart. "I can feel it."

Emma didn't really hear the prayer, couldn't focus on the words coming from Mary's mouth. But as soon as she started praying, the voices stopped again. And once more the feeling filled the room, working its way through Emma's fingertips and skin, easing its way to the center of her soul.

As the prayer ended, Mary looked up and took a deep breath. And in that instant, Emma suddenly knew what the feeling was—the sense she'd had from the moment she walked into the room. It was something she hadn't felt in four years, since she walked out on her mother and everything good about life. It was a feeling she never expected to feel again, foreign and welcome all at the same time.

The feeling was hope.

Chapter 3

There was no way to tell her story without starting at the beginning, back in the days before even Mary was aware that the story had started. From that vantage point, the pieces fit together and made a tapestry, a picture that belonged to the women God brought into her life. The first part had less to do with Mary and more to do with Grandma Peggy.

Peggy Madison, who was still closer to Mary than any other person, the only family she had.

Even so, Mary wouldn't spend a long time talking about Grandma Peggy. Emma was edgy, her eyes flitting around the room, checking the door every few minutes. Mary gripped the arm of the sofa. Urgency filled her soul and pushed her to tell the story—all the sad and unbelievable details—as quickly as possible without losing Emma along the way. She stood and poured cups of water for both of them from the pitcher on her desk. She looked at Emma as she took her seat on the sofa. "Comfortable?"

"Yes." Emma crossed her legs. She was still shaking, but she looked less likely to jump up and flee the building.

"Okay." She handed one of the waters to Emma. "You know what happened when I was fifteen."

"Yes, ma'am." Emma's cheeks got pink, and she looked at her feet for a moment. "I think everyone knows."

Mary nodded and took a sip of water. As she did she felt a prayer drift through her soul. *Let her hear me, Lord, and give me the words.* "I want to tell you about my grandma Peggy."

Emma settled back in her chair some. "Is she still alive?"

"Yes." Mary felt a flicker of pain. Grandma Peggy was sicker these days. Her doctor had said it wouldn't be long— a year, maybe two. "She's in a nursing home a few miles from here. We're very close."

Regret colored Emma's eyes, and she opened her mouth as if she might say something. But then her lips came together again. Mary let it go. Whatever Emma was feeling, it would come up later after the young woman learned to trust her.

"When I was a little girl, my grandma Peggy lived in New York City. I stayed with her until I was three. That's when my mother, Jayne, took me away from Grandma's home, to live with her on the streets." Mary melted into the sofa and let the memories come. "One day when I was ten years old, my mother called Grandma Peggy from an alley-way. It had been months since she'd heard from us." She felt the past coming to life again. "We were behind some restaurant. I can still smell the fish rotting in the trash can near the pay phone."

The story began to spill from her soul, and this time Mary didn't stop. . . .

❦

Mary's mother had told Grandma Peggy that she'd stopped taking drugs and she wanted to get Mary enrolled in school. She was tired of living on the streets. Four hours later she and Mary walked through the door of Grandma Peggy's small flat in Queens.

Grandma Peggy studied them. Mary guessed she and her mother were pretty worn-out looking, dirty from the streets, thin, and hungry. Her grandmother fed them as much as they could eat. They made small talk, but her grandma seemed worried about her mother the entire time.

When they were finished eating, her grandma took her hand and led her to the pink bedroom, the only bedroom Mary had ever known as a child.

The bedroom was like a wonderland to Mary after so many years on the streets. She made her way around the bed, marveling at the toys and photos; then she pulled eight picture books from the shelf near the bed and brought them to Grandma Peggy.

Grandma Peggy framed her small face and stooped so their noses were close together. "I missed you so much, honey." Her eyes shone with a love Mary hadn't understood then or for years afterward. Her voice was choked when she spoke again. "I thought about you every day."

"Me too!" Mary gave her grandma a long hug. Then she grabbed three titles from the stack of books. "These are my favorite ones, Grandma. Can you read them, please?"

"Of course. Want me to start with Dr. Seuss?"

Mary clapped her hands. "Yes! *The Cat in the Hat's* my favoritist of all. One of the ladies at the mission has a Cat in the Hat shirt, and I always remember you reading me that story."

Grandma Peggy pulled Mary close to her. "I wish I could read to you every day, sweetie." She took *The Cat in the Hat*, opened the front cover, and began to read.

Two hours later they were still working through the books, when Mary pointed to the picture of herself next to the bed, the one taken when she was three. "Is that me, Grandma?"

"Yes, honey. You're a very pretty girl; you know that, Mary?"

"That's what Mommy's friend says." Mary had been too young to know it might be strange that one of her mother's many male friends would make a fuss over her.

Grandma Peggy picked up on it, though. "Mommy's friend? Which friend?"

"Mr. Paul." That's when Mary had remembered. "I'm not supposed to talk about him."

Her grandmother leaned in close and put her arm around Mary. "Did Mr. Paul hurt you?"

"No." Mary's answer had been quick and adamant. She shook her head. "He never hurt me, Grandma. Never." It was true; the man hadn't touched her. But the subject had been uncomfortable for Mary at such a young age. She squirmed away and scampered across the room. "Look, Grandma! My pink teddy bear!"

Grandma Peggy closed the book on her lap and faced Mary. "Sweetie, you know Grandma loves you, right?"

Mary felt her eyes grow big and sad. "Yes." She swallowed and looked down at the floor. "I think about that sometimes when I'm scared at night."

"Really?" Tears spilled onto Grandma Peggy's cheeks.

Mary nodded and studied her grandma's eyes. They were full of a light Mary never saw in anyone on the streets. "Mommy says we'll be here for a while but not forever. But know what?"

"What?"

"I wish I *could* live with you forever, Grandma." She felt something sad in her heart. "But Mommy says that's a bad thing to say. She says I belong to her, and if I live with you she'll never get a chance to be my mommy again."

Anger colored Grandma Peggy's expression. She went to Mary and brushed her knuckles against Mary's cheek. "You know what I wish more than anything in the world?"

"What?" Mary blinked, her voice soft.

"The same thing you do. That you could live here forever. You and your mommy. Not just for a little while but for always."

"But what if my mommy goes away again?" A hint of hope sounded in Mary's voice. "Sometimes when she leaves me for a few days it's lonely without her."

Her grandmother looked surprised and worried. "Your mommy might go, but if I had it my way you would stay. I'd take care of you, and you'd never be cold or hungry or lonely again."

Mary leaned forward and planted a wet kiss on Grandma Peggy's forehead. "That would be my bestest dream in the whole world. Better than candy."

"Yes, 'cause we'd be together always. Just the two of—"

Suddenly there was a sound outside the door, and her grandma jumped. "Jayne?"

Mary moved closer to her grandma. Outside the bedroom door no one said anything.

Grandma Peggy went to the door, and as she did, Mary heard footsteps heading down the hallway. "Jayne . . . are you there?"

Even as a little girl, Mary understood why her grandma looked scared. If her mother heard them talking, then she might take Mary away again and never come back.

Mary had ordered her heartbeat to slow down. *Calm*, she told herself. *Act calm.* She watched as Grandma Peggy opened the door in time to catch the back of her mother as she walked past. "Jayne, didn't you hear me?"

"What?" Her mother looked over her shoulder. "Oh, sorry." She smiled, but her eyes didn't really look happy. "Just looking for something in the other room."

"Oh. Okay." Grandma Peggy pushed her hair out of her eyes. She motioned to the bedroom. "We're still reading if you want to join us."

Her mother shook her head. "No, that's okay. I'll put some pasta on for dinner."

Mary watched her mother turn and continue into the kitchen. Then Grandma Peggy shut the door and looked at her.

Mary felt scared about what her mother would do next. "Is Mommy mad?"

Grandma Peggy crossed the room and sat beside her on the bed. "No, baby, Mommy's not mad. No one is." She took Mary's hand and ran her thumb along the top of it. "It's good that you told Grandma how you feel."

Mary nodded, but she was distracted. She stood and wandered back to the bookcase. Then, from behind her, she heard her grandma take a loud breath. What happened next was something that had stayed with Mary every day since then.

In a quiet, almost desperate voice, her grandmother began to pray. "Please, God, be with my Mary. I know Your grace is sufficient for me, for her, for all of us. But I believe with everything I am that You have good plans for my Mary. Keep her here so she can grow and learn and become everything You want for her. She's safe here, God. Please . . ."

When she was done praying, Grandma Peggy came to Mary and ran her fingers through her little-girl hair. "I love you, Mary."

Mary still felt scared. But she looked away from the books to her grandma's eyes. "I love you too." She turned all the way around. "Were you talking to God?"

"Yes." Her grandma sighed. "Sometimes I can feel Him holding me, hugging me."

"Even when you can't see Him?" Mary was amazed.

"Yes. And something else." She smiled. "Sometimes I can hear Him talking back to me. Know what I heard Him say today?"

A warm happy feeling rose in Mary's heart. "What, Grandma?"

"I heard Him say that you, sweet child, are going to bring

glory to Him. He has a plan for you, Mary. No matter what happens, He has a plan."

The words wrapped their arms around Mary and gave her a hope she'd never known. Hope and security. "Really?"

Her grandma nodded and looked deep into her eyes. "Even when I'm not there to tell you, Mary, never give up. God is with you. Don't forget that."

Mary had known in that moment that she never would forget it. She would remember her grandma's words if she lived to be one hundred.

Later that night, after they had a quiet dinner, after her mother and grandmother whispered some words that convinced Mary there was trouble, and after she was already in her pretty pink bed, her grandma came to her again. In her hand she had a small red-beaded purse. It wasn't any bigger than a deck of cards, but right away Mary knew. This purse was very, very special.

Grandma Peggy held it out to Mary. "My grandma gave this to me when I was a little girl." She pressed it into Mary's hands. "Now I'm giving it to you."

A feeling like the wonder of a rainbow filled Mary's heart. She ran her fingers over the beads, her mouth open. "Thank you, Grandma."

"Look inside." Grandma Peggy opened the little buttons at the top of the purse. Then she carefully pulled a slip of paper from inside. It was covered with words.

Mary felt a moment of embarrassment. She was ten and she couldn't read. She swallowed. "Could you please tell me what it says?"

"Of course." Grandma Peggy's voice was kind. She took the paper and opened it. "It's a Bible verse. 'I know the plans I have for you,' declares the Lord, 'plans to prosper you and not to harm you, plans to give you hope and a future.'" She paused. "It's from the book of Jeremiah."

Mary wasn't sure what it was about those words, but they made her feel the way she'd felt earlier when Grandma had been praying for her. Every word felt sure and true. First her grandma had told her, and now the Bible said it. In that slice of time Mary became convinced that God really did have a plan for her life.

Her grandma folded the piece of paper in half and tucked it back into the purse. "Whenever you're sad, just know that the truth is in here." She patted the little purse. "Okay?"

"Okay." Mary held the purse against her heart. "I'll keep it for always."

Grandma Peggy's eyes grew soft. "You're such a pretty girl. Remember what Grandma always tells you? Who made you so pretty?"

Mary could feel her eyes glowing as her smile stretched across her face. "Jesus."

"That's right, baby. Don't ever forget, okay?"

"Okay."

"And you're the nicest little girl, Mary." Grandma Peggy took hold of her hands. They shared one last hug. "Let's pray." They bowed their heads, and their eyebrows touched in the middle. "Dear Jesus, thank You for bringing Mary home." A sob caught in Grandma Peggy's chest, and for a few seconds she didn't speak. "Whatever tomorrow brings for Mary, keep her close to You, Lord. Let her life bring You glory always. In Jesus' name, amen."

⟡

Mary stopped and drew a slow breath. "What happened next was the beginning of the real story—the one you and . . . well, the nation knows about."

Emma had been listening intently, sometimes with tears in her eyes. "Your grandma loved you very much."

"She did." Mary sniffed. Her throat was thick from the remembering. "She still does."

Emma's chin quivered. She opened her mouth, but no words came out, and she shook her head.

Mary waited. If Emma wanted to say something, she would give her time.

"It's just . . ." Emma swallowed hard. Her struggle was intense. "My mother and I . . . had something special like that before . . ." Her voice trailed off, and a pool of tears filled her eyes. She blinked, and the tears became little streams down the center of her cheeks. She shook her head again. "I'm not ready."

Mary wanted to rush ahead, tell the young woman that God had a solution for her and that she could find restoration and healing if she turned to Him. But she stopped herself. Victims needed utmost safety, not a lecture. Besides, that was the point of telling her story. So she could illustrate the power of God in a way no one could refute.

She sat back. It had been a while since she'd told her story, a year at least. "Anyway—" Mary kept her voice low, unthreatening—"my grandma tucked me in that night." She smiled as the memory returned. "I told her she was pretty too."

***

Her grandma had left the pink bedroom, and Mary fell asleep. But sometime in the middle of the night she felt someone grab her arm. She started to scream, but a hand came over her mouth. That's when she realized what was happening. Her mother was standing over her, whispering at her.

"It's okay, Mary. Come on, wake up." She looked like she was trying to smile, but her expression was full of pain. "We're leaving."

Mary felt a rush of fear. "No, Mama. Grandma doesn't want us to leave."

"We'll come back." Her mother's answer was quick. "I promise. Mama just has to get some things figured out first."

"But can't we—?"

"Now, Mary!" Her mother's tone said she was in a hurry and also a little frightened. "We belong together, you and me. You're coming whether you want to or not."

That had been the end of the discussion. Mary got dressed, and in just a few minutes she left with her mother. She never had a chance to grab her pink teddy bear or tell her grandma good-bye. In fact, she had time to take just one thing.

The little red-beaded purse.

Chapter 4

Mary thought about stopping there, saving the rest of the story for other sessions, but Emma was waiting, wide-eyed. Mary stood and filled their water cups. As she did, a silent prayer filtered through her soul. *God, should I keep going? Would it make things worse for Emma to hear the next part?*

This time there was no audible answer, no quiet resounding in her heart. But something came to mind all the same. Emma needed the truth. If she was ever going to be set free, she needed all the truth she could get. As long as she was willing to listen, Mary should be willing to tell her story.

And she was.

Mary handed one of the water cups to Emma. "Should I continue?"

"Yes." Emma slid to the edge of her seat. "Where did the two of you go? After you left your grandma Peggy's house?"

"I remember the other details like they happened yesterday, but I'm not sure where we went. Somewhere on the streets of New York." Mary took a swallow of water. She'd been so young at the time. Her whole life would've been different if only her mother had let her stay with Grandma Peggy.

She set her cup down and looked at Emma. "Right away my mother quit taking drugs, and after a few days the two of us moved in with a couple—Jimbo and Lou."

Emma set her cup on the floor near her feet. She never broke eye contact. "They're the ones? the people the news talked about?"

"Yes." Mary squinted against the glare of the past. "I remember one day in particular. About two weeks after we'd visited Grandma Peggy's house."

***

Mary's mother had her by the hand, and the two of them were walking along one of the lesser-traveled streets in Lower Manhattan, somewhere her mother called the Diamond District. Her mother was more talkative than usual.

"We'll be fine, you and I." She gave Mary's hand a squeeze. "You smile real nice and we'll pull in thirty, forty dollars an hour today. That'll be enough for pizza and a carton of milk."

"Pizza?" Mary was still sad about leaving Grandma Peggy. But it was nice seeing her mommy's eyes look normal. Not wide and nervous and red around the edges the way they were when she was taking drugs.

"Yes, pizza!" Her mama smiled at her. They walked the rest of the block without talking. Then her mother said, "Grandma doesn't think I can make it on my own, right?"

Mary didn't know what to say. She couldn't take sides. Yes, she wanted to be home with Grandma Peggy, but her mama needed her too. Mary shaded her eyes so she could see her better. "Grandma loves you. She wanted us to stay."

Her mother looked at the sidewalk for a few steps. Then in a quieter voice she said, "Maybe someday. When I pay off my debt."

"Debt?" Whatever a debt was it made her mama's shoulders slump. Mary felt nervous about that.

Her mother seemed to study the people in front of them. "I owe Jimbo some money. When I pay it off, maybe I can save up some cash and the two of us can stay with Grandma." She looked at Mary. "I won't do it if I can't pay my way." She paused. "Understand?"

Mary thought about that. Her mother had taught her it was wrong to steal, that people who stole were as bad as people who killed. Maybe if she didn't pay Grandma Peggy it would be sort of like stealing. She nodded. "I understand."

Her mama made a quick turn. "Tell me if you see the cops, okay?"

"Yes, Mama." That was Mary's job. They would find somewhere with people coming and going, and they'd make the people feel sorry for them. That's when the people would pull out money and hand it to her mother. The whole time Mary had to look for police, because police didn't like people asking strangers for money. That was something Mary didn't understand. But there was something called an arrest warrant on her mother for drug charges. Her mama always said she couldn't afford to be questioned by police.

They found a spot outside a diner, and for more than an hour her mother told people she was in trouble, that her wallet had been stolen.

It was getting dark when Mary finally said, "Mommy, can we go? I'm tired."

A couple with nice clothes was coming. Her mother smiled and squeezed her hand. "In a minute, honey." The couple spotted them and slowed their pace. Her mama took a step in their direction. "Excuse me, folks. My wallet was stolen." She looked at Mary for a long time. The longer her mama stared her sad eyes at her, the longer the people would do the same thing. And the more money they'd get.

The woman stopped, her face knotted with concern. "That's awful."

Her mother gave the woman the same look she gave every stranger she talked to. Like this was the saddest day of her life. "My husband left us." She raised her shoulders. "I think maybe if we got a little bit of help we might get back on our feet."

The woman had her pocketbook open before Mary's mother finished her sentence. The woman's husband nodded as the woman pulled out two twenties. "Here. Get a cab and a good dinner. Then get home before something worse happens."

Her mama took the money, and her eyes lit up with grati-tude. "Thank you." She smiled at Mary. "These nice people helped us. Isn't that wonderful?"

Mary knew her role. She nodded, though her expression felt blank and hesitant. She blinked at the couple. "Thank you, ma'am . . . sir."

"You're welcome, sweetie. Now get home." The woman patted Mary's head. "The street's no place for a pretty little girl like you."

It was the same every time. The way it looked to Mary, sometimes the people gave everything they had. Always they did two things. First, they commented on how beautiful Mary was. Never her mother, though she'd been very pretty before the drugs. Mary had seen pictures. But everyone talked about Mary. "My goodness, child, I've never seen eyes like yours." Or to her mother, "Take good care of her—she's a rare little beauty." Something like that.

And second, they'd assume Mary and her mother had a home, somewhere to go back to. As if the biggest problem facing them really was a stolen wallet.

As the couple walked off that late afternoon, her mama chuckled. "Good work, Mary." She slipped the twenties into her back pocket. "We can call it quits for the day."

"How much did we make?"

Her mother took a handful of bills from her pocket and looked at it for a minute. "Two hundred twenty." She beamed at Mary. "If we keep this up, maybe we can get back to Grandma's house in a few weeks."

Mary had been so excited about that news that she twirled

around and giggled and took her mother's hand. "That's the best news of the day!"

Her mother laughed—something she rarely did. "Maybe it is."

She led Mary to a diner, and people stared at them as they walked inside. People were always staring at them. Her mama told her it was because they were both so pretty. But the looks people gave them weren't always nice. Mary thought maybe it had more to do with their torn, dirty clothes and the fact that they asked for money.

Her mama stopped a few feet from the counter. "We have to hurry, okay? Jimbo doesn't like it when we're late." She smiled, but fear shone in her eyes. "Jimbo's not very nice to Mama when we make him mad."

Her mother was right. Jimbo could get mean in a hurry. But her mama said Jimbo wasn't all bad. He had bushy red hair and one gold tooth, a tooth that was easy to see because the man smiled all the time. Especially when he looked at Mary. A shiver ran down her arms. "Okay, I'll hurry."

They looked up at the counter, and her mother frowned. Mary thought she understood why. The place wasn't really a diner. More of a tobacco store with a counter display of rotating sausages. The smell of thick grease fought with the smell of cigars. For a minute, Mary thought her mother might take her somewhere else. But they didn't have time.

Her mama breathed out hard in the direction of the man at the cash register. "Where's the diner?"

The man snickered and adjusted a gold chain around his neck. "Got you in here, didn't it, doll?"

Her mother blew at a wisp of her bangs and reached for one of the twenties in her pocket. As she did, she grumbled in a quiet voice, "Why do I stay in this city? All crowded and dirty and full of places like this. It's enough to drive you back to drugs."

Mary must've reacted with alarm at that statement.

Her mama caught her eye as she pulled a bill out. "Don't worry, Mary." She gave a weak laugh. "Sober is sober is sober. Period. I'm just kidding." She looked at the money in her hand. "When I pay off Jimbo, you and me and Grandma will all move to the country."

Mary didn't say anything, but inside she felt relieved. In fact, she felt like twirling again.

"Listen, lady, you're wasting my time," the man behind the counter grouched. "You got an order, or what?"

Her mother put her hands on her hips and stared at the sausage display. "Not much of a choice."

The man was losing his patience. "Here're the choices, lady—cheesy sausage or spicy sausage. Take your pick."

Mary tugged on her mother's shirt. "Mommy?"

"What, honey?" She ran her hand over Mary's bangs.

"Cheesy, okay?" Her voice was small, but it was also certain. Mary knew her mind; she always had.

Her mother looked up at the man. "My girl wants the cheesy kind."

"Fine." The man tapped the display with a pair of bent-up silver tongs. "Cheesy sausage coming up."

Mary expected it would be served in a bun, but it wasn't. The man simply tossed a yellowish sausage—one with plastic-looking cheese leaking out the sides—into a little cardboard dish.

Her mother brushed her knuckles against it. "It's cold." She shook her head and laid a twenty on the counter. "You rip people off, buddy, know that?"

The man gave her an exaggerated shrug. "Everybody rips off everybody, lady. You too."

Her mother looked like she was about to say something in reply, but she must've changed her mind. Maybe she was thinking about the wallet story and that possibly the guy had a point. Either way, she led Mary to a small table and sat across from her. There was a layer of sticky grease on the Formica finish. "Well, this is dinner." The corners of her mouth lifted some. "Sorry it's not better."

"Thank you, Mama." Mary sniffed the cheesy sausage and wrinkled her nose. "It smells like cat food."

"It's fine, baby." Her mother nudged her arm. "Go ahead and eat it."

Mary waited. "Can I pray?"

"Pray?" Her mother's mouth hung open for a few seconds. "You mean like Grandma does?"

"Mmm-hmm."

Her mama looked frustrated, but she nodded. "Sure, go ahead."

Mary bowed her head and folded her hands. "Dear Jesus, it's Mary. Thanks for the food. I love You, and—" she opened one eye and looked at her mother—"Mama loves you too." She paused. "Right?"

"Right." Mama looked at her watch. "You need to start eating." She drew a slow breath. "Honey, tonight Mama's going to need more work than what we get from strangers."

Mary felt a little sick to her stomach. "Night work, you mean?" Night work was when her mother dressed in short skirts and high heels and went away for the night with a man. She wasn't sure what went on with the men, but her mother was always quiet and sometimes angry when she came home. Plus Mary had to spend time alone with Jimbo and his wife, and nothing about that felt safe.

"Yes, night work." Her mother leaned her elbows on the table and looked into her eyes. "It'll help us get back to Grandma faster."

Mary tried not to think about that. She chewed her first bite, but she felt her face scrunch up the way it sometimes did before she started to cry. She reached into her sweatshirt pocket and put her fingers around the little red purse, felt the tiny beads and the buttoned clasp.

Her mama looked at her. "What do you have?"

"The purse Grandma gave me." She held it up. She'd carried it with her every day since leaving Grandma Peggy's house. The purse felt good in her hands, better than thinking about her mother's night work. "It makes me feel happy when I look at it."

No more questions came from her mother.

Mary hurried and finished the cheesy sausage; then the two of them went back to Jimbo's apartment.

"You're late!" Jimbo towered near the front door as they walked in.

His wife, Lou, took hold of his elbow. "Ah, give the girls

a chance." She pulled him away so Mary and her mother could walk past.

Jimbo shook a fist at her mama. "Don't make me teach you a lesson, Jayne. I need you back here early if you're gonna get work. The customers expect you to be available."

Mary knew what Jimbo was talking about. He wanted her mama to get night work, and that meant she had to be dressed in her short skirt and outside on the sidewalk before it got dark. Mary felt sicker than before, but she wasn't sure whether it was the cheesy sausage or the fact that her mother was going to be gone most of the night.

Her mama tucked her into bed in the room the two of them shared. "See you in the morning." She bent down and kissed Mary's forehead. "I'm sorry about things, Mary. It'll get better."

"I know." Mary reached out and put her hand on the back of her mother's head. "Be careful."

She left then and when she was gone, Mary got an idea. Her mother met up with the men out front on the sidewalk. Maybe if she opened the window she could spy on her mama, make sure she was okay. Mary tiptoed out of bed and opened the window. It stuck halfway up, but it allowed her to see outside. After a few minutes, her mama came into view. She wore a black skirt and black stockings. Her shirt was cut low, and her hair was different than before, bigger.

Mama was out on the street just five minutes when a man crossed the street and walked up to her. He was one of those businessmen who walked up and down the sidewalks of the city, the kind dressed in stiff suits.

Mary watched him stop a few feet from her mama. He looked her up and down. "Hey, baby, you for sale?" He took a step closer. "You look it."

"Maybe." Her mother studied him. In the glare of the streetlight, Mary could see that the man had a fancy watch and nice shoes.

"I got some business associates in town for a three-day meeting." He leaned his head back. His look said he knew her answer before he asked the question. "You up for a three-day job?"

She tapped the toe of her spiked heel and hesitated a long time. "What's the pay?"

The man shrugged. "Fifteen hundred."

Her mother must have worked hard not to react, because she raised her brow and gave him a half smile. "Two grand."

The man laughed. "You're not that pretty, lady." He started to walk past her, but he stopped and pursed his lips, as if maybe he was reconsidering. "Tell you what . . . eighteen hundred, but you do whatever we ask. All five of us." He winked at her. "Got it?"

Her mama's expression changed. She looked sick, the way she did when she drank too much wine. "I have some arrangements to make." She took a step back. "I'll start tomorrow."

The man thought for a minute. "Fine. I'll come for you at eight." He winked at her again. "Be ready . . . if you know what I mean."

As he walked off, her mother watched him go. Then she came back inside. Mary heard the door, and real quick she shut the window. Jimbo didn't like the windows open. Bad guys could get in. Mary hurried to the bedroom door, opened it, and listened. Her mother was talking to Jimbo.

"I got a job. Three days straight. Starts tomorrow night."

Jimbo did a slow laugh. "Now that's more like it."

Mary's stomach rumbled, and she couldn't catch her breath. Her mama would be gone for three days? That was too long. Jimbo and Lou couldn't watch her for three whole days. Who would find her something to eat? And where would her mama go? Maybe she wouldn't be safe. She quieted her thoughts and listened.

Her mother was talking. "When I get back I'll pay you what I owe you." Her voice sounded angry. "Then I'm through with you. No more junk, no more tricks. I'm going home."

"That's your choice, baby." There was still a laugh in Jimbo's voice.

For a little while there was no talking. Then her mother started in again. "One more thing." Her voice was different. Sadder, maybe. "I need you to watch Mary."

"Mary?" Jimbo made a loud whistling sound. "Okay, baby. Might even make some money off her." He chuckled hard. "Those blue eyes and that mop of blonde curls." He laughed again. "Honey-colored skin smoother than caramel ice cream."

"Stop, Jimbo!" Her mother sounded mad.

"Pretty thing like her could probably make more money than you."

"That's not funny!" Her mother was louder now. "You leave my Mary alone, hear me?"

Mary squirmed in the doorway. Maybe her mother would

take Mary with her. Or maybe take her to Grandma Peggy's house.

They were still talking downstairs.

"Let up, Mommy." Jimbo wasn't laughing anymore. "Your baby angel's safe with me."

The talking ended, and Mary scrambled back to bed. She slid under the blanket and forced her eyes closed. *Please, God . . . no! Don't let her leave me with Jimbo, please!* She reached onto the table near the bed and took hold of her red-beaded purse. Grandma Peggy told her that God had good plans for her. So her mama would have to think of something better than leaving her with Jimbo, right?

She lay there a long time waiting for her mother to come to bed, but finally she fell asleep.

The next day, after they spent another afternoon taking money from strangers, her mother bought her a piece of pepperoni pizza.

Her mama looked her in the eyes and took a long breath. "Mama has to go away tonight, okay? I have some night work, only this time—" her voice cracked, like maybe she was going to cry—"this time I won't come home for three days."

Since her mother hadn't mentioned the work all day long, Mary had hoped maybe it wasn't going to happen. She set her pizza down. "Three days?" She blinked twice, and her chin quivered a little. "Who's gonna watch me?"

Her mama reached across the table and patted her hand. "Jimbo and Lou."

"Jimbo scares me." Mary could hear the whine in her voice. "He always scares me."

"He's teasing you, baby. Jimbo'll take good care of you."

"But, Mommy—" she stuck her lower lip out—"if you need someone to watch me for three days, how 'bout Grandma Peggy? She'll watch me anytime. That's what she said."

Her mother looked tired and maybe a little angry. "We'll go see Grandma when I get paid. After this job we can move back there, and you can go to school. All right?" She made her voice stern. "No whinin', Mary. Mama doesn't have any choice." She pushed back from the table. "Bring your pizza. We have to get going."

Mary shook the whole way home. What if Jimbo was mean to her? What if he tried to scare her or hurt her? *Be brave,* she told herself. *Be brave and when Mama's done working we can go back to Grandma Peggy's.* She could go to school and learn how to read, and one day she would be able to read the books in her pink bedroom all by herself.

They walked a long way, and when they got home her mother sat her on a chair in front of the television. "Stay here while I get ready." She didn't sound scared anymore, but nervous. Like she was in a hurry.

Mary was too scared to say anything.

When her mama was gone, Mary noticed Lou across the room, stretched out on the broken sofa, snoring. A baseball game was playing on the screen, and Mary stared at it. If only there was a way to crawl through the box and wind up in the sunny seats on the other side.

A little while later her mother came back wearing the same short black skirt she'd worn the night before. Her face was made up with extra black around her eyes. She looked at Lou.

An empty bottle of wine lay on the floor beside the sofa. "Lou . . ." Her mother shook the woman, but nothing happened. Lou slept most of the time. When she was awake she was always talking about smoking joints. Mama tried again. "Lou, wake up. You're watching Mary tonight, remember?"

A low growl came from Lou's throat, and she mumbled something that barely made sense. She opened her eyes halfway. "Leave me alone."

"Lou, get up!" Her mother shook her one more time. "I have a job."

Lou pushed herself up and rubbed her face. When she was more aware of what was happening, she dropped the corners of her mouth. "You're leavin' your kid with me for three days; is that it?"

"Jimbo said it was okay." Her mother tapped her toe. Only then did she notice Mary, huddled in the chair on the other side of the room. Her mama gave her a weak smile and the okay sign.

Tears welled in Mary's eyes, but she held up her fingers and gave her the okay sign back.

"Ah, baby." Her mother came to her and bent down so their eyes were at the same level. "It's just three days, okay? I'll do the work, get the money, and come home." She smoothed Mary's bangs. "I'll be back before you know it."

Mary tried to talk, but her throat was too thick. She could feel her chin shaking, and her tears ran down her cheeks. She started to nod, but then she jumped to her feet and threw her arms around her mama's neck. "Don't go . . . please." Sobs rose in her chest, and she held tight. Maybe if she never let go . . .

"Baby, shhh." Her mama rocked her. She smelled like strong perfume, and her hair was stiffer than usual. But her voice felt good all the same. "It's just three days."

While her mama held her, she spoke to Lou. "Mary's had dinner. Just make sure she stays inside and give her three meals a day. I bought a box of Cheerios." She motioned to the kitchen. "It's in the cupboard, and there's milk in the—"

The door flung open, and Jimbo burst inside. "I'm late." He threw his hands in the air. "My fault, I know it. Don't gripe at me, Lou." He looked at Mary and her mama. "What do we have here? A sad little good-bye?"

Her mama pulled back and flashed angry eyes at Jimbo. "I was just saying I bought Cheerios." She took Mary's hand. "Make sure you feed her."

Jimbo took a few steps closer. He looked at Mary in a way that made her feel like running. "You and me are about to have some fun, kid."

Mary hid behind her mother, burying her face in her mama's back.

"Don't worry." Jimbo laughed a little softer this time. "I'll take real good care of you."

"Stop!" Her mama crossed the room to Jimbo and shoved his shoulder. "That's no way to talk to a little girl. You're scaring her."

"Listen." Jimbo held his hand up high as if he might hit her mama. His laughter stopped. "Don't tell me what to do."

Lou stretched out on the couch again and closed her eyes. "I'm going back to sleep." She raised her arm a bit. "I'll make breakfast in the morning."

"Don't worry about it." Jimbo slapped her feet and chuckled again. "I'm the babysitter. For the next three days Mary's mine."

Something was wrong with Jimbo. Mary noticed it about the same time her mother did. He was too happy—strangely happy.

Her mama put her hands on her hips. "What're you on, Jimbo? Don't tell me you're babysitting my girl when you're on drugs."

"I'll take whatever I want!" His shout shook the small apartment. He leaned against the wall, and his face relaxed. "Go, Jayne. Your job'll be here in a few minutes. Everything'll be fine."

Mary gave the slightest shake of her head, but she didn't cry out. She didn't dare. A ribbon of fear worked its way around her heart. It was really going to happen; she was going to stay with Jimbo.

Her mama backed away from him and returned to Mary. She opened her arms, and Mary ran to her. For the sweetest few seconds she allowed herself to feel safe, lost in her mother's arms. Then she felt her mama pull back, and their eyes connected. "I'm sorry, baby. This is the best I can do."

Mary wanted to ask one more time about Grandma Peggy, but there wasn't time. Her mama would be gone in a few minutes. Instead she sniffed twice and nodded.

"Be a good girl, okay?"

Another few sniffs. "I will."

Her mother ran her thumb along Mary's brow. "I'm doing this for you, Mary." Her eyes looked watery. "I love you, baby."

"Love you too."

Her mother picked up a grocery bag full of what looked like clothes.

On her way out, Jimbo shouted, "Work hard, Jayne. We'll be waiting for you."

The last thing her mama did before she walked out the door was look at Mary. In her eyes Mary could hear everything her mother had just told her all over again: *"I'm sorry, Mary. It's just three days . . . just three days."*

Then, in a rush, she was gone.

⁂

"That was the last time I ever saw her." Mary blinked, and she felt the memory lift like patchy fog. "Jimbo and Lou did a lot of secret talking that night, and in the morning they packed up the apartment and we left."

Across from her, Emma was still rapt, her expression anxious. "For the remote cabin? the one in Virginia? I think I read something about that in the newspaper."

"Yes. My mama made a lot of bad choices." She lifted her chin. "But she loved me." Mary wanted Emma to understand this part. "She just didn't know how to go home again."

The words seemed to hit Emma hard. She sat back, unblinking. Her eyes filled and she shook her head. "Me neither."

Mary felt her expression soften. This was what she wanted, what she was praying for. That Emma would see herself in the story, and that along the way she would come to know the truth. If Jesus could rescue Mary, He could rescue Emma. No matter how terrible her life was today. She reached out and patted Emma's hand. "I had a feeling."

Emma wiped her fingers beneath her eyes. "It's complicated."

Mary sat back. "It always is."

"What happened to your mother?" Emma reached for her water. Her hand shook as she took a sip, but she never broke eye contact. "That's the part . . . the part the news never talked about."

"I've tried to piece it together from the police reports." Mary felt an ache in her heart. Her mother had never found her way off the streets, never figured out how to free herself from the abuse. It was the reason Mary was driven to help women like Emma. She drew a slow breath. "After three days she must've come back for me and found the apartment empty. The three of us gone."

"She must've been crazy with grief."

"I think so." Mary closed her eyes for a few seconds. She could still feel her mother's arms around her, the way she'd felt safe in her embrace the last time they were together. She blinked and looked at Emma. "She must've figured there was no way to find me, and the guilt . . . it must've been too much." She paused long enough to rope in her emotions. "The police . . . found her in an alley a few blocks away. Dead from an overdose."

Emma was shaking. She covered her face, and for a moment she looked like she might break down. "That could've been me." Her words were muffled, but they rang in painful honesty through the room. "So many times that could've been me." After a while she wiped a few errant tears. Her eyes met Mary's. "I'm sorry. About your mama."

"It's been a long time." They were words she said easily now, meant to release people from feeling sorry for her. She was okay—she really was. Healed of so many horrors. But still, on certain late-spring days, she would remember her mother, the feel of her arms, the feel of her hair that last time. Only Grandma Peggy knew how much the loss still hurt.

"What happened next?" The moment Emma asked, a shadow fell over her face. "I mean, if you don't mind talking about it."

"I don't mind." Mary tried to look past the walls in Emma's heart. "There's a reason I tell this story."

Emma hugged herself tight. She was still shaking, partly because of the story, no doubt. But at least some of her jittery behavior had to be from needing a drug fix. She took another sip of her water. "It can't be easy."

"It isn't."

She raised one bony shoulder. "So why do it? Why tell it?"

"For you, Emma." Mary's throat was thick. "So you don't wind up like my mama. If maybe someone would've found her on the streets and told her the truth about Jesus, maybe . . . maybe everything would've turned out differently."

Emma didn't say another word. Her silence allowed Mary to fall back into the story, back as deep as she'd been before.

The part just ahead was one of the saddest of all.

Chapter 5

Jimbo and Lou had lied to her. They told Mary they were packing up their things and loading them into the back of Jimbo's truck so they could go find Mary's mother. Because her mama wasn't coming back, and they needed to go where she was.

"Why are we taking the couch and the dishes?" Mary had been ordered to stand along one of the walls so she wouldn't be in the way.

"I told you, kid." Jimbo gave her a mean look. "We need to find your mother."

"But why are we taking the stuff?"

"Because," Jimbo yelled from the doorway, "we ain't comin' back." His face was red, and sweaty drops ran down it. He and Lou were holding a chair between them. It looked like they might drop it.

Mary took a few steps toward them. "After we find my mommy, you mean?"

"Quit askin' questions. You'll have your answers soon enough."

When they finished packing, Jimbo grabbed her and pulled her toward the truck. Before they climbed in, he stopped and looked at her. His face was still red, and he smelled like dirty clothes. He put his hand on her cheek and smiled at her. Only something wasn't right about his smile because the bigger his mouth grew, the more his eyes got scary.

"You know what, little girl?" He moved his face close. His breath smelled like cigarettes.

She didn't want to answer him, so she turned her face. Where was her mama? How would Jimbo know where to find her? And how come her mother never said anything about Jimbo and Lou going away and taking all the chairs and beds?

Jimbo was still breathing at her. "Okay, don't talk to me." He laughed quietly. "I'll do the talking. One of these days real soon you're gonna make me a fortune. You know that, kid?"

She stuck her chin out. "What about my mama?"

"You'll see her soon enough." He put his hand on the back of her head and shoved her into the truck.

Not until they were an hour out of New York City did Jimbo look over his shoulder at her sitting in the backseat of the extended cab. He flashed her that scary smile and said, "Did we say we were gonna find your mama?" He glanced at the road and then back at her again. "Oops, I was wrong."

"Wrong?" Mary's voice was the smallest squeak. She scrunched herself against the seat and searched Jimbo's eyes through the rearview mirror. The red-beaded purse was in her lap, and on the seat next to her was a small bag of her clothes.

Lou took over. "Kid, what he's sayin' is your mama's gonna have to find us." She looked at her husband. "We're relocating."

Relocating? Mary had no idea what they were talking about. How could they move when her mama was coming back in just two more days? And how would she know where to find them? Fear circled her and squeezed her chest so she couldn't draw a full breath. She started to cry, and for a minute she got mad. Really mad. "Take . . . take me back to my mama!"

Jimbo shot her a look. "You're comin' with us, so quit your sniveling."

Mary continued to cry, but she kept herself quiet except for the pitiful sobs that slipped out every now and then. If she couldn't talk to Jimbo or Lou, she'd talk to God. The way Grandma Peggy would do if she were trapped in a truck heading away from everything she loved. *Dear Jesus, it's me, Mary. I don't know where they're taking me or what's happening. Please bring my mama back to me. She just had one more job, and then me and her were going back to Grandma Peggy's. Please, God.*

As she said the silent prayer, her fear faded. What had Grandma Peggy said? God had plans for her, plans for a good future, right? He would bring Mama to her, probably as soon as she was finished with her job.

Mary felt herself settle down. If her mama didn't come, she'd wait till Jimbo and Lou were asleep and she'd leave. She'd find her way to a nice family and ask for a ride back to her mama or Grandma Peggy's house. She clutched the little red purse more tightly. God would work it all out.

A lot of time passed. The tall buildings disappeared, and she started seeing trees and grass. Mary tried to think how long they'd been driving. At least long enough for one day's walk into the city, maybe two. It was a long time, more than she ever thought they'd drive. How would her mother find her, way out here in the country?

In the front seat Lou whispered something to Jimbo. He was still driving, and he looked at Mary over his shoulder. "That's a good girl. Nice and quiet." His lips came up in that sort of smile again. Only this time the light from the sun hit his golden tooth, and he looked *really* scary. Like a pirate.

She stared out the window again. So many trees. Never in all her life had she seen so many trees. They were pretty, but they made her tummy feel sick and rumbly. Because where would she find a friendly neighbor if she needed to leave in the nighttime? There were hardly any houses way out here in all the trees. Mary checked to see if Jimbo and Lou were watching her. They weren't. She looked down at the little purse, the tiny red beads.

The reason she had the purse was because she was wearing her shorts, her only ones. These were the best shorts of all because they had a deep pocket where she could hide her red purse, and that way Jimbo couldn't make her leave it behind.

For a while she ran her fingers over the outside of the purse and remembered what her grandma had said. That she would take care of Mary if ever her mama couldn't. Mary stared at the purse, and a thought came into her head. Maybe she would have to find Grandma Peggy first. Because where would her mama live, anyway? She would come home from her job and the apartment would be empty. She might go to Grandma Peggy's too. Maybe they could all meet there tomorrow.

Mary squinted at the little red purse and tried to remember the exact words her grandma had written on the piece of paper inside. She moved her quiet fingers slowly as could be so Jimbo and Lou wouldn't hear her. Then she opened the little purse and pulled out the note. She looked at it. Her grandma had said that it was special and that the words on the paper would always be important for her.

She unfolded it and studied the letters. They were strange and jumbly, and they reminded her of the sad truth: she couldn't read. But one day she would, because this year she was going to school. Grandma Peggy said so.

She sneaked another look at Jimbo and Lou, but their eyes were looking straight ahead, and when they talked it was too quiet for her to hear. Her eyes dropped down, and she looked at the note again. It felt special in her hands, but if Jimbo saw it he might take it away, and Lou might want her beautiful purse. So she folded the paper again and put it back where it belonged. Then she closed the purse and hid it in her pocket.

They drove and drove and drove, and after a while the roads got smaller and there were even more trees but fewer cars. Once they stopped at a gas station, and Jimbo gave her an apple and a candy bar. Mary had been very hungry, but she didn't want to say anything. The farther they got from the city the more she wasn't sure.

What if her mama didn't know where she was or how to find her? And what did Jimbo mean when he said she was going to make him a fortune?

After the gas station they drove a long time again, and finally Jimbo slowed the truck down. He turned onto a bumpy, rocky kind of road. It was skinny too. Mary was sure that only one car or truck could fit on it. They drove on the road until it went up high onto a hill, and that's when Mary thought of something. There were no other houses, no apartments or neighbors or buildings or anything. At the top of the hill there was just a little square building.

She had another thought, and she leaned forward. "Is this where my mama works?"

Jimbo climbed out of the truck, opened the back door, and pulled her out by the hand. "No, little girl." He smiled that mean smile again. "But it's where you'll work; that's for sure."

"What . . . what about Mama?" She slipped her hand into her pocket and felt the little beads brush against her fingers. "How will we find her?"

Jimbo opened his mouth like he might say something, but then he stood straight, shook his head, and pulled her along.

She didn't want to go, so she dug her heels into the ground a little. But Jimbo was stronger than her. A lot stronger. He yanked her hard, and she fell onto her knees. In a flash she got back on her feet because she didn't want the little purse to fall onto the ground. When she was standing, Jimbo dragged her along behind him. Lou followed with a bag of stuff from the truck.

When they reached three little steps, Mary had the most scared feeling ever. "What is this place, Jimbo? Where are we?"

He stopped and looked at her, and even with the outside air she could smell his stinky mouth. "This, little girl, is your new home." He took her inside and sat her in a corner. The cabin was small, even smaller than the apartment. It had a little room and a kitchen, and that's all she could see. It felt dark and lonely and cold. Then Jimbo pointed at her, and his dirty fingernail came real close to her face. "Don't go talkin' about your mama. Don't say a word or I'll slap your pretty face, got it?"

Mary put her hand over her cheek and pushed herself back against the wall. She slid down to the floor and nodded, but she didn't say anything else. Because what could she say? Jimbo said not to talk about her mother, and that's all she wanted to talk about. Instead she pulled her knees up really close to her chin and wrapped her arms around her legs. Then she put her head down and closed her eyes and thought about everything her mama had said, about how she was just going to work and she'd be back in three days.

But as darkness came and Jimbo and Lou brought all their old stuff inside, Mary heard Lou say something that was even scarier than the feeling she had when she walked inside this place. She said, "When're you gonna tell the kid her mama ain't comin' back? Maybe then she'll quit buggin' us."

Mary lifted her head and stood up. Her arms and legs were shaking, and she leaned against the wall so she wouldn't fall. "What?" She was scared but not so scared that she was going to sit still. Not if her mother wasn't coming back. "What'd you say?"

Jimbo and Lou stopped and turned so they could see her. Jimbo waved his hand in the air. "You heard Lou . . . your mama ain't comin' back. Okay?" He let his arms fall to his sides. "What'd you think? That she had a receptionist job out here in the hill country?"

Hill country? Was that where they were? And what was the hill country, anyway? Was it a place her mama could find? If not, then how were they going to find each other again? She started crying. Not loud, but with lots and lots of tears. Her body felt hurt or broken. Or maybe it was her heart.

"What ya cryin' for, ya brat?" Jimbo came three big steps closer. "You'll have all you need here." He looked at Lou, then back at Mary. "Besides, your mama, well . . . she died. She got hit by a car in the city, so don't go cryin' about her anymore. She ain't comin' back."

Mary shook her head. Her mouth opened because she wanted to scream at Jimbo and tell him he was a liar. Her mommy was at work, and she'd be looking for Mary in the morning. "No . . . no, she's not dead!"

"Shut the brat up." Lou waved in Mary's direction and took a drink from the refrigerator, something in a silver can.

"Fine." Jimbo came closer and took her hand. "If this is how you want it, we'll show you to your room."

He pulled her to a door, opened it, and showed her a long row of stairs that led to the basement. Once her mother had taken her to stay with one of her boyfriends, and they had made her stay in the basement.

But that wasn't where she wanted to go. How would her mommy ever find her down in the basement of this little boxy house in the trees? Wait, not in the trees . . . in the hill country? "Jimbo, stop!" She squirmed, but she couldn't get free. "I don't wanna go down there!"

"You're going! This is where your room is," he growled. When they reached the bottom, Mary saw a dirty couch against the wall. Jimbo brushed off some leaves and maybe a few spiders. Then he yanked her arm and threw her onto the middle cushion.

"Why are you doing this?" she screamed. Her tears came so hard she couldn't see, but she wasn't even sad. She was mad—very, very mad. Jimbo and Lou had done all of this. "Take me back to the apartment so I can see my mommy."

"Shut up!" Jimbo slapped her hard across the face, so hard her teeth hurt. "Shut up or I'll give you something to cry about." He spread out his fingers and pushed her face so she fell back against the couch. "Don't say another word." He stood straighter, and his eyes got a funny look. The one that scared her every time. "Get a good night's sleep and don't turn on the lights. Tomorrow's your big day, little Mary. The first day of the rest of your life, and you know what?"

Mary turned her face from him.

"You're gonna make me a rich man." He leaned in and touched her where no one was ever supposed to touch her. "Rich and happy."

The first thing Mary did when he pounded up the stairs was reach into her shorts pocket. The purse with the red beads was still there. Even though her whole life felt like it was going crazy, she knew she would be okay. As long as she had the purse. Because that purse had the words that told her God loved her and that He had plans for her. It was proof that her Grandma Peggy loved her too. Her mother might not know where to find her, but her grandma would know, because her grandma was smart. She knew everything.

She pressed the purse to her chest and had a thought. She had to hide it; otherwise Jimbo or Lou would take it for sure. But first she wanted to hold it and remember how it felt to be in her pink bedroom, the one at Grandma Peggy's house. That's where life was happy and good and safe, and that's where she wanted to be right now. There with her mama's arms around her. She brought the purse up to her cheek, the hot one where Jimbo had hit her. It felt soft and cool, and she felt the fear start to leave her.

She was alone in the basement of a house she didn't know, but tomorrow . . . tomorrow her mother and her grandma would find her. They would find her and yell at Jimbo and take her away. She lowered the purse and looked at it once more. "I miss you, Mama." Tears started to come, and she blinked them away. "You too, Grandma." She closed her eyes and thought about God. *Jesus, it's me, Mary. I'm lost and I need some help, okay? Maybe You could find my mama and my grandma and tell them where I am.*

A noise happened upstairs. Something loud, like a book hitting a wall.

Mary gasped and looked around the dark basement. There was one window, and through it a bit of light came in. Just enough so she could see things around her. Where should she hide the purse? It had to be somewhere she could reach, somewhere Jimbo and Lou wouldn't find it.

Mary shivered. The basement had nothing in it really. Just the couch and a few boxes. Someone could move the boxes, so she decided on the couch, the place where she was sitting. That would be the best spot. She slid the purse down behind the seat part, deep down into the crack. Then she pulled her hand back and looked. It was too far down to see, but what if it was too far down to get again? She quickly reached into the crack and there it was. Safe and sound.

"Stay there, little purse." She left it hiding in the crack of the couch, and then she lay down. She thought about her mother and her grandma and all the things she'd tell them when they found her. She'd tell them how awful Jimbo was and how he'd hit her. They'd be very mad about that. Then she thought about school, how nice it would be to learn about the letters and words and how to read.

It was getting colder, and Mary wasn't sure she could sleep. She could never sleep well when she was cold. She stood up and looked around again, and that's when she spotted a blanket on the back of the couch. She pulled it down and spread it out so it covered her. Finally, just before she fell asleep, she thought of something else. Jimbo's words: *"You're gonna make me a rich man . . . rich and happy."*

Mary thought and thought and thought, but she couldn't figure out what Jimbo meant by that. What could she do that would make him rich and happy? She was still wondering when morning came and Lou brought her a bowl of oatmeal and a banana. "Leave your dishes on the bottom step," Lou told her. "I'll get 'em later."

It was a new day, Mary told herself. The day when her mama and her grandma would come. Maybe when she was finished eating. But when she was done and she put her bowl on the stairs with the banana peel inside, Jimbo opened the basement door and stared at her. He came down.

His face had that strange look, and when he reached the couch he smiled at her. "Today's the day, Mary."

"What are you—?" But Mary never finished her question.

He came closer, and he did unspeakable things to her that made her scream—even after he stopped. She felt dead, inside and out, and she threw up her breakfast. Lou came down and cleaned it up.

For three days no one came down to the basement except when Lou brought her food.

Then one afternoon another man came. A man she'd never seen before. He took one look at her and grinned the way the devil grinned in cartoons. Then he gave Jimbo a handful of dollar bills.

Jimbo smiled. "She's all yours." He thudded back upstairs, and now it was the new man's turn.

"This is our special visit, little girl," the man told her. Then just like Jimbo, he hurt her and did awful things while she screamed for her mama and her grandma. "Help me!" She scratched at the man. "Someone, help!"

But no one came and helped, not that day or the next or the day after that. She tried to think of a way to escape. But where would she go and how would she find her way home to her grandma's house? Was this what Jimbo had meant when he said that tomorrow was the first day of the rest of her life? her new life? If so, then she wanted to die.

Mary had no answers, nothing but a sick emptiness. And by the end of the week—with Jimbo and the other man making special visits to the basement—she didn't have to wonder how she was going to make Jimbo a rich and happy man.

She already knew.

Chapter 6

Emma felt like she was going to pass out. She slid forward and steadied herself on the edge of her chair. "I . . . I have to go."

The voices were back. *Yes, go, Emma. Go buy the drugs and get it over with. No one loves you, no one'll miss you.*

The fog in Mary's eyes cleared. She was a counselor again, sharp and in control, no longer lost in the sickening days of her tenth year. "We're finished for today." Her tone was firm but tender. "You can get your girls and go to your room. We've assigned you to one on the third floor. We have a library on the first floor and a craft table off the kitchen. If you and your children want to watch a movie, there's a den with a television and a VCR on your floor."

Crafts and movies? Emma shook her head. "I don't know."

That wasn't what she wanted, was it? She looked out the window. Clouds had gathered, and it was starting to rain. That was okay; she could still find a dealer, still get enough junk to be dead in an hour.

And everyone'll thank you for it, Emma. Your life's been a waste for years now, so leave . . . go get it done. You're trash, and trash needs to be taken out and—

"Emma?"

The voices stopped. Emma shot a look at Mary. "I'm not sure about anything." She needed to flee. The girls were better off without her. If she hadn't wound up here at the women's shelter, she would've been on the streets. And then something terrible could've happened to her girls, the same way it had happened to Mary. The thought was too much to bear. They'd all be better off if she left through the front door and never—

"You promised me you'd come back for the rest of the story." There was a depth to Mary's words that stopped Emma's thoughts in their tracks.

She *did* promise that, didn't she? But wasn't it obvious where Mary's story went from there? Mary was abused for years, and then she managed to pull herself up from the grime and trouble of the street, get herself educated, and make something of herself.

It was a Cinderella story, not something that could bring any real hope for Emma and her girls. They'd still be better off without her. She shrugged. "You were trampled by that guy, and after you grew up, you made good for yourself, right?"

Mary's smile fell. "No. My story gets worse. And in the end—I wasn't strong enough to save myself from any of it."

Emma sat back. Not strong enough? Mary Madison? And how could her story get worse? It was enough to convince Emma to end it all. If Mary's story got worse, then her story was bound to get worse too. It was more than she could stand, more than she could imagine going through, especially with two little girls who—

"Emma, are you hearing me?" Mary touched Emma's knee. "I know what you're thinking." She smiled, and in it was that same hope Emma had felt earlier. "My story gets worse, but it isn't finished. Yours isn't either."

Yes, it is, Emma. You're finished. Take the drugs and be done with it.

"I need time." Emma hugged herself and pressed her arms against her middle.

"You need more than that." Mary eased back and folded her hands. "But you're not ready."

Emma's heart raced. "I won't ever be ready. I'm not like you."

"Battered women, abused women—inside we're all alike." Mary's voice seemed to get quieter, calmer even as the tension in the room built. "Our story is the same, and freedom can only come one way."

A drug overdose, Emma thought. *That's the only way out of this nightmare.*

"Can I be blunt?"

Emma swallowed hard. She wanted to bolt from the room and the building as fast as she could. Instead she exhaled hard. "Go ahead."

"Taking your life isn't the way out."

What? The voices had nothing to say. How could Mary have known what she was thinking? what she wanted to do? She felt the blood leave her face. "How . . . did you know?"

"I told you." Mary lowered her chin, her gaze direct. No one had ever talked to Emma this way before. "I've sat in your chair before. I almost believed the lie that killing myself was the only way to find freedom. But it isn't, Emma." Her tone grew more stern. "You do that, and the nightmare will continue as long as your daughters live. Every day of their lives they'll wonder why their mama didn't love them enough to live."

The shock was sharp and immediate. Emma had been telling herself that a drug overdose would set her daughters free. Someone could take them and raise them or give them to her mother, Grace. Everyone would be better off. But now . . . what if it happened the way Mary said? What if they went through life angry and hurt because their mother wasn't around? They might end up worse than if she lived.

Emma kept her lips tightly pressed together, but inside her heart she felt something change. The desperate urge to run began to dissolve, and in its place came a knowing. She *could* get through the day. Maybe take the girls to the craft table or watch a movie with them. Something to pass the time until she could be back in this room again, hear the rest of Mary's story, and find out if she was right.

If the two of them really did share the same story.

The look on Mary's face said she knew she'd won. She stood, took Emma's hand, and helped her to her feet. "I'll see you at nine tomorrow morning."

"Okay." Emma drew back and hugged herself again. She wanted to see her girls. But first she looked hard at Mary.

"Thank you. For taking the time." Before Mary could say anything else, Emma turned and left. As quickly as she could, she took light running steps to the day-care room.

The same old woman was there, sitting on a small sofa reading to Kami and Kaitlyn, who were sitting on either side of her. When she heard Emma, the woman looked up. "Hi." She closed the book and grinned at the girls. "We'll finish reading tomorrow."

Kami noticed her first. Her eyes lit up. She jumped off the sofa and ran toward her, arms open wide. "Mommy!"

Behind her, Kaitlyn eased herself down and came running too.

The older woman smiled and set the book down. "I have some paperwork in my office. You three look like you'll be just fine without me," she said before she quietly left.

Emma immediately dropped to her knees. The girls came to her, and she pulled them in close to her chest. Her precious daughters. How could she overdose and leave them alone, without their mommy? The voices were wrong. Her girls needed her. A chill passed over her spine, and she felt a wave of nausea. She'd come so close. If Mary hadn't said something at the end, she might be buying the drugs right now.

Kami pulled back enough so they could see each other. "We missed you, Mommy. Where have you been?"

"Talking to a nice lady." Emma's words stuck in her throat. Looking into Kami's eyes was like looking into Mary's, the way they must've looked when Mary was a little girl. Not that they shared any physical resemblance, but there were inno-

cence and trust in her daughter's eyes that must've been in
Mary's at one time.

Until she had been kidnapped and locked in that basement.

Without warning, tears flooded her eyes and spilled onto
her face. What sort of life had she made for her girls? At every
turn she'd gone against her mother's wishes. Gone against
God. In the process she'd exposed her girls to violent abuse
and drugs.

She buried her face against them as her sobs came in
waves. How many nights had she been so high that she didn't
feed them dinner? And how many of Charlie's friends had
been around them, holding them and teasing them? It was
a miracle something hadn't already happened to them.

"Mommy—" Kaitlyn stroked her hair and dabbed her
fingertips against Emma's face—"why sad?"

Kami took a turn, brushing her soft knuckles against
Emma's cheeks. "Mommy's having a hard day."

Mommy's having a hard day were words she'd told her girls
hundreds of times. *Mommy can't make breakfast. . . . Mommy can't
take you for a walk. . . . Mommy can't see out of her right eye. . . .
Mommy can't lift you up. . . .*

Because she was too wasted on drugs or too exhausted
from all she'd consumed the day before or too beaten up to be
the mother they needed. And always she said the same thing:
"Mommy's having a hard day." Her girls must've heard that
nearly every day of their lives.

She pushed her sobs down to the deepest part of her heart,
the part that never stopped crying. "Girls . . . Mommy's sorry."

Neither girl said anything, but Kami patted her head and

kissed the tip of her nose. Kaitlyn drew closer, her head on Emma's shoulder.

They were the sweetest girls. If she hadn't come to the shelter, she might've lost them by now. Maybe she would've taken enough junk that she lost track of the girls. They could've been kidnapped or sold into slavery. Anything was possible. "God . . ." His name was a cry, a quiet moan on her lips. "I'm sorry."

The girls sensed somehow that this was different than any other time their mother had been upset before. They clung to her, and Kami started to whimper. Emma closed her eyes and savored the feel of her precious daughters in her arms. What if she'd lost them? What if she'd killed herself the way she'd planned to do? She would never have had a moment like this again. Instead here she was, and suddenly the sorrow and fear and heartbreak that represented her life cleared long enough for her to feel one very real, very clear emotion.

Gratitude.

However it had happened, she was here. Despite her fear and the fact that every inch of her body screamed for a fix, she was here. She had her girls and her life and her hope because Mary had more of the story to tell. What was it Mary had said? Her story wasn't finished, and neither was Emma's.

Finally as she dried her tears and kissed her girls' cheeks, as she took their little hands in hers and led them to the craft table, she was overwhelmed by one single possibility.

Maybe Mary was right.

Chapter 7

Grace Johnson had never missed her husband more. If Jay were here, he would've known how to find Emma and the girls, how to reach them and bring them home. Instead, she wandered alone around her small three-bedroom house across the river from the nation's capital.

How could God have allowed this, and how had everything gotten so bad? Grace hadn't gone a day without blaming herself since Emma left home years ago.

The last time Grace had dropped by to see Emma she had realized how bad things really were when she'd seen for herself the bruises on Emma's face, the finger marks on her arms. The way the girls had cowered behind Emma even after they saw that the person at the door was their own grandmother broke her heart.

Grace could still see the horror on Emma's face. "Mama! I told you never to drop in without calling!"

The situation had been horrific, so much worse than Grace had ever imagined. Not only was Emma battered, she was painfully thin and her fingers trembled. Sure signs that she'd found her way back to taking crack. Grace wanted to take her and the girls home and never let them back on the streets again. But that wouldn't work any better than it had worked when Emma first moved out.

Grace had taken a step inside the apartment and let her gaze dart around the room. There were broken windows and dents on the wall. Pieces of a vase lay near one of the baseboards. "What—" she'd looked at Emma, her mouth open— "what has he done to you?"

Emma didn't answer. The look on her face told the obvious—she couldn't answer. Instead she shook her head and blinked fast. "I'll figure it out myself, Mama." She put her arms around the girls and pulled them to her sides. "It's not like it looks. Everything's fine."

Fine? Grace took a step closer. "Look at your arms." She brushed her fingers across her daughter's bruises. "How could he do this?" Her eyes lifted to Emma's. "It *is* like it looks."

For the next five minutes she had begged Emma to leave Charlie and come with her, to get help and counseling and a new start.

But Emma had shrieked at her, pointing at the door. *"You're the problem, Mama! Leave me alone."* She pushed herself past the girls and opened the front door. "We'll figure it out ourselves."

But they hadn't, of course. Grace left and called the next morning. When no one answered, she went back to the apartment and knocked on the door.

Charlie answered, his eyes bloodshot.

Grace wanted to spit at him. Instead she looked into the room, peering around him. "Where is she?" Her tone was beyond angry. She wanted him in jail for what he'd done to her daughter.

Charlie was scraggly with dark hair and unkempt facial hair. He reeked of cigarette smoke and something else—something strangely sweet. Drugs, probably. He took a step back and shut the door all but a few inches. "She's gone. Took the girls."

"Fine." Adrenaline raced through Grace. "I'll stay outside until she gets back."

"Look . . ." Charlie flung the door open and gestured toward the apartment. The smell of smoke grew stronger. "She's gone. She ain't comin' back. She's a crackhead, and she needed a fix." He shrugged. "She'd sell her soul for a fix."

Sell her soul? Fear reached up and grabbed her around the throat. If Emma was that far gone, maybe Charlie was right. She'd been through bad bouts with drugs before. They made her crazy, desperate. Grace pinched her fingers against her temples and squeezed her eyes shut. *Think . . . please, God, help me think.*

She blinked and looked at Charlie again. "Where'd she go? She must've told you." Her daughter had no family in the area, no one except her. No matter how she'd messed up, regardless of her poor choices, Grace had always known where to find her.

Until now.

"Listen, lady, she's gone. If you see her, tell her I'm looking for her. She owes me a thousand dollars." Charlie slammed the door in her face.

Grace left, not sure where to go, what to do. She called the police the next day and filed a missing person's report, but no one was going to put man-hours on a case like Emma's. Women left their men all the time. It didn't necessarily mean that something bad had happened to her. But still . . .

What if Charlie had let things get out of hand? What if he'd hurt her and the girls . . . or worse? Where would Grace or the police begin to look then? In all her life she had never imagined her daughter living with a man—not when she'd been raised to believe such a thing was wrong. But to think she lived with an *abusive* man who hit her and threatened her and raged at her . . .

Finally, several days after she disappeared, Emma had called from a pay phone. "Mama, don't worry about me and the girls." Her voice was cool. "We're fine."

"Thank You, God!" Grace's heart pounded so hard she could barely hear her own whispered voice. "Are you back at Charlie's?"

"No." Emma sounded rushed. "I don't want to get into it. I just didn't want you thinking something bad had happened to us." There were soft voices in the background. "Look, Mama, I gotta go."

The phone shook in Grace's hand. "Call again soon, all right? I'm worried about you."

Emma said good-bye, and that was it. Whatever had happened between them back along the trail of years, the chasm was a mile wide, too far to cross. Somewhere between pigtails and prom dresses, Grace had lost her only daughter, maybe forever.

Half the time Grace felt as if she were stuck in some horrible nightmare. As if she'd stumbled into someone else's life. And nothing—not prayer or phone calls to the police or walks through the heart of Washington, DC—helped her find Emma and the girls. She had to rely on the information from that one call, had to believe what her daughter had said.

Emma and the girls were safe.

It still didn't make sense that Emma would choose a life of abuse and drugs over a life of love and safety back at home. That and her good friend Terrence, of course. Terrence had loved her since she was a sophomore in high school. He was still single and plodding through medical school now, trying to figure out why Emma left, why he hadn't been enough for her.

Grace grabbed a can opener from the top drawer beneath the microwave and tapped it on the counter. She'd had no appetite since Emma and the girls left Charlie, but she had to eat. Otherwise she wouldn't have the strength to keep looking, to always keep looking. She opened the cupboard and stared at a shelf full of canned goods. She decided on two— a small can of diced chicken and a can of black beans. The can opener fit neatly on the edge of the bean can, and the lid was off in a few twists of the handle.

Life's done that to me, she thought. *Cut into me and sliced off the top layer. Now my heart's bare for everyone to see. Right, God?* She emptied the can into a glass bowl. *Right?*

I am here, daughter. . . . Your ways are not My ways.

"Stop!" Grace slammed the can on the counter. Her breaths

came fast and hard. "If You're here, then where are Emma and
the girls?" Maybe the quiet voice in her soul was God talking
to her. Maybe not. But every time she thought to pray lately
it was there. God was here; He had everything in control.
Her ways were not His.

But as long as her girls were missing, she didn't want to
hear the voice of God traipse across her heart delivering
false hope. If God had something to say to her, then how
about handing over Emma's whereabouts? That would be
something useful. A bunch of pithy platitudes weren't
enough anymore, not when the people she loved most
were living on the streets.

Grace opened the other can and dumped the chicken
over the beans. The mess looked like something she
might've found in the disposal or gathered at the bottom
of the trash can. She shuddered. It would be better warmed
up. She heated it in the microwave and took it to the small
dining room. The table was slightly lopsided, but it was
the same table she'd had for fifteen years and it would do.
No matter how frustrated she was at God, she still bowed
her head. "Thank You for the food, God. You know the rest.
Amen."

Emma and the girls were all she had left. Didn't God
understand that?

The window in the kitchen was open, and she looked
toward it. The sunshine had been constant since Memorial
Day, and now that it was the end of June, the temperature
matched the season. Hot and humid and drawn out, day after
day after day. Most grandmas worried about whether their

grandchildren had sunscreen and enough water on a day like this one. Not Grace. She worried about whether Kami and Kaitlyn had a place to sleep and enough food.

She pulled her spoon through the chicken and beans and ate a few bites. They went down like so many boulders. If only Jay were still alive. He'd been everything to her. He was the one who had told her about Jesus. She ate another bite, chewing slower than before.

Jay Paul Johnson had been Grace's knight in shining armor. Yes, he'd worn a leather jacket and driven a Harley, but he was her knight all the same. Without him, she might've gone the same route as Emma. She had been headed that way after all. Her own parents had left her for a life of crime, and both wound up in jail. She had been raised by her aunt and uncle in Jersey, and by the time she was seventeen she was sick of their rules and curfews and distrustful glances.

Seventeen was supposed to be wonderful. She felt free and fun-loving and anxious to find her way. Sure, she hung out with a wilder crowd, and sometimes she came home stone drunk. But she wasn't that bad, and she didn't appreciate her aunt and uncle giving her lectures.

Grace took another bite of chicken and shook her head. She was lucky her aunt and uncle hadn't kicked her out. No matter how she viewed herself back then, the reality was clear. She'd been wild and rebellious. The summer before her eighteenth birthday, her attitude had been terrible—especially toward her aunt.

One night she had a visit from Lindy, a girl her age who lived at the end of the block. . . .

"Let's take the train into the city," Lindy suggested. "I met a guy there." She was smacking her gum, and her mascara was thicker than usual.

"I don't know . . ." Grace sucked at the inside of her cheek. Going into the city could mean trouble for two girls alone at night.

"Live a little, Grace. Come on." Lindy was black, like her. The two of them shared hairstyles and clothes, and both turned heads wherever they went. Now Lindy's eyes shone with excitement over the possibilities that lay ahead. "This guy told me about a place where we can make a lot of money—" she looked over her shoulder to make sure Grace's aunt couldn't hear—"fast money."

Grace had a pretty good idea where girls dressed like Lindy might make a lot of fast money. The idea scared her, but at the same time she didn't want to spend another night with her aunt and uncle. Finally she tossed her hands in the air. "All right. But if it feels dangerous, let's come back."

Lindy rolled her eyes. She took hold of Grace's hand and shoved her in the direction of her bedroom. "Get ready. Hurry up."

While Grace was dolling herself up, she thought about what she was doing. Maybe it would be exciting out on the streets at night. It was a way out of the house, and if it brought in enough money . . . well, then in time she could leave and start life on her own.

But when they got downtown to the place where the guy

was supposed to meet them, there was Jay instead. He spotted them and revved the engine of his bike. With a nod in their direction, he pulled up, parked his Harley, and approached them. "You ladies look awful young for this neighborhood." He was a white guy, and his face was covered with hair. But his eyes—kind and warm and deep and blue—would haunt Grace until the day she died.

When they didn't respond, he spoke louder. "I said, you ladies look awful young for these parts."

"What's it to you?" Grace stepped up to him, chin raised, voice defiant. "We can do whatever we want. Age doesn't matter."

"Actually, it does." He straightened, and she guessed he was well over six feet tall. "It matters because once you start working these streets, you leave one of two ways. Hard and old and used, an old lady at thirty."

Lindy smacked her gum and gave Jay a sarcastic look. "And the other?"

He leveled his eyes straight at her. "In a body bag."

Something about that image had snapped Grace's cool exterior. She turned to Lindy, struggling to stay in control. "Maybe he's right. Who needs the street stuff? Let's go home."

"That's my good girls." He crossed his arms and smiled. "Go home and don't ever come back."

Just then a car screeched to a stop a few feet away. There were four young guys inside—one white, two black, and one Hispanic. They were loud and drunk, and they hooted at Grace and Lindy. "Hey, girls, wanna take a ride?" The driver honked his horn, and the other three burst out laughing.

"The ladies aren't working, fellers." Jay planted his hands on his hips and took three strides toward the carful of guys. "Be on your way."

"Wait!" Lindy ran to the car before Jay or Grace could stop her. She looked over her shoulder once. "I'm going to do things my way. You can come or you can go home, Grace. Your choice."

Grace looked at Jay, and there they were again—those amazing eyes.

He lowered his voice so only she could hear it. "Anyone ever tell you about the Bible? about a God who loves you and wants to be your friend?" He nodded at the car and at Lindy, who had already climbed into the backseat with two of the guys. "God wants more for you than that." His voice was soothing, like healing oil for the cracks in her soul. "Believe me. Come on."

The driver of the car yelled at Grace, "You comin' or not?"

Next to him, another guy was peeling off twenties from a pile in his hands and handing them to Lindy. "Come on, pretty friend." He held the bills up. "Plenty to go around."

Jay took gentle hold of her arm. "I'll take you home. Let's go."

She looked at Lindy and the guys and then at Jay and back at Lindy one more time. Then she took a step in Jay's direction, just one single step. And it was a step that changed her life. Jay helped her onto the back of his bike, and for the next forty minutes she clung to him as if she were clinging to the only hope she had. She had no reason, really. Nothing to prove he was honest or that he really wanted to help her.

But when they reached her aunt and uncle's house, they stayed outside and talked. Jay was twenty-two, a few years older than her. He was part of a motorcycle group that called themselves Christ's Motor Angels. They rode through the worst parts of town a few evenings each week looking for people who needed a way out, people like Grace and Lindy.

"Usually we bring 'em home, give 'em a little tract about salvation in Christ, and leave it at that," Jay told her. He took off his jacket and laid it over the back of his Harley. He had on a cut-off T-shirt.

Grace saw a tattoo on his shoulder that read *All or Nothing*. She looked hard at it and ran her finger over the letters. "All or nothing?"

"That's what God wants. Give Him our all or give Him nothing." He shrugged. "Pretty simple."

Something about Jay stirred strange, mysterious feelings in Grace's heart. He was a rebel—or at least he looked like one. That meant her aunt and uncle definitely wouldn't approve. They were straitlaced and went to potluck dinners. Sunday services and Wednesday church nights. A motorcycle man— even a motorcycle man for Jesus—would never be acceptable to them.

Maybe it was that or the way he made Jesus seem so real. Whatever it was, Grace couldn't get enough of Jay Johnson. At the end of the night she told him yes. Not yes to the sort of question most men asked, because Jay wanted nothing sexual from her, not at all. Rather she told him yes about Jesus. Yes, she wanted to be cleansed from her sins, and yes, she

wanted a relationship with God and yes—most of all yes—
she wanted a Savior.

When Jay started to leave, he turned to her and grinned.
"Can I call you sometime?"

And Grace said yes to that too.

Jay called her the next morning, and after that they were
inseparable. She told her aunt and uncle about Jay's faith and
that he was the nicest guy she'd ever met. But still they were
suspicious.

Her uncle pulled her aside after meeting Jay for the first
time. He raised an eyebrow at her. "Doesn't look like your
type, Grace."

"He's a Christian, remember?"

"So you've said. Still . . . I'd keep a close eye on him."

Her aunt was even worse, saying only a few words to Jay
and making it obvious by her expressions that she didn't
approve. A week later Grace found out why. "White guys
want one thing from black girls, Grace."

"Are you kidding?" She was furious at her aunt. "That's a
horrible thing to say! All my life you've taught me that color
doesn't matter and it's wrong to be judged because of your
race. Color this and color that." Her voice was louder than
she intended. "How dare you think Jay's like that just because
he's white." She anchored her fists on her hips. "Maybe *you*
should stop judging people by their color."

Her aunt backed off then. "I'm sorry." She made her tone
calm again. "I . . . I guess I didn't see it that way."

After that, her aunt and uncle gave Jay more of a chance.
They didn't like motorcycles or beards or tattoos. But after a

month they liked Jay. He had that way about him. At the end of their first year of dating, two things happened that Grace would remember all her life.

First, Lindy overdosed on drugs on the very street where Jay had first found them. She'd been making money as a prostitute, hiding the fact from her parents. The double life caused her so much pain inside that nothing helped ease it—not even Grace's pleas. Finally—as it did with so many girls who sold their dignity—the desperation drove Lindy to drugs, and the drugs killed her.

The second thing was that Jay Johnson asked her to be his wife. "You're young, but I don't need another year or five years to know you're the one for me." He had been so careful with her, kissing her only once in a while and never asking more of her than what God would've allowed. Now he merely cradled the side of her face with the palm of his hand. "Please, Grace. Marry me?"

She couldn't answer him. Not because she had any doubts, but because the emotion in her heart had spilled into her eyes and down along her throat, and she couldn't talk if she'd wanted to. She threw her arms around him, her wonderful prince. And when she found the words she whispered them into his muscled chest, "Yes, Jay, I'll marry you."

Jay was a mechanic by day—and a good one. He made enough money to pay for a beautiful church wedding. Most of Christ's Motor Angels attended and filled up one side of the pews, while her aunt and uncle and their nicely dressed conservative friends filled up the other.

"I don't think anyone's ever had two more different sets of

guests at a wedding," Jay told her as they danced in the church hall after the ceremony. "But you know what?"

"What?" The hall might as well have been the queen's ballroom, because Grace had never felt more like a princess.

"It's good for them." He leaned in and kissed her forehead, showing the tenderness that had marked their relationship. "Because people can't be judged by their clothes or their hair or their skin. But only by the way they love Jesus."

It was a good motto, one that drove Jay back onto the streets to rescue young girls even after the two of them had settled into a house and begun experiencing the thrill of married life. And it was thrilling. Night after night, knowing the safety of Jay's arms, the height of his passion for her. And days spent working at Patty's Preschool down the street, coming home to make dinner. Pot roast was Jay's favorite. He'd come into the kitchen, kiss her on the mouth, and pull her close. It didn't matter if he smelled like sweat and grime and car grease.

She would've stayed in his embrace forever.

A year after they were married she was pregnant. Jay was in the hospital room when Emma was born. She had light brown skin and enormous blue eyes, a perfect mix of the two of them. Emma was the name Jay picked out, so it was the only name Grace ever considered. Because Jay was the best man she'd ever known. The best person. If their daughter had half his traits she'd be an angel in her own right.

The first time Jay held their daughter, he had tears in his eyes. "God is so good!" He nuzzled his face against hers and looked into her eyes. "Daddy's going to be here for you, baby. Forever and ever. I'll protect you the way I protect all little girls."

But it wasn't to be.

Three months later Jay was out with two other Motor Angels when they ran across a frightened teenage girl and a gang of guys hassling her on the street. Grace was never quite sure what happened that night, but the police figured that Jay and the others pulled up and tried to scare the guys away.

Only this wasn't just any group of guys they were messing with. It was a pimp and his cronies, the ones who ran the prostitution ring along that entire city block. Whatever happened next, the pimp ended up pulling out a .45 and shooting two of the Motor Angels dead on the spot.

Jay Johnson—hero and prince, father and husband— had been one of them.

Grace poked her spoon into the chicken and beans, and she realized that her cheeks were wet. She was crying, so caught up in her own memories that it was like they were happening all over again.

When the police officer had knocked on her door late that night, the night Jay went out with the Motor Angels, Grace knew. She had known it as surely as she could hear her infant daughter suddenly wailing in the other room.

Jay was dead.

She tried another bite of the chicken and beans, but the mixture was cold and it struggled on the way down her throat. Enough. She pushed the bowl back, and her eyes found the photo that had hung on the wall every day since she and Jay were married. The one that would hang there until she died. It wasn't a traditional wedding photo, the kind most people had with the white dress and dark tuxedo and floral bouquet.

Rather it was the two of them on Jay's bike, him with a leather jacket over his suit coat and her with her wedding dress hiked up to her knees, her arms tight around Jay's waist. It was a picture of everything he'd meant to her. Because that was how he'd rescued her in the first place, on the back of his bike. And that was how he wanted to take her into the future. Him leading the way, telling her more about Jesus every day and always finding time to live out the things he told her.

"Jay Johnson . . . I miss you," she whispered, and a few fresh tears blurred her vision. "If only you were here."

Grace stood and put the bowl of mush in the sink, washed it down the disposal, and returned to the photograph once more. If only there were a way back to yesterday, a long string of yesterdays.

She wouldn't go back to the day Emma had left home and moved into Charlie's place or even back to the days before Emma started taking drugs. She would return to that evening when Emma was three months old. This time when Jay Johnson kissed her and told her good-bye, she would grab him by the arms and beg him to stay. Because if anyone ever needed a Motor Angel it wasn't the strangers on the street.

It was their very own daughter.

If Jay had lived, Emma never would've left home. She wouldn't have gotten pregnant as a teenager, and she wouldn't have started taking crack. Jay's mesmerizing power would've captivated their daughter, and she would've grown up doing everything right, as right as a teenager possibly could. Grace had no doubts. Emma would be married to Terrence, and Kami and Kaitlyn would have a wonderful home.

If only Jay had lived.

Chapter 8

Emma woke early the next morning and felt her little girls on either side of her. She hadn't had crack for two days, and her body screamed for a fix. But the noise dimmed compared to the sweet breathing sounds her girls made beside her.

How long had it been since she'd had a morning like this, where she and the girls were safe and warm and she wasn't hungover from the effects of drugs? She ran her fingers gently over first Kami's forehead, then Kaitlyn's. Somehow in the light of day, her troubles didn't seem nearly as bad as Mary's had been.

The idea of running and finding a dealer, overdosing on junk, and leaving her girls alone in the world seemed ludicrous now in the morning light. Her girls were safe, and despite years of bad decisions on her part, they'd been spared the sort of childhood Mary had suffered through.

Forget about the drugs. It's Charlie you need, Emma. Go back to him today. Don't wait another hour.

Emma yawned. Yes, that was it. She would climb out of bed, wake the girls, and get everyone dressed. Then she would thank the women at the shelter for their help and go home to Charlie. She loved him, didn't she? Yes, he had an anger problem, but he was trying to work through it.

He might take you back, if you're lucky. You aren't worth having someone love you, not even Charlie.

The voice was there, but it was quieter than it had been in months. Charlie would take her back if she handled herself right. She could promise to pay him everything she owed him and ask him to ease up a little on her. Then he'd see what she was seeing—how precious and wonderful the girls were—and he'd want a normal life like other families. A life where he didn't rage at her or hit her, one that included romantic dates and family outings to the park, where the girls could play on the swings.

That could happen, couldn't it?

She slid her feet onto the floor and stretched. As she did, she caught a glimpse of her reflection in the mirror. Her entire left cheek was still splotched with dark smears from the bruises Charlie had left on her the last time they were together.

He won't hurt you again, Emma. Go back to him. Leave the shelter and the crazy ideas about God and change. You don't deserve that. You're wasting their time.

Emma held on to the windowsill and closed her eyes tight. *Stop! God, please make the voices stop!*

She held her breath for five seconds . . . ten. She opened her eyes and glanced at the bed, where the girls were still sleeping. Again she looked at herself in the mirror. What was she thinking? She couldn't go back to Charlie, not now. Not until he got help for his problems. In the meantime, she had to stay at the shelter because she wasn't finished hearing Mary's story.

She woke the girls, dressed them, and met two other women down in the cafeteria over breakfast. One of them looked calm and peaceful. If she had bruises, they didn't show.

"I've been coming here for months," she told Emma. "Mary's story . . . it saved my life."

Emma set her piece of wheat toast back on her plate. "Mary talked to you too?"

"She talks to all the tough cases." The woman smiled. "She says it's the reason she's here. So she can tell her story and share the power with us."

"The power?" Beside Emma, Kami and Kaitlyn were eating cereal, happier and more relaxed than she'd seen them in years.

"Yes." An otherworldly peace filled the woman's face. "The divine power of Jesus. It's the only thing strong enough to save us."

The words sounded foreign. Emma knew about Jesus from her mother. But divine power? Power to do what?

The woman must've sensed her confusion. She patted Emma on the back and smiled again. "You'll find out soon enough. You're meeting with Mary today, right?"

"Right."

"Just keep your promise, and one of these days you'll know about the power personally."

"How do you know about the promise?" Emma took a napkin from the center of the table and dabbed at Kaitlyn's mouth.

"Mary makes us all promise the same thing. That we'll stay long enough to hear her story. By the end—" the woman stepped back from the table with her empty plate—"you'll know everything you need to know about the power."

Not for you, Emma. There won't be power for you. The power of God isn't wasted on trash. . . . The voice was there, but it was still quieter than usual.

Fifteen minutes later Emma was sitting across from Mary Madison once again. The confidence she'd felt earlier this morning faded. She needed a fix in the worst way. Maybe the voices were right; maybe the power that helped Mary and the other women wouldn't work with her.

"You're here." Mary smiled, but it didn't hide the loss in her eyes. "I told you the story would get harder."

Emma shifted in her seat. Why *was* she here? How could Mary's story—an even worse part of the story than she'd already told—help either of them?

Mary crossed one leg over the other. She was dressed casually today. Black jeans and a short-sleeved pullover. Even so, she was stunning. "Let go of your doubts, Emma."

Mary's words took her breath away. How could she know? She was right every time. The voices had nothing to say in light of Mary's understanding of the situation. Emma sat back and nodded. "I'll try."

Mary had been up most of the night praying for Emma. God had made it clear: the battle for Emma's heart and soul was one of the fiercest Mary had encountered yet. She was up against some of the same bondage and horrors that Mary herself had gone through years earlier. There was hope for Emma, of course, but she needed to keep coming to the sessions.

When Emma walked in this morning, Mary had whispered a prayer of thanks. They still had much of her story to work through before Mary could introduce a solution for Emma. Otherwise Emma would never understand.

She took a deep breath and let herself drift back. "Jimbo let me out of the basement only a few times every month. Otherwise I stayed downstairs."

Emma squirmed. "I couldn't stop hugging my babies yesterday." She studied her hands, shame etched into the corners of her eyes, her mouth. She looked up. "They could've wound up like you, but they didn't. I'll never stop being thankful."

"I'm glad." Mary angled her head. "My mama didn't know about the dangers, I guess. She wouldn't listen to my grandma Peggy, and no one else told her." She hesitated. "Anyway, Jimbo kept making special visits to me, and once in a while one of his favorite customers would come down."

The nightmares started before summer was over that first year. It would take Mary hours to fall asleep, and as soon as she did, she would have the most terrifying dreams.

In one of them, she was locked in a cage near a deep, fast-moving river. Her mother spotted her and screamed her name. Then she came running toward her. "I'll help you, baby! I'm coming!" She held out her hand, and in it was a key. The key to the cage.

But just as her mother was about to reach her, Jimbo appeared and pushed the cage into the river. "That'll teach you to try to break free!" He laughed at her, and the sound of it hid the sound of her mother's voice.

"Mama! Help me. . . ."

But the cage began to sink. Water rushed in through the bars, swirling higher and higher until it covered her face. With every second that passed, the cage sank deeper. Finally, when Mary couldn't hold her breath another moment, she gasped and water filled her lungs. She shook and kicked the bars and tried to scream, but it was too late.

The instant before death took her, she would wake and bolt up straight in bed, gasping for air.

Another dream had her running from Jimbo and the other men, running for her life. They would be chasing her with knives and guns, shouting at her to stop. But still she ran, terrified, her heart bursting in her chest. Finally . . . finally she would see Grandma Peggy's house. She could feel the men behind her—ten steps, maybe fifteen.

"Grandma, help!" She threw open the door, but inside nothing was the same. Instead of Grandma Peggy's house it was a roomful of cobwebs and skeletons. In one corner were her mama and grandma, but they were sleeping.

Jimbo reached her and grabbed her hair, but she pulled

away. "Mama, wake up!" She shrieked and ran to them, but when she made her way through the cobwebs and tried to touch them, she realized it was all a cruel trick.

It wasn't them. They were stuffed dolls, made to look like her mother and grandmother. Mary screamed and turned around, and all the men—each of the ones who visited her in the basement—were inside coming closer . . . closer. . . .

She would scream again, and this time she would wake up.

There were a few other dreams, four in all. They repeated themselves in no special order. She might have the dream about being in the cage ten straight nights, and then she'd have the one with the cobwebs and skeletons. It didn't matter which one happened, because once she was awake, she couldn't fall back to sleep.

So she went through the day exhausted, sleeping in fits and starts between meals, hoping that day wouldn't be one when Jimbo would come downstairs. She was so tired that she felt sick to her stomach most of the time. Once in a while the fear from the dream would stay with her all day, and when nightfall came she'd lie in the basement shaking, imagining things in the dark corners. Men with knives or cages.

Jimbo's friends continued to come see her. By the end of her first year in the basement, no one bothered to call them special visits anymore.

They were work.

The old couch was still in the basement, but Jimbo had brought in a bed a few weeks after setting her up down there. "Treat the men nice, Mary, ya hear?" He handed her an oversized bag. "These are for you. Men pay top dollar. You need to look the part."

The part was ugly and shameful. See-through nightgowns and panties that didn't fit right. She felt like a doll being dressed up and then used for sport. And that's what she was, nothing but sport to the men who came down the basement stairs.

One time she asked Lou about the visitors. "There are no neighbors, no other houses." She rubbed at a bruise on her right cheek. Jimbo had slapped her the night before. "Where are the men from?"

"They come for the stuff, the junk." She made a face at Mary as if she were stupid. "They pay more for the drugs if they get a little action on the side." She chuckled. "A lot more. Makes it worth the drive."

Mary was eleven when she said something under her breath, words that changed her life yet again. "See if I'm still here in the morning." She blurted the threat at Jimbo as he finished with her.

His eyes blazed instantly, and he pushed her down onto the bed. With all his weight he pinned her shoulder to the mattress. "Meaning what?"

Mary was too angry to back down. She sucked up whatever was in her throat and spat it in Jimbo's face. The spit hit him square in the eyes, and before he had time to wipe his face, she answered him. "It means I'm running away. I'll be gone before you wake up."

Jimbo's face grew deep red, and for a minute she thought he was going to kill her. He slapped her cheek hard and shouted something obscene at her. He probably would've finished her off except Lou opened the basement door.

"Quiet down," she shouted at them. "I got a customer waiting."

That night Jimbo tramped down the stairs and studied Mary. "You're a fool. You think you can run from me, do you?"

That's when he brought out the handcuffs. He clamped one cuff around her hand and one to the bedpost. "There." He laughed again. "You should be quite a sight trying to run away with a bed flying behind you."

***

Over the next few years, Mary pieced together enough information to understand her lot in life. She was a slave, really. She wasn't sure how much money she was making for Jimbo and Lou, but the last time they let her out of the basement she saw a fancy car in the driveway and a big-screen television in the living room. She could only guess about the money Jimbo had locked away somewhere.

When she was old enough to have a woman's body, sometime around her fourteenth birthday, Jimbo sent more of his customers down to her. Ten or fifteen of them were regulars. Lots of the visits were from men who came over and over again. They would tell her all sorts of things. "No one's like you, baby. . . . You're the prettiest girl in the whole world."

That's when she began lying.

Not just an occasional lie here and there, but lying about

everything. She'd tell the men nice things about themselves, and when one of them would talk about setting her free, taking her for himself, she'd correct him.

"I'm not here because of Jimbo." She'd give the man a practiced smile. "I'm here because I want to be."

Lying that way gave her a sort of false control over her life, and it made her less frightened—at least in the daytime. After a while, her lies seemed to make life easier for her, less of a fight all the time. And as the years passed, the things Jimbo's friends said to her began to feel like love. Because real love—the way Grandma Peggy and her mama had loved her—was so long ago in her past that she couldn't remember what it was like.

So maybe love was only a physical thing. That was all anyone ever really liked about her, so maybe it was okay if it felt like love. Though no one ever explained it to her, she figured a lot of it out on her own. She had power over men. Even Jimbo. If she treated him nice when he came down for a session or lied to him about her feelings for him, then he might let her upstairs for dinner or a walk outside. Even then, he stayed close beside her.

"Can't have you runnin' away on me." He'd chuckle, and the sound would send chills down Mary's spine.

When she wasn't lying, she rarely talked. Anything she might say would come across as rude, and rude meant Jimbo would pay her a different sort of visit. One where he'd throw her across the room and hit her. She hated the beatings, so she stopped being rude. And that meant she stopped talking.

Except for the lies.

Mary stood and went to the coffeemaker in the corner of her office. "It went on that way until one night when I was fifteen. The nightmares, the lying." She held up her hands and looked at them. "Sometimes Jimbo would handcuff me to the bed, and I'd smash my wrist against the metal. Over and over until it bled."

She poured a cup of coffee for Emma and another one for herself. She crossed the room and handed Emma her cup, then sat down and closed her eyes. The story was so hard to tell. Every time she told it she felt the same way, as if all of it had happened only the day before. The pain of the beatings, the cool handcuff against her wrist, the emptiness of the lies, and the dreaded fear of nighttime—all of it came rushing back at her. *God, give me the strength. You know how hard this is for me. . . .*

I am with you, daughter. My Spirit is in you, leading you even now.

Mary opened her eyes and took a sip of coffee. The warmth felt good. "Sometimes if I hurt my wrist on purpose, the pain would give me a distraction. A reason not to feel the pain of my life, I guess."

Emma ran her hands over her forearms. "I've . . . felt that way before."

That's when Mary noticed something she hadn't before. Along Emma's arms were tiny scars and a few scabs. Classic signs that she, too, had found a way of manifesting the pain into something tangible. Emma hadn't tried to free herself of handcuffs, but clearly she had an issue. "What's that, Emma?" she asked gently. "What happened to your arms?"

Tears filled her eyes. "Sometimes . . . after Charlie hits me, I . . . I cut myself." Emma shrugged. "It takes away the other pain for a few minutes."

Mary could feel her heart breaking. No wonder God had brought Emma to her. They had even more in common than she'd thought. "I understand."

"Sometimes I'll be cutting my arm, and all of a sudden I'll realize what I'm doing." Emma wiped the back of her hand across her damp cheek. "It's like I can't help myself."

Mary felt the burden of the young woman's pain. "The horrors that come with abuse are not always explainable. It's bondage."

And it was. As strong as if Emma, too, were in handcuffs.

Chapter 9

They were too far into this part of the story for Mary to stop.

Emma settled farther back into her seat and nodded. "Continue, please. You were saying . . . something about one night when you were fifteen."

Mary could still see it all vividly. "It was evening, and I was already afraid of the nightmares, wondering which one would come and how long I could stay awake so it wouldn't happen." She took another sip of her coffee and set the cup down. "For some reason, that night I started thinking about God."

***

Mary still had the little red-beaded purse. But she hadn't gone to it or opened it in a very long time. What was the point? What sort of God would let a child be chained up in a basement?

As usual, Mary had no answers, but she had something that didn't make any sense at all. Deep inside, where the tiny trickle of life still flowed in the underground caverns of her heart, she had hope. She knew because that night when she thought about God, there was still the flicker of a thought that maybe—just maybe—He really did have plans for her. But the hope God brought was so slight that Mary let it pass.

Besides, it was a hope that didn't make sense. Obviously God was finished with her, and He certainly didn't love her. No one did. Sure, once in a while the men would tell her they loved her. Their whispered words made her sick. But at least they acted like they loved her. And sometimes it was enough to convince herself—for a short while—that they really did. Or maybe love was just another lie, like the ones she told everyone Jimbo sent down the stairs.

Mary rolled onto her side. She had furniture now. A dresser and a nightstand. Pretty clothes in a cardboard closet Jimbo had built for her. The clothes were all see-through and silky, and the underwear was lacy and colorful. Mary figured any girl her age would be thrilled to have such pretty things.

She had something else too. She had the memories of her mama and her grandma Peggy.

She'd thought about her poor mama and her sweet, loving grandma every day since she'd been kidnapped by Jimbo and Lou. A few weeks after they brought her here she understood what had happened. Her mother was dead—Jimbo said so. If it was true, then she wasn't coming back for her. Mary didn't hope much about seeing her again. And she didn't pay much heed to God either. Because God had let Jimbo and Lou bring her here.

But Grandma Peggy . . .

Her grandma would do whatever she could to bring Mary home to live with her. She'd promised that, right? That even if her mama left or ran off or died, her grandma would take care of her forever. All she had to do was find her, and the two of them could be together always.

The night grew darker and Mary shifted, restless. The handcuff was cold on her wrist, and the cuts there never quite healed. Over time she got used to sleeping with one wrist locked to the bedpost, but it was never comfortable, never like it should be. She reached with her free hand and soothed her fingers over the cuts.

Maybe this was normal, this life she lived. Maybe being chained to a bedpost and having men visit her throughout the week was what any girl her age might go through. Not every girl, but lots of girls.

Jimbo had explained it to her many times. "God made women so that men could have their needs met and everyone could get along just dandy."

These thoughts of how her life must be at least somewhat normal were lulling her into sleep when suddenly there was the sound of cars on the gravel drive outside the basement window. Mary opened her eyes, fully awake. How many cars were there? Three or four? And why were they here so late? She didn't have a clock, but it had been dark for a long time. Jimbo had left her hours ago, and usually after he attached the handcuff she was finished for the day.

She lay still; her heart beat so loudly she could hear it. Outside came the crunching sounds of people walking over the rocky drive, heading for the front door. Mary's chest rose and fell faster than before. *I can't breathe . . . help me breathe.*

There was a crash, and in the same instant she heard a man shout, "Police . . . freeze!"

Police? Panic hit hard. What had Jimbo always told her about the police? That if they ever came, they'd haul all of them to jail and throw away the key. Wasn't that it?

Mary turned over and jerked her wrist, the one cuffed to the bedpost. "Come on!" She pulled at it some more, yanking her hand hard against the metal until her wrist throbbed from the pain. A familiar warm sticky wetness ran down her arm. She was bleeding again, and somehow the feeling was freeing. It gave her somewhere to focus her fears.

Upstairs she heard Jimbo yell a bunch of cusswords and a few threats at the officers. "Where's your search warrant?" There was pounding across the floor above her. Probably Jimbo, moving toward the policemen. "You can't do this without a—"

An explosion rocked the house, and Mary jumped up. They were shooting! Jimbo must've run at the police, and they'd shot him and killed him. Lou would be next and then her. She rolled off the bed and cried out when her bloody wrist twisted in the cuff.

The cement was cold on her bare legs, but she didn't care. They could come for her, but she wasn't going to give up without a fight. She cowered beside the bed, hidden except for her one wrist still chained to the post. She looked fast and hard around the room. There had to be a way out—there had to be.

Someone kicked the basement door. "What's down here?"

"I don't have to tell you nothin'." The voice belonged to Jimbo. He wasn't dead after all. Maybe they'd only used the gun to wound him, knock him down, and keep him from fighting.

For the first time in her life, she was pulling for Jimbo. *Fight at them; come on! Get them out of the house!* Jail terrified her, made her sick with fear. They would take her and lock her up, and she'd never see daylight again, never find Grandma Peggy. *Fight, Jimbo. Come on! Fight for all of—*

The door burst open, and two officers stood at the top of the stairs, both shining flashlights. "It's a basement," one of the men said. "This where you keep the drugs, Jimbo?"

Mary yanked at the cuff on her wrist again and again, and when she looked up, in the light streaming down the stairs she saw that the blood was running down her arm. She pulled one more time, but the cuff wouldn't budge. All she could do was keep low and hope the officers didn't see her hand.

One of the cops flipped on the light, and two sets of foot-steps sounded slowly down the stairs, stopping partway down. From her hiding place, Mary could barely see them. They were looking at the bed, staring at it in confusion and then in a surprised and angry sort of way.

"Who's there?" The taller officer took the rest of the stairs, his gun drawn.

Mary was trembling so hard she was sure the bed was moving. *They're going to kill me. I'll make one move, and they'll shoot me or catch me and send me to jail. Please . . . not jail. Please.*

"You . . . by the bed." The short officer had black hair and a mustache. He fell in beside his partner and shone the flashlight on her hand that was cuffed to the post. His tone was gentler than before. "Get up and tell us your name."

She wanted to think him mean, but there was nothing mean about his eyes. They reminded her of someone from a long time ago. And then in a flash she remembered where she'd seen eyes like that before. They were like Grandma Peggy's eyes. Kind and warm and safe. But that didn't make sense, because he was a cop, and cops would only hurt her. Jimbo had always said so.

The tall officer crept around the foot of the bed, and when he could see her fully, he stopped, lowered his gun, and whispered, "Dear God . . . what have they done?"

His partner came up and saw her too. "Sweetheart . . ." His voice cracked. He shone the flashlight on the wall beside the bed, the one she was cowering against. Then he found the light switch. He turned it on, flicked off his flashlight, and took another step toward her. "Everything's okay." Another step.

"No!" She shook her head, letting her wild mass of loose curls fall over her eyes. An awkwardness came over her. Maybe the see-through nightgown she was wearing was somehow not right, not the sort of thing a fifteen-year-old should wear. She bent over her knees and lay as flat as she could. *Stop shaking*, she ordered herself. "Leave me alone! Don't take me to jail!"

The tall officer held out his hand and stopped his partner. Then he cupped his hands over his mouth and turned back toward the stairs. "There's a victim down here. We need backup."

"No!" Mary screamed. "Leave me alone! Please!"

"Listen—" the voice belonged to the man with the mustache—"you haven't done anything wrong. You aren't going to jail." He breathed out and muttered something about not believing this. "Look at me."

She sorted through the things he'd just said. She hadn't done anything wrong, and she wasn't going to jail. Was that the truth? She'd mistrusted police since she was a little girl, but now the police officers standing a few feet away sounded honest, like maybe they really were here to help her.

She lifted her head a few inches and looked at them. Was it possible? What had they called her? A victim, wasn't that it? Mary wasn't sure what a victim was, but it didn't sound like a bad thing.

"We're telling the truth." The tall cop took a small step closer. "We're here to help you." He paused and bit his lip. Horror and pain muddied his eyes, and again Mary felt ashamed at how she must look. "How long . . . how long have you been like this?"

Mary sat up a little more. Her wrist was throbbing, the blood still dripping down her arm. She had no reason to believe them, nothing to prove they were telling the truth. But she had no choice either. She crossed her chest with her free arm, covering herself as best she could. She thought about lying, but something told her that would only make things worse. "Since . . . since I was ten."

The officer with the mustache dropped down to the edge of the bed. He looked like he was about to cry, but he blinked a few times instead. "How old are you now?"

She kept her knees beneath her, her arm across her chest.

"Fifteen." Her cheeks were hot from shame, hot in a way that they never were when Jimbo's friends came down the stairs.

The tall man moved slowly around to her arm. "Just a minute. Let me free you; then we can talk." He took a ring of keys from his pocket, working them around until he found a small narrow one. He slid it into the handcuff, where only Jimbo's key ever worked, and the metal snapped off her wrist.

She pulled her hand to her chest and rubbed at the blood; then she shrank back into the corner and waited. They weren't going to shoot her—she could tell that much. And if they were going to take her to jail, now was the time they'd make their move. She shook worse than before, and her stomach hurt.

The shorter man with the mustache looked around the basement until he spotted her cardboard closet. He went to it, flung it open, and grabbed a heavy silk robe. It was one of the only things she owned that wasn't sheer enough to see through. He brought it over and handed it to her. "Here."

She worked it over her shoulders, staying low to her knees so they couldn't see her. When the robe was on, she sat straighter. They weren't going to take her to jail. Otherwise they'd already have her halfway up the stairs.

And that could only mean one thing: Jimbo had lied; all the time she'd been living here he'd lied.

"Can you tell us your name?" The tall officer crouched down so he was eye level with her. His voice was soft, but not the sort of soft that most men had when they came to visit her. His was more like a daddy or a grandpa, like someone trying to help her.

"Mary." She brushed her long hair off her face and looked straight at him. The fear was leaving her. "My name's Mary."

"Mary what?" The cop with the mustache pulled a pad of paper out of his back pocket. "Do you know your other name?"

Her other name? Yes, she knew it. Jimbo called her by that name all the time. "Mary Margaret."

"Margaret?" The officer wrote something on his pad. "That's your last name?"

Mary felt another wave of shame. "I think so. I . . . can't remember." Her head was spinning, and her heart beat fast inside her.

The tall officer leaned against the wall and ran his fingers hard through his hair. "We need to ask you a few questions, Mary, but first let's take care of that wrist." The muscles in his jaw flexed as he gently wrapped his clean handkerchief around her bloody wrist. "These questions might not be easy," he warned her.

"Okay." She pulled the robe tighter around her waist.

He nodded at his partner, then looked back at her. "Has anyone ever hurt you while you've been living down here?"

Hurt her? The question was harder than she thought, not because it made her sad, but because she wasn't sure how to answer him. "Jimbo, you mean?" Her voice was quiet, timid.

"Yes. Him or anyone else."

Mary sucked at the inside of her cheek. Without thinking about it, she brought her hand to her face and rubbed her cheek. "Sometimes Jimbo hits me." She jerked back, because in that instant she could picture him raising his hand to strike her. Her eyes closed for a moment, and when she opened them, she could feel the strangest thing. They were wet and blurry. She was crying—something she hadn't done since her first year here. She nodded. "Yes, he hurts me."

The tall man kept asking the questions, and the one with the mustache wrote things down—her answers probably. He leaned over and pulled in a long breath, as if it were hard asking her questions and learning about her life. "I'm sorry, Mary." He gritted his teeth as he straightened. "Jimbo will never hit you again." He looked at her, and again his eyes were sad. "How 'bout anyone else? Does anyone else hurt you?"

Mary lowered her chin to her chest. "The customers do once in a while. Jimbo's friends." After so many years of lying, it felt good to tell the truth.

The officer with the mustache lowered the pad and pencil to his sides. He looked from his partner to Mary. "The customers?"

Surely they knew about the customers. They were men, and all men had needs. Wasn't it obvious that's why she was here? To meet the needs of men? But the look in the eyes of both officers told her that whatever needs men had, this was not a normal way for them to be met. She swallowed hard. "Jimbo takes the money, and he sends the customers down here for visits. It's not a lot of men. Fifteen, maybe. The same ones come all the time."

"How long has he been doing that?" The tall man crossed his arms and pressed them against his middle. His face looked pale.

Mary lifted one shoulder and felt it poke through the opening in her robe. She pulled the ends tight once more. A realization hit her. None of this must be normal. Otherwise the officers wouldn't look so surprised, so shaken. She looked up at the ceiling, and some of the wetness in her eyes slid down her cheeks. "Since I first came here. When I was ten."

"Every day?" The tall officer didn't have to say so; it was obvious how he felt about her having customers since she was ten. He was disgusted.

"No." Her voice faded some. "Most days, though."

The one with the mustache was writing notes again. Twice he rubbed his eyes with the back of his fist. Was he crying? Was her story that sad and broken that a police officer would cry? He made a fist around his pencil and pressed it to his lips. He whispered, "I'm gonna kill that guy."

"Wait—" the other officer shook his head at his partner— "not in front of the girl."

And in that moment, no one had to tell Mary what *victim* meant. She knew what it was because she felt it deep down to her soul. A victim didn't have any choice about the things that were done to her, and the things done to her were the most awful things of all.

The officer with the mustache relaxed his hand and looked at her. "I'm sorry, Mary. No one—" he clenched his teeth, and the words sounded trapped between his lips—"no one will ever hurt you again. I promise you."

He was about to say something else, but there was the sound of more cars pulling into the driveway. Cars and something else, something in the sky.

She pressed herself farther back into the corner. "What's that?"

"Great." The man with the mustache lowered his notepad

again. "Backup's here and the media with 'em. They must've heard the call and come for the news."

The *media?* Did that mean the television people? Mary wanted to hide under the bed until everyone went away.

"Not many news stories come out of Virginia hill country." The tall officer pinched his lips together and blew out hard, so hard his cheeks filled up. "I'm sorry about this, Mary. We need to get you out of here and somewhere safe. But there's going to be a lot of confusion, a lot of people asking questions as we leave. You don't have to answer any of them, okay?"

She nodded. What was he talking about? They were taking her somewhere safe? Where would that be? An idea hit her, and she felt her eyes light up. "Could you take me to my grandma Peggy's house? She lives . . . she lives in the city. In New York."

The faces of the officers changed, and they looked less shocked and sad. The officer with the mustache almost smiled. "You have a grandma?" He raised his pencil over the pad of paper. "Tell us her name, and we'll call her right now."

The tears were back. They stung her eyes and made it hard to see. "I'm sorry. I . . . can't think of it."

"We can figure it out later." He reached out as if he might touch her arm, but then he stopped himself. Instead, he walked to the bed and picked up a blanket. Without touching her, he put it carefully over Mary's shoulders and nodded toward the stairs. "We're going to take you out now. Stay between us, okay?"

"Okay." The shaking was back. How would she get up the stairs if she couldn't get her legs to move? "What about the other officers?" She looked from the tall cop to his partner. "Will you tell them not to shoot?"

The tall officer's shoulders slumped. "Mary, no one's going to shoot you. You haven't done anything wrong, understand?"

She nodded and took a step toward them. As she did she rubbed her wrapped wrist and looked back at the bed one last time. The bed where she had worked and slept and had nightmares for most of the past five years. How could she have thought any of it was normal?

The tall officer nodded toward the bed, then gestured toward the rest of the basement. "Is there anything you want to take?"

Mary didn't hesitate. She moved past the officers and over to the old couch against the wall. With practiced ease, she reached in behind the center seat cushion and pulled out the only thing that mattered to her at all—the small red-beaded purse. The single thing in all the world that she would keep with her, wherever the officers took her. It mattered to her for the same reason it had mattered when she was a little girl.

It reminded her that someone, somewhere, still loved her.

Chapter 10

Mary took a slow breath and finished her coffee. Sometimes when she told her story, she stopped here. The details of her life were hard to take in big sections.

Across from her, Emma was wiping tears off her cheeks. "Did they take you to your grandma Peggy's?"

A heaviness settled in Mary's chest. The answer was never easy. "No. I couldn't remember my last name." She stood and stretched. The room was stuffy, and outside the sun had broken through the clouds. She opened the window and took in a deep breath of the air that rushed in. "Even in the heart of the city you can smell the blossoms. Even in June."

Emma nodded, but her eyes never left Mary. "What happened? Where'd they take you?"

Mary sat back down on the sofa. "We can pick up again

tomorrow, or we can take a short break and I'll keep going. You decide."

Emma didn't hesitate. "Please, Mary. I want to know what happened. If you don't mind."

They agreed to meet back in Mary's office in ten minutes, long enough for Emma to check on her girls and use the restroom.

When they met again, Emma was anxious and fidgety.

"Are you okay?" Mary had poured water for both of them. She was settled back in her place on the sofa.

"No." Emma covered her face with her hands for a few moments. Then she looked at Mary again. "I can't help but think . . ."

"Yes?"

"It wasn't fair, what happened to you." Her voice held a cry, as if it was taking all her energy not to break down.

"Abuse is never fair. It leaves its mark on everyone involved."

"But . . ." Emma leaned her head back and stared at the ceiling for a few counts. Her struggle was so real it filled the room. "This story is supposed to involve God, right? God's power?"

"Yes. Like I said yesterday, it isn't finished."

"But why did God allow it?" She ran her right hand over the scars on her left forearm. "Don't you ever ask yourself that?"

It was a universal question, one every victim asked at some point or another. "We'll talk about that at the end of the story, okay?"

"Promise?"

Mary smiled. "You keep coming every morning, and I promise I'll answer that question at the end."

Emma relaxed her hands, but she sat at the edge of her seat. "Okay, then, go ahead. What happened next?"

A breeze filtered through the room and took Mary back. "Well, most of the time I was so scared by my new life, I wondered if maybe I was better off before."

A shadow fell over Emma's face. "This morning I thought about going back to Charlie."

"I'm glad you didn't."

"Me too."

A red flag shot itself through Mary's consciousness. This was the first detail Emma had shared, and it proved she was still so much at risk. Charlie was the man who had abused her. If Emma went back to him, he would be angrier than ever. Angry that she'd left him, angry that she waited so long to come back home. That sort of rage could lead to his most violent act yet.

Mary swallowed and kept her thoughts to herself. Emma was waiting for more details. "I spent two nights in a hospital, and then a social worker explained that I'd be paired up with short-term foster parents."

<hr />

At the hospital there were machines, people poking Mary with needles and taking blood from her arm, and doctors and nurses whispering to each other, sometimes right in front of her. They'd look up and catch her watching, and sometimes they'd give her a nervous smile.

"Tests, honey," they told her. "We're discussing the tests. We need to make sure you're okay."

On the second day, a doctor gave his report to Mrs. Campbell, Mary's social worker. "Mary is surprisingly healthy," he told her. "She has traces of disease, but nothing life threatening. We'll give her strong antibiotics for a few weeks, and she should be fine."

"Physically." Mrs. Campbell lowered her voice, as if maybe Mary couldn't hear her.

"Yes." The doctor frowned. "Physically. The rest . . . well, that's up to your department. She will need counseling."

Mary understood. Her body was going to be okay. But her dreams, her hopes, her reasons for believing in tomorrow . . . all of them were diseased and dying. She still couldn't read, and there were so many things about life that she didn't understand. In some ways she was still the same child Jimbo and Lou had kidnapped and taken to the basement five years earlier.

But her heart felt like it was a hundred years old.

When they let her out of the hospital, Mrs. Campbell took her to a building called Social Services. She waited for her short-term foster parents in a room with a couch and a television. The air inside was warm and stale.

Mary eased forward on the couch and ran her hands over the thighs of her jeans. They were her first pair in a long time, and they felt stiff and soft all at the same time. Mrs. Campbell had given them to her with a few shirts and underclothes— her first in years that weren't sheer and lacy.

She looked around the room. There were two small children at the opposite end on the floor in front of the television. *I'm no older than them, really. I never got to be older than them.* What had they been through that would bring them to this Social Services building? Were they waiting for foster families too?

Like an old friend, she could hear Grandma Peggy's voice: *"Your mommy might go, but if I had it my way you would stay. I'd take care of you, and you'd never be cold or hungry or lonely again. If I had it my way . . . if I had it my way . . ."* Her words were distant now, hushed by the passing of years.

Mary closed her eyes and willed the sound of her grandma's voice to fill her mind, her senses. *Are you still looking for me, Grandma? Don't you know where I am?* She breathed out hard.

The little red purse—that's what she needed. She reached into her back pocket, and her fingers felt the tiny beads. Somehow through all the craziness of the past couple of days she still had it. She opened the buttoned clasp and gently took out the yellowed note that she still couldn't read. Some of the letters looked familiar—an *i* and a *p*.

Once, a long time ago, her grandma had read that note to her. But this was where her grandma's words got too tangled to hear. Something about God having plans for her life, right? Or was it that Mary was supposed to make plans for her life? She wasn't sure anymore. She brought the paper closer and squinted hard at it. Why couldn't she remember this part?

She was still looking at it when she heard the door open behind her. As quickly as she could, Mary pushed the note into the purse and slipped the purse back into her pocket.

Mrs. Campbell walked up and sat down beside her on the couch. "Mary, your foster parents are here."

A sensation came over her then, the same terror she'd felt when the police officers rescued her. Mrs. Campbell was waiting for her to do or say something. She cleared her throat, stood, and looked down. Her knees were shaking so hard they were hitting each other.

"Are you ready, Mary?"

She nodded but didn't look up. In her new life, she tried not to look at people's eyes. The looks they gave her made her feel like more of a victim.

Mrs. Campbell's expression said that she was sorry and that she also doubted Mary. Finally she slumped a little and turned. "Follow me."

From the moment Mary saw the older couple waiting in the lobby outside the door, she felt herself relax. Ted and Evelyn were their names, and they were young and old at the same time, like her. The difference was that Ted and Evelyn were old in years, with small bunches of wrinkles on their foreheads and around their mouths. But after talking with them for a few minutes, she discovered that they were young on the inside, because kindness was in everything they said, every look they gave her. Suddenly Mary recognized where she'd seen old people like Ted and Evelyn before. Grandma Peggy had been like that. Her eyes were like theirs.

Ted and Evelyn took her to their country home half an hour from the Social Services building. Mary felt hope stir within her. There were no handcuffs, no see-through night-gowns, and no talk of working from the bedroom.

Instead, Ted and Evelyn sat her down right after she got settled and talked about the same things her grandmother had talked about. "Mary," Evelyn told her, "we want you to know about Jesus. He has a plan for you, and He wants to give you a future with Him. A future filled with promise."

Mary liked the way Ted and Evelyn talked, even if their words didn't feel like they belonged to her. She was a victim, right? What hope was there for someone like her, someone who had grown up in a basement and chained to a bed?

That night she waited for Ted to visit her and explain about how she needed to earn her keep, but he never came, and she wondered if maybe Ted didn't have the same needs as other men. He looked at her differently too, at her eyes and her face and not at her body.

On her first morning Ted made breakfast, and Evelyn brought out a yellow-and-white cardboard box. Inside were books and tapes and sets of little cards with letters on them. Evelyn sat across from Mary at the kitchen table and spread the items out in the space between them.

"These tapes and cards will help you know your letter sounds." She smiled. "You're a smart girl. We'll have you reading in no time."

Reading became the focus of every one of their days together. Ted would fix eggs and toast or hot oatmeal with brown sugar, and Evelyn would get out the tape recorder and flash cards and tapes. "We're working on vowels today." She'd smile and pat Mary's hand. "Vowels are the foundation of every word."

Mary loved learning. Every day she felt a little smarter, a little more like maybe the nice words Ted and Evelyn told her might actually come true. By the end of the first month, Mary knew all her letters and the sounds they made, and at the end of the second month she could read the books in the first packet. Simple books, but books all the same.

Mary found Evelyn in the living room one morning. "When I learn how to read, can you help me write a letter to my grandma? She's trying to find me."

"Of course." Evelyn took her hand. "Maybe we could send a letter to the city officials in New York, and they could help us find her."

They'd already discussed the fact that Social Services had been unable to locate Mary's grandma.

But Ted told her to never give up. Never. "If she's looking for you, there has to be a way to find her."

Ted and Evelyn taught Mary more than reading. They told her about calendars and money and checkbooks and the names of animals and stars and historical figures like Abe Lincoln and Thomas Jefferson and Franklin Delano Roosevelt. She learned to drive Ted's pickup across the back acreage when the horses needed hay, and she learned about the Gospels of Matthew and Mark and Luke and John and how Jesus came to save everyone.

She went to sleep every night with her head too full to think about Jimbo and Lou and the handcuffs and customers, and every morning she woke hungry for more. And something else: her nightmares stopped, and she could finally get a full night's sleep.

Ted and Evelyn always reminded her that her place in their home was temporary. "We're only licensed to do short-term foster care," Evelyn told her several times. "You understand that, right, Mary?"

"Right. You're going to help me find Grandma Peggy; then I'll go live with her."

"We all want that, honey. Mrs. Campbell at Social Services is trying every day to find her."

"But . . ." Mary was filled with a sudden fear.

Evelyn touched her shoulder, her eyes sad. "But there's a chance you'll have to move to a different family before we can find her. Do you know that?"

"I guess." Mary would cut the conversation short. She loved living with Ted and Evelyn. If God had a plan for her, then she'd stay with these nice people until someone found her grandmother. Then she'd go live with her in New York and keep learning and growing, and she would send letters to Ted and Evelyn thanking them for all they'd done.

Mary couldn't imagine going anywhere else. Whenever her heart tried to remind herself that any day with Ted and Evelyn could be her last, she shut out the voice. She wasn't leaving.

Once in a while she'd talk to Evelyn about her life in the basement, but only briefly. "They told me my job was to meet the needs of the customers," Mary told her one night before bedtime.

"They were wrong." Evelyn never sounded angry, but in that moment there was something intense in her tone. She looked deep into Mary's eyes. "You are a child. Children need to be loved, not used."

Mary looked down at her sweatpants, the ones she slept in. A thought filled her heart, one she couldn't share even with Evelyn. Back when she was chained to the bed in the basement, sometimes being with the customers felt like love.

They would tell her they loved her and stroke her hair and her forehead and say wonderful things to her, things Jimbo and Lou never said. "You're my beautiful angel" or "You don't know how much I love you." Things like that.

That was all she'd ever known of love.

But somehow she knew that the love she felt from the men in the basement wasn't the sort of love Evelyn was talking about. "That's why the police took me away, right? Because children shouldn't be used?"

"Right." Evelyn's eyes told Mary that she knew there was more to be said, but she wasn't going to push. She smoothed Mary's hair and smiled. "We can talk about it some other day. When you're ready."

But in the end, time ran out on them. The bad news came at the end of Mary's third month with the couple. Evelyn brought her into the living room and sat next to her on the sofa. "Honey, Mrs. Campbell called." The older woman's eyes were watery as she took hold of one of Mary's hands. "They've found a long-term foster home for you." She bit her lip. "You'll be leaving in the morning."

Mary wanted to scream or hide under the bed or lock the front door or beg God to stop the sun from moving so morning would never come. But she'd spent most of her life hiding her feelings, and as much as Ted and Evelyn had taught her, they hadn't taught her how to open her heart and spill out the contents in a moment like this. She felt her lips part, but no words came out.

"The couple is younger than we are. They have two little

boys." Evelyn gave her a half smile, but it faded before it reached her eyes. "You'll have little brothers."

"Tell me again . . ." Mary swallowed. Her throat was thick, so she brought her fingers to her neck and rubbed it. "What does *foster* mean?"

The light in Evelyn's eyes dimmed.

Ted entered the room and sat next to his wife. "*Foster*—" his voice was quiet, sad—"*foster* means it isn't forever." He brought his hands together and looked down for a moment. When he found her eyes again, she could see he was hurting. "A long time ago God told us to help kids like you, kids who have a crisis in their life and need a safe home for a short time. It's how we're licensed with the state."

That was the part Mary didn't understand. She squinted, and the words made a slow climb up her throat. "But we didn't find my grandma yet."

"I know." He took his wife's hand. "Mrs. Campbell will keep looking for her."

"But . . ." The walls of her new little world were falling one after another. "Why short-term?"

Ted's face was kind, but his answer was certain. "Because lots of children need a safe place, Mary, and there aren't enough places. We want kids in crisis to know God's love as the first part of the rest of their lives."

"It's what we do." Evelyn covered her mouth with the back of her hand and shook her head. Tears were on her cheeks. "It's never easy, but, honey, I told you this would be short-term. We'll let you go believing God, trusting that He has a plan for you."

Mary nodded, but inside she felt herself closing down, felt her feelings running for cover, back to the cold dark places of her heart. Her back stiffened. "Fine." She stood and gave Ted and Evelyn a look that said she understood. "I'll pack my things."

The tears came once she was alone in her room. She'd been a fool to believe it could last, that she could stay with Ted and Evelyn and keep learning, keep letting them make her feel a little more normal every day. They'd bought her a few more pairs of jeans, more shirts, and a flannel nightgown, and she stuffed them all in the white plastic bag, the one she'd gotten from the hospital.

The rest of the day she kept to herself, even when Evelyn tried to talk to her.

Mrs. Campbell, the social worker, came for her just after breakfast the next morning.

"Mary—" Ted put his hands on her shoulders—"stay with God, follow Him. He has all the answers, honey."

She willed herself not to cry. "You and Evelyn have the answers."

"Because He gave them to us." Ted took a step back. "Remember what I'm telling you. Stay with God."

Evelyn was next. She took Mary in her arms and hugged her for a long time, rocking her back and forth and making small crying sounds. When she pulled away, her eyes were red and swollen. She wiped her hands across her cheeks and held up a single finger. "Wait here."

They stood there—Ted, Mrs. Campbell, and Mary— waiting in awkward silence until Evelyn returned. She was carrying the cardboard box with the books and tapes and flash cards. She held it out to Mary. "Take this. You're half-way through."

Mary started to shake her head, but the gift was too great to pass up. She took it and held it tightly to her chest. "Thank you."

Evelyn brought her hand to her mouth and nodded.

"Mary, we need to go." Mrs. Campbell stood by the front door. "The new family is waiting at the office."

Mary looked over her shoulder at the social worker and then back to Evelyn. "When I'm older—after I find my grandma, when I can read and drive—I'm coming back." She hugged Evelyn again. "I want you to meet her because the two of you . . ." Her voice cracked. She pressed her lips together for a moment, then looked deeply into Evelyn's eyes. "The two of you would be friends."

Then, with her plastic bag in one hand and the cardboard box clutched to her side, she turned and followed Mrs. Campbell out to the car.

Into whatever the next chapter in her life might be.

Chapter 11

Mary was willing to stop, but Emma didn't budge.

"I have nowhere to go, Mary." Emma stood and helped herself to a cup of water. The easy way she had about her now made her look more comfortable. "The girls were just lying down for a nap when I checked on them."

"Okay, then . . . tell me if you have to go." Mary shifted in her seat so she could feel more of the breeze. If Emma was willing to listen, she'd keep telling the story.

Ted and Evelyn had been right about the new family. Mr. and Mrs. Lake were younger, and they had two little boys—

Trevor was six and Ty was four. The Lakes must've been rich because they had a pool and a two-story house, two cars, two televisions, and even two dogs in the backyard.

For the first couple weeks, Mary said little to them. She stayed in her room, working with the contents of the cardboard box—the flash cards and tapes. She could feel herself becoming a better reader every day. They invited her to the table for meals and talked about getting her enrolled for school in the fall, but they didn't push her. If she wanted to stay in her room, that was okay with them.

And that was exactly what Mary wanted. Every night before she fell asleep, Mary would reach to the bottom of her white plastic bag and find the little red-beaded purse. By the end of the second week there, when she pulled it out, unbuttoned the clasp, and took the note from inside, something amazing happened. She could read the words—or at least most of them. For the first time, she could actually make sense of what Grandma Peggy had written on the slip of paper.

The first part was something the Lord wanted her to know. That He had plans for her, plans to give her hope and something else, something that started with the letter *f*, and then a word that told her where she could find those words in the Bible. Mary wasn't sure, but she thought she understood. It meant God had hope for her not just today, but tomorrow and all the tomorrows she might ever have. The last part she could read without missing a word: *Mary, I will always be here for you. I love you. Grandma.*

It was late enough that the Lake family was already sleeping, but Mary's joy filled her senses. She could read! She covered her mouth and made the softest squealing sound. She could really and truly read. Not only that, but the message was wonderful. Her grandma loved her, and she was waiting for her. Now all Mary had to do was find her way to the little flat in New York City where her grandma lived. Maybe she'd talk to Mrs. Lake in the morning.

She slipped the note back in the purse and hid it under her pillow. Now that she could read, she wanted it close by so she could take it out and look at it anytime she was missing her grandma and wondering how to find her. When the purse was safely tucked away, she turned out the light and thought about her grandma's voice, her face. Sometimes the memory of her seemed so distant that Mary worried it would disappear forever.

Maybe if she spent more time getting better at her reading, she could learn to write. Then she could write down all her memories of her grandma so she wouldn't forget them. She sat up and looked at the corner of her room where she kept her cardboard box of reading supplies. But the corner was empty. Her eyes followed the edge of the room around the entire perimeter. The box was gone.

Strange. The box was always in her room. Maybe Mrs. Lake had borrowed it for one of the little boys. She lay back down, and gradually thoughts of her reading box faded. She'd talk to Mrs. Lake and find it tomorrow. Sleep was beginning to find her when there was a noise at her bedroom door. She sat straight up, startled. Sounds in the middle of the night reminded her of the basement and the men who would sometimes make their way down later than usual. For a second she thought maybe she was back there, and maybe the past few months were nothing but a dream.

But then the door opened, and there stood Mr. Lake. He wore a frown and concern around his eyes. "Mary?"

She clutched the bedcovers to her chest, her eyes wide. "Yes?"

"Did you yell?" He took slow steps into the room and looked once over his shoulder. Then he shut the door very quietly, so it didn't make a sound. There was a streetlamp outside her window, so there was still enough light to see his eyes as they found hers. "Is everything okay?"

Mary pressed her back into the headboard. "I'm fine." She remembered her reading box. "Do you know where my box is? the one with my reading stuff?"

He laughed and leaned against the wall near her bed. "That's baby stuff. I found it in here this morning and threw it out with the trash. You're way too old for that."

Mary's mouth hung open. He'd thrown away her precious box of reading supplies from Ted and Evelyn? Now how would she get better with her letter combinations and with the words at higher levels? She folded her arms against her chest. "Those . . . those were special to me."

He brushed off her comment. "You don't need them." He sat at the foot of the bed. "I can teach you everything you don't know." Another glance at the door. His smile became thin and mean. "But you already know more than most girls twice your age." He paused, staring at her. "You sure you didn't scream?"

What was wrong with him? Mary studied his face. There

was something familiar about the look in his eyes, and gradually she understood. His expression was sort of glazed over, and every few seconds he ran his tongue over his lower lip. He didn't look like Mr. Lake at all, but more like one of Jimbo's friends. She slid to the back corner of the bed, as far away from him as possible.

"Everything's okay."

He wasn't going to touch her, was he? Mrs. Campbell said these were nice people. Safe people. She swallowed hard. "Good night."

Mr. Lake let his eyes move from her face down to her feet and back again. "Can I ask you something?"

"I'm . . . I'm tired." She glanced at the window a few feet away and then at the door. If he made a move she would run—she'd have to. But how would she get past him? And where was her grandma through all this?

"What I want to know is this." Mr. Lake slid along the mattress until he was only an arm's length from her face. "They brought men to you every night?"

She was trembling now, and her stomach felt tight, like someone was punching her over and over and over. "Mrs. Campbell said I don't have to talk about it."

"Yeah, but you must miss all that attention." He leaned closer, put his fingers on the shoulder of her flannel nightgown, and ran them down her arm. "Pretty girl like you."

Mary jerked back. This wasn't supposed to happen. Her days of meeting men's needs were over. Wasn't that what Mrs. Campbell said? *"The Lakes are nice people; you'll do real well there."* But then why was Mr. Lake doing this? Why was he touching her? She pressed herself against the wall and whispered, "Please . . . don't touch me."

Mr. Lake frowned again. "I want to get to know you, Mary." He stopped his hand near the small of her waist and rubbed his thumb along her side. "This is what a girl like you wants from men."

"Not anymore." Her voice was low, the words trapped by fear. How could she explain that she'd never wanted that sort of life? She hadn't, right? Even though sometimes the customers said nice things, it wasn't what she really wanted. She shuddered. "Things are . . . different now."

"Girls like you never change." He came a few inches closer. "We can make it our secret. . . . You won't be sorry."

Mary felt herself gag, but she swallowed whatever wanted to come up. Was this how it was with the men who had visited her in the basement? Did they have wives and families at home, and was she their little secret? If so, then . . . then she was something awful and wretched. A horrible, horrible girl.

Mr. Lake was waiting. If she told him no, he could force himself on her. Some of the men had done that, and the bruises lasted for days.

She glanced around the room, but there was no way past him. If only she could get him out of her room. She could call Mrs. Campbell in the morning and get a ride back to Ted and Evelyn's house. If it came down to lying and acting, so be it. Whatever it took. She lowered her chin to her chest and forced the slightest smile. "I feel sick tonight." *Don't look scared . . . he'll see through you.* She willed her arms to relax. "Okay?"

Mr. Lake's expression eased. "Does that mean I'd have a better chance tomorrow night?"

"Maybe." A shy shrug. "If it's our secret."

That was all it took. Mr. Lake stood and gave her a mock salute. "Tomorrow, then." He was smiling, but his voice sounded ice-cold. "You won't be sorry."

After he left, Mary lay back down and stared at the ceiling. Her heart was pounding so hard the noise filled the room. *Ba-boom . . . ba-boom . . . ba-boom.* She watched her clock, watched the time go from 11:45 to 12:25, and only then—when she was sure Mr. Lake was asleep—did she creep out of bed.

She packed her clothes into the white plastic bag and buried the little red-beaded purse near the bottom. Mrs. Campbell had given her a small card with her phone number on it. "Use it anytime you'd like," she said. "If you're having a problem, I want to know about it."

Mary found the card in the top drawer of the nightstand, and she pressed it into the palm of her hand. Then she lay in bed, shaking and waiting for daylight. It was summer, so the Lakes expected her to sleep in past eight o'clock. Instead she used the phone in the office down the hall and called Mrs. Campbell.

"Social Services, how can I help you?"

She coughed. Terror and exhaustion fought for position. "Mrs. Campbell, please."

"Sorry—" the man at the other end sounded distracted— "she's out for the week."

"But . . ." Panic kicked her in the gut. "I need to talk to her."

The man sighed. "Can I get another social worker for you?"

Another social worker? Mary pushed her fingers into her long hair and shook her head. How could she tell another social worker what was happening? "No, that's okay." She was shaking so hard she could barely hold the phone. "I'll call back." She hung up the receiver.

If Mrs. Campbell was gone, she had only one choice. She would take her things and run away, find a ride to New York City, and go to the nearest police station. The police who rescued her from Jimbo and Lou's basement had been so nice to her. Certainly all policemen would be willing to help. And once she was in New York, a police officer could help her find her grandma.

Determination welled up inside her and made her feel strong. She wouldn't stay another night with the Lakes, no matter what she'd done in the past. Her feelings before had been wrong. Meeting the needs of men wasn't love; it never would be. But love was out there. It was at Ted and Evelyn's house and wherever Grandma Peggy was. She would leave, and she would find love if she had to spend the rest of her life looking for it. The fact that she had no money would make her search harder, but that was okay. She'd lived on the streets most of her childhood, and she'd survived. She could live there again if she had to.

She ate breakfast late that morning when she was sure Mr. Lake was at work. After Mrs. Lake and the boys left for the supermarket, Mary was ready. There wouldn't be a better time. It was hot outside, but she wore her jeans and a sweatshirt. She stepped into the bathroom and looked at the mirror. As ugly as she felt on the inside, her outside more than made up for it. But for a fifteen-year-old runaway, being pretty would only make life more dangerous.

Working quickly, she grabbed a ponytail holder from the top drawer—the one that held Mrs. Lake's things. She pulled her hair back tight and put it in a ponytail. Then she went to Mr. Lake's closet and found a baseball cap. It was big, but that was okay. The back band fit over her hair better that way. Near the front door, she grabbed her overstuffed plastic bag and left as fast as she could.

She never once looked back.

The Lakes' house was right off the freeway, so it didn't take long to walk to the boulevard and find a spot just before the on-ramp. She stuck out her thumb and made eye contact with every driver who passed by. She'd seen a guy do that in a movie she'd watched with Ted and Evelyn.

The third trucker swung his rig over and pushed open the passenger door of his cab.

"I need a ride to New York City," Mary shouted at the old man behind the wheel.

"Get in." He gave her a quick nod. "I'll pass right through it."

Mary's heart was thudding hard, but she ignored it. She pushed her things up into the cab and climbed in after them. Tough girl—that was her image now. She looked straight ahead. *Come on, Mary . . . sound old.* She cleared her throat. "Thanks." She shot him a look. "I don't have much money."

"That's okay." The man had white hair and a white beard. His brown eyes were warm and kind. "Call me Big Dave." He saluted her. "God tells me who to pick up. I just listen and obey."

Mary felt her pretenses fading. God? Again? Why did she keep running into people who wanted to tell her about Him? She looked out the windshield. At least this man wouldn't hurt her, not if he was anything like Ted or Evelyn or her grandma. She kept her voice deep anyway. "You'll have to thank God for me."

The man was a talker. He asked about her past, and she kept her answers vague.

Good, she thought. *He doesn't recognize me.*

Because of her public rescue from Jimbo's basement, she had a face people often looked at twice. After her first week at Ted and Evelyn's, they told her that the story of her rescue had been played across the nation on television. She was bound to be recognized. It was why she liked to stay inside and learn.

During the whole trip Big Dave talked about God being his copilot and the Lord's will this and praise Jesus that. He was nice, and if she hadn't felt the need to play the role of a tough street girl, she would've enjoyed talking to him. As Dave drove, Mary remembered something her mama had told her: *"If you're going to live on the streets, you need to be invisible."* Yes, the tough-girl image had to stay, along with the baseball cap and ponytail.

"Well, little lady, we got about an hour left." Big Dave broke the brief silence and pulled his truck off at the next exit. "Let's get some dinner and get you where you need to be."

Mary was ready to run, just in case Big Dave wasn't the nice man he seemed to be. She kept her fingers tight around the door handle as he drove his truck into what looked like a gas station and restaurant.

As soon as he parked, he nodded at the door. "You can go now, missy. The bathrooms are inside."

Mary felt herself relax. Everything was going to be okay. Big Dave was safe, and in an hour she'd be in New York City. She was closer to her grandma—and maybe even her mama—than she'd been since she was ten years old. She could hardly wait to feel her grandma's arms around her, hear her voice telling her that she was never out of her thoughts for one minute.

Before she climbed down the steps she reached into her bag, took the red-beaded purse from the bottom, and stuffed it into her back pocket. She gave Big Dave a smile. "Thanks."

She hopped down and walked through the front door. Two police officers stood at the counter, visiting with a waitress. When Mary walked up, they stopped talking and looked at her.

The waitress was punishing a piece of gum. "Table for one?"

"No, thanks." Mary adjusted her baseball cap. The way the officers stared at her made her feel uncomfortable.

"Hey . . ." One of the officers squinted. He took a step toward her. "You look familiar." Another step closer. "What's your name?"

Mary's mind raced. "Jane." She gave a nervous laugh. "Sorry." She pointed toward the restroom. "I need to go."

Neither officer said anything as she walked down the hall, her steps as quick as she could make them without looking suspicious. What could they know about her? Had her foster family already reported her missing? And if so, would police this far away know about it? She didn't think so.

She stepped into the restroom, found a stall, and leaned against the door. *Breathe, Mary. Breathe.* The officer was just making conversation. She took her time, and ten minutes later she dried her hands, tossed the paper towel in the trash, and headed back down the hall toward the front counter.

What she saw stopped her in her tracks. The lobby was full of police—the original two and at least four additional officers. Big Dave was standing in the middle of them shaking his head and shrugging. From where she stood, she was hidden from their view, but not for long. If one of them took a few steps toward her they'd all know where she was. In that same instant Big Dave caught her eye and immediately looked back at the policemen. He gave a quick shake of his head and, without looking at her, he waved his hand in the air.

Was he using his hands to talk or giving her a signal? She took a step backward and looked over her shoulder. There was a door at the end of the hallway, and a sign over it read Exit. She had no time to thank Big Dave or think of a way out. There was just one. If she didn't take it now she'd be caught by the police and taken . . . where? Back to the Lakes' house? A shudder passed over her arms and down her spine.

She'd rather live under a bridge.

Moving slowly so she wouldn't gain their attention, she moved back until she was out of view. Then she turned and pushed her way through the emergency exit. Outside was a parking lot, and on the far side were long stretches of cars. She squinted at the sign above them. She wasn't sure about the first line, but the bigger words at the bottom read Used Cars. She blinked. The cars lined up in rows must've been for sale.

She sucked in her cheek. If only she could get a car. Then she could drive to New York, find a safe place, and park the car. The owners would find it eventually. It wouldn't exactly be stealing, would it? She could drive after all. Ted had told her that all farm kids learn to drive young. And she wouldn't hurt the car. Once more she looked over her shoulder. Whatever she did, it had to happen fast. They would be looking for her any minute.

Her heart raced, but her feet moved even faster. In a few seconds she crossed the back parking lot of the restaurant and headed for the rows of used cars. When she reached them, she felt her fear triple. There were people everywhere. Couples walked around looking at cars, and scattered throughout the rows were people dressed in nice clothes. Salespeople, probably.

With everyone around her, she couldn't exactly walk up and take a car, could she? She looked back at the restaurant. No one was coming after her, but it wouldn't be long.

The cars on either side of her were locked and had no keys in the ignition. She hurried down a row of vehicles until she came to a section of pickups. Trucks like the one Ted and Evelyn used to let her drive. The first one in the row had an open window and . . . she leaned in . . . yes, there were keys on the front seat.

She swallowed hard. *You can do this,* she told herself. *Take the truck, get to New York, and find Grandma Peggy. Then you can give the truck back.* She glanced around, and out of the corner of her eye she saw police officers spill out the back door of the restaurant. She had maybe a minute to pull it off.

She slipped into the front seat and grabbed the keys. Her hands shook as she slid the largest key into the ignition and turned the engine. It was too late to back out now. From not far away she saw one of the well-dressed men turn and head toward her, his hand raised. Terror wrapped its arms around her, squeezing the air from her lungs. She had to get out of here fast.

The gearshift was just like the one in Ted's truck. She put it into drive and peeled out of the parking space. The squeal was bound to get the attention of the officers, but she had no choice. If she didn't move they'd catch her for sure.

She would only have the clothes on her back and the red-beaded purse, but that was okay. She had all she needed. Her mouth was dry, and she ran her tongue over her lower lip. "I'm coming, Grandma. . . . Please be waiting for me."

The aisle ahead was clear, but in the rearview mirror she could see people running after her. "Come on," she yelled at herself. "Go, Mary . . . move it." She wasn't sure where the entrance to the lot was, but it didn't matter. Trucks could take a curb. As soon as there was a break in the row, she turned and sped up to the sidewalk. She looked to the left. No traffic. Behind her the men were catching up, and in the far distance the police were heading toward the car lot. "Okay." She grabbed a quick breath. "Here goes."

The truck dropped down over the curb, and she was off. The freeway was just ahead. She'd paid close attention while Big Dave was driving, so she knew which way he'd been going. Without slowing, she entered the freeway heading the same direction as before.

There. She settled back against the seat. She'd done it. Her breathing returned to normal, and even her heartbeat slowed down. No one would know where she was going, so everything would work out just fine.

It took a few minutes to get used to the flow of the freeway, but it was easy compared with what lay ahead. She had to find her grandma as soon as possible. Grandma Peggy would explain the situation to the police and the Social Services and the people who owned the truck. No one would be mad at her—not once they understood.

She passed one exit, then another and another. With every mile she could feel herself getting closer to her grandma, feel the past falling away. Never again would someone chain her to a bed in a basement, and never, never would someone use her to meet the needs of men. Never.

The minutes passed, and no one seemed to be chasing her. Her back melted into the seat, and she loosened her grip on the steering wheel. Tears filled her eyes, and she blinked so she could see the road. "Grandma . . . I'm coming." She could hardly believe it was actually happening. She was going to find Grandma Peggy, maybe even today. Every exit she passed took her closer to the place where she had spent her first years, the place where she still had a safe home and a pink bedroom and a pink teddy bear and a stack of books that finally . . . finally she could read.

A smile lifted the corners of her mouth, and she rolled down the window. It was wrong to take the truck, but what choice did she have? She'd leave it somewhere safe, and her short loan wouldn't hurt anyone. The summer wind felt wonderful on her face, washing away the dirt of her past, the grime of every ugly yesterday that had scarred her heart and soul and seared her memory. Her grandma would be waiting, and she could live with her and maybe one day her mama would join them. Because if Jimbo had lied about the police, maybe he'd lied about her mama. Maybe she wasn't dead. Maybe she'd joined up with Grandma Peggy, and they were both looking for her.

They could all live together once Mary found them.

Yes, it was all going to work out. She could already imagine the smell of her grandma's house, already feel her arms around her. Soon, very soon. She pressed her foot to the pedal, but as she did she saw flashing lights in her rearview mirror.

Her eyes fell to the control panel. She wasn't speeding. *They're not coming for me,* she told herself. *I'm way too far ahead of them.* Just in case, she changed lanes until she was on the far right. In the mirror the police were gaining ground. Two cars, both with their lights flashing. They changed lanes, and Mary felt her heart fall to the floor of the truck. One more lane change and they were right behind her.

She was wrong. They were coming for her after all. Sweat broke out on her forehead, and she pressed the gas pedal to the floor. She wasn't going to give up without a chase, not when her grandma was so close. At the next exit, she whipped the truck down the ramp. But up ahead was a red light. Two lanes of stopped traffic blocked her path, and the shoulders weren't wide enough for her truck.

The police were right behind her. A booming voice came from one of them. "Pull over!"

She thought about sideswiping the cars on the right and squeezing past them. But that would never work. The police would get through easier than her, and she wouldn't lose them. Besides, she might hurt someone. Slowly, all life and hope and promise leaked from her. She pulled over, put the truck in park, and sat back in the seat.

The officers were on her in seconds, their guns drawn. "Put your hands on your head," one of them shouted at her.

In that instant Mary knew it was over. Over the next ten minutes, when she put her hands on her head and stepped out of the truck, and while strangers stared at her from their cars, and officers searched her and read her something called rights, and as they slapped the familiar handcuffs on her wrists, all the while she couldn't stop thinking about one very sad thing.

It was the same thing that haunted her for the next three years after she was convicted of grand theft auto and placed in a juvenile detention center in New Jersey, and when she was caught sleeping with the math teacher while there. While she studied hard enough to get her high school equivalency certificate and when she was placed in a work program doing clerical tasks at the New Life Center on the streets of inner-city Washington, DC.

Mary allowed only one thought to dominate her heart and soul. It was the saddest thing of all.

Grandma Peggy would never know how close she'd come.

Chapter 12

*E*mma wanted to cry for Mary. "Did your grandma have any idea where you were or that you were trying to find her?"

"She had an idea." The pain in Mary's eyes colored everything about her face. "She saw the newspaper the day after I was rescued from Jimbo's basement. She called the police and told them she thought I was her granddaughter."

"So . . ." Emma tried to contain her frustration. "Why didn't the police get the two of you in touch?"

"For a long time I couldn't remember my last name. The information Grandma Peggy had didn't match what was in my file. I guess a lot of people called after my picture ran. If the caller's details didn't match, then the police dismissed the call.

My grandma said my name was Mary Madison, but my file said I was Mary Margaret."

Emma slumped. "That's terrible."

"Yes." Mary's eyes grew damp. "My grandma loved me so much. She still tells me all the time how much she prayed for me back then. No matter what she did, she couldn't find me, but she could talk to Jesus. And Jesus could talk to me."

"But . . ." Doubt breathed on Emma's neck. "Jesus doesn't really talk. I mean, not out loud." She thought about her mother, how faithful she'd been checking up on her and the girls after she'd moved in with Charlie. "That's what my mama says too. She can talk to Jesus, and He can talk to her."

"He talks to us through His promises in the Bible." Mary blinked back the tears in her eyes. "And through other people." She hesitated. "I can look back over my story and see lots of people who, in a sense, were like Jesus to me. My grandma, of course, and Ted and Evelyn, and even Big Dave, the truck driver. But more than anyone else He used my friend Nigel." She smiled. "I'll save that part for tomorrow."

Emma stood. Her heart was torn in a dozen different directions. If Jesus had come to Mary through the people in her life, then maybe He'd done the same for her. Maybe she'd missed it somehow. She was amazed at Mary's strength and her willingness to tell her story even when going back in time was obviously painful for her.

Mary rose and put her hand on Emma's shoulder. "Are you seeing yourself yet? the pieces of your story woven into the pieces of mine?"

"Yes." Emma felt her chin quiver. "I never thought anyone would understand."

Mary hugged her, just a quick hug, but for a moment it reminded Emma of everything safe and warm and good that she'd walked away from. An ocean of sobs began to build in Emma's heart.

Her mother had tried to hug her that way, but ever since she was a teenager, Emma had always pulled away, kept her distance. Now she ached to feel her mother's arms around her again. How come she hadn't listened to the people in her life, the ones who were trying to be like Jesus to her?

She couldn't speak, so she gave Mary a nod and a hurried wave. As she picked up her girls and took them to the cafeteria and afterwards as she read the girls a book and patted their backs as they fell asleep, she stuffed the sorrow that grew inside her.

Finally when the girls were sleeping, she took a pad of paper from the desk drawer in her room and sat in the chair by the small window. Only then did the tears come and with them a review of her life, every bad choice and missed opportunity. . . .

Emma was an only child. Her mother had worked nights as an X-ray technician and delivered newspapers before sunup. Together they shared an apartment and got by, but never with very much. Emma had worn secondhand clothes, and birthdays and Christmases were sparse. Even so, Emma thought her life was wonderful. Her mother was kind and bighearted, with an easy laugh. Faith was everything to her mother, and as a child, faith had been a comfortable given for Emma—Sunday school every weekend, church classes every Wednesday night.

She and her mother found ways to stretch their money. They'd visit the library and check out books together. Her mother would read the tougher ones aloud, and Emma would read the simpler ones, like *Stuart Little* and *Charlotte's Web*. When they reached the funny parts—when Stuart was nearly washed down the kitchen sink or when Wilbur, the pig, tried to fly—they'd set the book down and laugh, sometimes so hard they got tears in their eyes.

Her mother taught her how to make homemade modeling clay from flour and water and food dye, and on rainy Saturdays they'd make crafts together and sing to country songs on the radio.

Emma had heard stories about her father, Jay, and the way he had rescued her mother from the streets of Washington, DC. But she never really knew how much her mother had loved him until one day when she was twelve. Emma walked into her mother's room in search of toothpaste. But there was her mom, sitting low in her chair, crying as if her heart had broken in half.

"Mom . . ." Emma approached her, and only then did she see the scrapbook in her lap. It was something her mother had showed her years earlier. "You're looking at pictures of Daddy?"

Her mother didn't answer. She put the scrapbook down and opened her arms. "Baby . . ."

Emma came to her, dropped to her knees, and hugged her mother for a very long time.

"I loved him . . . so much." Her mother's sobs went on for another few minutes. When they finally eased up, she drew back and studied Emma. "He should be here to keep you safe. You're getting older and . . . and you need him."

Emma wasn't sure what to say. She'd never known her father, so she couldn't relate to his death the way her mother could. But that afternoon, lost in her mother's embrace, her cheeks wet from her mother's tears, she had felt an over-whelming sense of loss. What if he'd lived? How different would her life have been with a daddy like Jay Johnson watch-ing over her, taking care of her?

Looking back, Emma was pretty sure the change in her heart happened that day—the one that ushered anger into her soul, slipped it in between the complicated layers of adoles-cence and left it there to simmer and grow. How dare God take her father from her? How dare her father leave her and her mother alone, her mother scraping by with two jobs, always tired and anxious and overworked?

Even with her work, her mother had tried to be everything to her—both mother and father in one. When Emma was thir-teen, the neighbor lady no longer came over and slept on the sofa so Emma wouldn't be alone at night. The extra money Emma's mother paid the woman was the difference between buying teenage shirts and jeans for Emma or keeping her in secondhand clothes.

"You'll be safe, Emma. I'll lock the doors, and you'll never know I'm gone."

But Emma knew.

She'd lie there at night, eyes wide-open, and jump at every sound. The wind was like a scary voice whispering to her that she was all alone, the creakings of the old building like bad guys trying to break in and hurt her. Eventually she'd fall asleep.

In the morning—after her mother delivered her newspapers—she would get home and hug her tight. "It makes me so happy to be here in the morning, Emma."

Before she left for school, she and her mother would hold hands, and her mother would pray for her. "Protect Emma, help her be a light to others, and help her fall more in love with You every day. In Jesus' name, amen."

Emma liked the closeness with her mother, but the words of her prayers always fell flat. Protect Emma? God had already taken her father, the man known for his ability to protect girls. Why would her mother think God would have any interest in protecting her now? The part about being a light didn't fit right either. The picture that had come to her mind was one of an advertisement, as if her mother wanted her to go around shouting with her actions, "Have faith in God! It'll be good for you."

But having faith hadn't helped her mother, and it certainly hadn't helped her father.

As for love, Emma wanted more than some talked-about emotion from an invisible God. By the time she was in high school, the only love that made any sense to her was the love being offered by boys her age.

Her mother thought by working nights and early mornings she was making herself more available for Emma. But early in her fifteenth year, Emma figured out a way to work her mother's absence to her favor. She took up with a boy three years older than she was, a boy whose parents had little control over him.

When she told the guy she was home alone every night, he raised his eyebrows. "Every night?"

"Yep." Emma angled her head and gave him a coy smile. "Gets awful lonely."

The boy figured out a way to ease her loneliness the next night. He showed up an hour after Emma's mother left for work and stayed until the sun came up. A new pattern took shape in her life. Her daddy wasn't there to take care of her, but there was never a shortage of boys who were.

⌘

The memory dimmed, and Emma felt the ache of the years build in her throat.

Her mother had trusted her, prayed for her all those years. How could she have turned her back on everything that mattered to her? Fresh tears slid down her cheeks, but she kept her crying quiet so Kami and Kaitlyn wouldn't wake up.

⌘

It was no surprise halfway through her fifteenth year when she realized that she no longer felt close to her mother. They both noticed it, because her mother had pulled her aside one Saturday morning and taken gentle hold of her shoulder. "Maybe we need a craft day, huh, Emma?"

She rolled her eyes. "I have homework, Mom."

And that was that.

Of course the reason there had been distance between them had little to do with the fact that they didn't read aloud anymore or make crafts on rainy Saturday afternoons. By then, Emma had trouble even looking at her mother without feeling guilty. And even stronger than her guilt was the feeling of lying in a boy's arms, safe and taken care of, not every night but lots of nights.

The boys changed names and faces, but always there was someone sneaking through the front door after dark.

Her tenth-grade year she met Terrence Reid, a quiet football player with dreams of being a doctor someday. Terrence lived a block away, and that year he started walking her home from school.

"It's not out of the way." He shrugged. "Besides, I like the conversation."

Terrence was a church boy, one of the few on the football team who didn't drink or stay out late on Friday nights. "If I want to be a doctor someday, I can't mess up," he told her once. "I have to stick with my plan."

Emma thought him a curious boy. He was funny and kind and safe. He had none of the dashing good looks or daring personalities of the other boys who paid her attention, and over time they became friends. Every topic was open for discussion on their walks home from school, all but one.

The other boys in her life.

Terrence never asked, and she never volunteered information. Emma figured Terrence knew about the other boys.

Whether he knew or not, they were there. And though
Terrence stayed her friend until the day she moved in with
Charlie, the two of them never dated, never even explored the
idea.

Once in a while the boys who spent the night would
offer Emma drugs or a cold beer, but she always turned
them down. She might've been a sinner for having boys
spend the night, but she wasn't low enough to turn to drugs.
Not even close.

But one decision had a way of naturally leading to the
next. The summer before Emma's junior year, she stopped
attending church with her mother because it made no sense
to keep pretending. "I don't believe the way you do." Emma
put her hands on her hips, her tone ruder than she intended.
"Don't make me go, Mom. Nothing could be worse than pretending I believe when I don't."

"What happened to you?" Her mother's voice was strained
and louder than usual. "When did you stop being the girl
I knew?"

Emma had no answer for her. She simply turned and ran
from the room.

Before her mother went to work that night she knocked
on Emma's bedroom door. "Emma?"

With everything in her she wanted to open the door and
run into her mother's arms, cling to her the way she'd clung to
her when she was twelve and she had found her mother crying over her father's scrapbook. But the road between then
and now was a long, crooked one, too complicated to walk
back down.

She'd made her decision when she began having boys spend the night. That night she squeezed her eyes, shut out the tears blurring her vision, and shouted at her mother, "Leave me alone! You don't understand!"

The doorknob turned, and for a moment it seemed her mother was going to come in anyway. Emma half hoped she would. But then there was the sound of her mother letting go and walking back down the hallway.

After that Emma didn't go to church, and her mother never asked again. They'd taken their positions, set up in opposite camps. The battle line was drawn, and neither of them made more than a halfhearted attempt to cross it.

The fall of her junior year, Emma wound up pregnant. Two boys had been keeping her company the month before, and she had no idea which one was the father. The pregnancy clinic down the street was very willing to set up the abortion and the one that followed it six months later.

By then, Emma no longer felt alive.

She'd stopped the visits from boys, but nothing could stop the nightmares, the faces of babies that haunted her at night. The voices started not long after. She'd be brushing her teeth at the bathroom sink and look in the mirror.

You're a killer, Emma. You're worthless. You should take your own life, the way you took the lives of those babies. Worthless . . . trash, Emma. Nothing but trash.

Sometimes she'd put her hands over her ears to stop the noise, but that didn't work. The voices didn't come from somewhere outside herself. They came from inside.

A month later she went back to having boys stay the

night, and this time when one of them pulled out a rolled-up cigarette and offered it to her, she hesitated.

"Come on," he told her. "You'll be on another planet in fifteen minutes."

Take it, Emma . . . who are you kidding? You're no better than a drug user . . . you're not above it. It's what you need, Emma. Try it; you'll see.

The voice taunted her, pushed her, and she put the cigarette to her lips. "Light it for me?"

"You got it, baby." The boy did, and it was just like he told her. In fifteen minutes she was on a different planet.

Being high was better than anything she'd tried yet, better than having control over her life and better than boys. Because when she was high, the voices were utterly silent. At least at first.

When she reached her senior year, her mother found a box of joints in her dresser drawer. "What are you doing to yourself?" She held up one of the tightly rolled cigarettes. "Is this who you've become? Is this all you want for yourself?"

Her mother's anger was fierce, but it had burned out quickly. By then her mother was too tired to fight with her. A month later she'd stopped Emma in the hallway. "I know what you're doing, and I won't stop you."

"What's that supposed to mean?" Even though Emma's tone was cruel, again she had the urge to take her mother in her arms and break down, tell her she was sorry for all the things she'd done, and beg her to take her to the library. Just one more time. But the idea left as quickly as it came.

"You know what it means." Her mother was calmer than she'd ever been, but her eyes held a world of pain. "You're sleeping with boys when I'm gone. The neighbors have told me. I'm praying for you, but I can't force you to live the life I want for you." She found a sad smile, but it didn't last for more than a few seconds. "I love you. I always will. But I'm turning you over to God. Only He can help you now." Her mother held her gaze a few moments longer. Then she turned and headed for her bedroom.

Emma had wanted to shout at her mother to stop, to turn around. She wanted her mother to put up more of a fight before she let her go. She didn't want to be turned over to a God she didn't believe in. *Wait, Mom . . . come back. . . .*

But the words died on her lips, and the voices kicked in.

See? You're beyond help, Emma. Worthless. The sooner you're out of this house, the happier your mother will be.

And that became the message day after day after day.

Chapter 13

The frightening part of Emma's story came next.
Everything about her life with Charlie had been terrifying. Emma's heart skipped a beat and slipped into a strange
irregular rhythm. What if Charlie knew she was here at the
shelter? What if he was coming for her right now?

*He is coming for you, Emma. He's on his way here, and he's going to
kill you! Just like you killed those two babies and all your mother's hopes
and—*

"No!" Emma waved her hand, fending off the voice.

Behind her, one of her daughters stirred. She looked, but
neither of them was awake. She pressed her fingers to her
mouth and looked out the window. She forced herself to
exhale slowly. Charlie wasn't coming for her. If he knew she
was here, he would've already come.

An ache filled her chest as she glanced at the pad of paper on her lap. Why hadn't she listened to her mother in the first place? So her father had died. Lots of kids lose their parents. She wouldn't have had to turn her back on everything her mother stood for. What had that done for her, anyway? She might as well have lost both parents—all by her own choosing.

She picked up the pen, and her mother's sweet face came to mind.

> *Dear Mom,*
> *I'm sorry. I'm so very sorry.*

That was as far as she got before the tears came again. Her mother had done so much for her—working two jobs, praying for her, and trusting her even when she had acted in direct defiance to everything her mother asked of her, everything she believed in.

The letter was pressing in on Emma's heart, filling her mind with things she wanted to say. But she'd allowed the memories to take her this far. Maybe she needed to relive the rest of it first before she could explain what she'd done and take the next step with her mother.

Emma closed her eyes. . . .

A month after she graduated from high school she took a job at a diner a few blocks from home, and the next week she met

Charlie. He was Hispanic, a bouncer from the bar across the street, and everything about him exuded power and intensity. He wasn't quite six feet tall, but he was thick with muscles and he had an angry stare that made people keep their distance.

But not Emma.

Around Charlie she felt safe. He kept coming around, and when she had a break she'd slip outside into the back alley and the two of them would kiss.

"You're the most beautiful girl I know," he'd whisper in her ear.

And she'd melt in his arms. "You know what I feel when I'm with you?"

"What?" He kissed her neck, her collarbone.

"Protected." She grinned at him. "No one would mess with me when I'm with you."

"Because I'd kill him."

Emma would laugh, flattered that Charlie's feelings for her ran so deep.

But after a few weeks one of the other waitresses cornered Emma in the kitchen and pointed a finger at her. "He beats his girls. Stay away from him."

"You're just jealous."

"No, I'm serious. His last girl worked here until he put her in the hospital."

But Emma had dismissed the warning. Charlie would never beat her. He was strong, but he would use that strength to protect her. She was convinced. Two months later when he asked her to move in with him, she didn't hesitate.

At home, her mother had stood in her bedroom doorway,

tears streaming down her face, and watched Emma pack her things. "Was it something I did? something I missed along the way?"

Emma kept packing.

"If it doesn't work out, I'll be here, Emma. I'll always be here. I never meant for things to turn out this way."

"Look." Emma exhaled hard. "It isn't you, Mother. It's me. I need my freedom." Again she felt the strange twist of conflict in her soul—the desire to stop and beg her mother to hold on to her, to never let her go, versus the desire to push past her without stopping to say good-bye. It was the anger, of course. The anger that had wedged itself in her heart back when she was twelve.

In the end, Emma had stopped only long enough to give her mother a stiff hug. "I'll be in touch."

"I need an address or a phone number." For the first time that afternoon her mother got angry. "If you leave like this, then maybe I'm wrong. Maybe you shouldn't come back."

"Fine." Pierced by pangs of guilt, Emma walked past her mother into the kitchen, grabbed a pad of paper near the phone, and scribbled a number on it. "There. Now you can call me." Even as she said the words she wondered why she was acting so cool toward her mother. Why the angry tone? How had she gone from feeling like her mother was her best friend to treating her like an enemy?

The answers wouldn't come, and Emma barely stopped long enough to say good-bye on the way out the door. She had made a promise to herself as she climbed into a cab and headed for Charlie's place: no matter how bad life got, she wouldn't come back to her mother's house. Not until she had made a life for herself. Got some college or skill training, found a job and some stability. Then maybe they could find their way to common ground once more.

But for all Emma's intentions, none of them had materialized. The first time Charlie hit her, she was already six weeks pregnant with Kami. She'd gone out for milk and bread and come home with an extra jar of peanut butter.

He pursed his lips and snarled at her. "I said . . . milk and bread. Nothing more."

"Charlie, we're almost out." She gave him a nervous laugh. "I'm saving us a trip."

"You don't know about my money." He'd shoved her across the kitchen, and the corner of the vinyl countertop dug into her back. "You're sucking me dry."

She got mad then—fighting mad. Without thinking, she rushed at him, screaming. "How dare you lay a hand on me!" She gave him a sharp shove, but it didn't budge him. "They warned me about you, and I defended you!" She shoved him again.

Throughout her tirade, the anger in his eyes grew. Now that she was inches from him, he reared back and brought his hand full force against her face. The blow knocked her to the floor, and then, her face throbbing, she'd had the most difficult realization.

The warning about Charlie had been right on.

She lifted her head and felt the skin around her right eye. It was already swollen and tender, but it wasn't bleeding. "Charlie . . ." Tears clouded her vision. She reached out to him, her voice as weak as a child's.

Sorrow and regret filled his eyes. "Emma—" he dropped to his knees and took her hand—"I'm sorry. I . . . I didn't mean it."

She was in his arms before she had time to think the decision through. That day, after his apologies and whispered promises, Emma convinced herself that everything would be okay. Charlie might have an anger problem, yes. But he loved her. They were going to be parents together, after all. If anyone could change him, help him let go of the rage, it was her.

It was the same thing she'd told herself every few weeks for the next four years, through the births of Kami and then Kaitlyn, while she went to the emergency room for stitches and CAT scans more than a dozen times, through the days when she wouldn't leave the house because her bruises were too dark to cover with makeup—even on her caramel-colored skin.

Charlie didn't mean it. Charlie loved her. Charlie could change.

All those years she did everything she could to avoid her mother. She scheduled her rare visits between her beatings, and when her mother acted suspicious she would make up a story. She'd fallen down the stairs or tripped going up the slide at the park. Conversations were always awkward, because deep down, Emma doubted that her mother believed her.

After each visit, her mother would collect her purse and car keys, hug and kiss the girls, and give Emma a sad, longing look. A look that found its way to the darkest places in Emma's heart, even if she didn't let on that it did.

"I love you, Emma." Her mother would take tender hold of

her shoulders and kiss her forehead. "You can come home anytime. You and the girls."

Emma would toss her hands into the air and exhale an exaggerated breath. "I'm happy, Mother. How many times do I have to tell you?"

Her mom would study her a moment longer, say one last good-bye, and leave without looking back. Time after time after time.

But the awful truth was this: Emma had been wrong about Charlie. Nothing was going to change him, not her love or her determination or her decision to stay with him. When she told him she was pregnant with their third child, his rage grew and so did the violence and strength of his attack.

"Get rid of it." He grabbed her arm and pressed his fingers deep into her flesh. "I don't want another kid; you hear me?"

She'd lifted her chin and looked straight at him. "I won't, Charlie." She was still haunted by the memory of the babies she'd aborted when she was a teenager. The babies she'd destroyed. No matter what Charlie did to her she wouldn't take the life of another child. "You can kick us out, but I'm keeping the baby."

Charlie shook her hard and then stormed away. Emma's willfulness made him angrier than ever because he had no intention of letting her go. "You're mine," he told her almost every day. "I'll never let you out of here alive."

By then, Emma was convinced that Charlie meant what he said, that if she tried to leave he really would kill her. Her and the girls, no doubt. So in her final weeks with Charlie, she began to make a plan. She would run away with her girls and her things and move some place safe, where Charlie wouldn't find her and hurt her.

The problem was, she had no money, and her only friends were the drug dealers who kept her and Charlie supplied with the best pot and crack and a handful of people they used with. Drugs remained very much a part of Emma's life—one way to shut out the voices that still plagued her, a way to drown out the noise of Charlie's fury. But she never used when she was pregnant, not at all. The moment she learned about her third child, she quit on the spot.

So how could she take her girls and move in with a drug dealer? She'd been working on her plan the day her mother dropped in without calling. It was the first time her mom had seen for herself how bad the bruises were.

What her mother didn't know was that Charlie had been home, laying low in the bedroom. When her mom left, Charlie came out of the room, his steps slow, eyes locked on hers.

Emma still wasn't sure what set him off that day, whether it was her pregnancy or the fact that her mother knew about the beatings. Whatever it was, Charlie grabbed the girls and locked them in their bedroom. Then he turned on her.

"Charlie . . . don't!" she screeched, holding up her hands to fend off his blows. "I love you. Please . . ."

But he didn't stop. Not then and not when she was on the floor fifteen minutes later. This time her abdomen took most of his attack. He would've killed her; she was sure of it. But a car pulled up outside. One of his druggie friends honked.

Charlie stepped back. His eyes were bloodshot, and his

chest heaved from the exertion he'd meted out on her. "I'll finish you later," he hissed, and then he was gone.

Emma had lain on the floor weeping and bleeding and missing her mother with every fiber of her being. Why had she turned her back on her mother's love? All those years her mother had only wanted the best for her, and what had she given in return? Sarcasm and deception, heartache and isolation.

In the other room, the girls were screaming, terrified from the sounds that had filled the apartment. She struggled to her feet and swayed, forcing herself to breathe, to survive long enough to reach her girls. As she took her first painful steps and realized there was blood between her legs, she was sure about two things.

First, she'd lost the baby.

And second, it was the last time Charlie was going to beat her. For the next hour she thought about calling a cab, getting a ride to the nearest bridge, and jumping with her girls in her arms. *Yes, Emma,* the voices told her. *That's exactly what you should do. End it all . . . it's the easiest way out.*

But for the first time in her life she didn't want the easy way out.

The girls were still whimpering, clinging to her legs, and looking to her for comfort. Emma shut her eyes and did the only thing she knew to do. With tears streaming down her battered face, she cried out to the God of her mother. "If You're there, if You're really there, help me now, God. I can't make it on my own!"

There had been no loud response. The building didn't shake, and she didn't feel an immediate transformation. But as she opened her eyes she had a very sudden, very clear memory. She'd seen a television talk show the week before, and on it they featured a woman Emma had heard about before.

The woman was Mary Madison.

Mary Madison, who testified on behalf of abused women before Senate committees and political hearings, ran shelters throughout the city and talked about the power of God being strong enough to change lives and cities and even the nation.

The most powerful woman in Washington, DC.

* * *

And now Mary's story was helping Emma remember her own. But there was one problem. As much as she was sorry for what had happened between her and her mother, and though Mary's story was giving her more hope every day, it didn't erase the way she felt about Charlie.

The way she still felt.

For every time he'd hit her, there had been a hundred times when he'd loved her. No one had ever made her feel so beautiful and cared for, not ever. A picture of Terrence came to her mind, and she dismissed it. Terrence had been her friend, nothing more. But Charlie loved her. He wanted to protect her and give her a wonderful life. His anger problem was just that—a problem. It was something they could work through, right?

She opened her eyes and looked at the beginning of the letter to her mother. Her thoughts were as scattered as fall leaves on a windy day. She wasn't sure what to do about Charlie, but she could at least finish the letter to her mother.

She picked up the pen again and put it to the page. But as she did, she heard Kami's voice behind her. "Mama . . . what are you doing?"

Emma turned around just as Kaitlyn sat up from her nap and stretched her arms toward her. "Drink, Mama?"

A protective love welled up inside her, filling her beyond anything she'd known before. These were her daughters, and they'd been through far too much in their few years. But they were here with her now, safe and well, learning to wake up without being afraid. It was a victory, and it was the direct result of Mary's story, Mary's survival.

Emma set the notepad and pen down on the windowsill. She went to her girls and hugged them, kissed the tops of their heads. This love—the love she felt for her girls—was a miracle. And only then did another possibility take up residence in her heart. Maybe the change wasn't from Mary or her story or the time she was giving to Emma. Maybe it wasn't any of those things at all. What if instead the change really and truly was coming from an all-knowing, all-powerful God?

The same one her mother tried to tell her about all those years ago.

Grace Johnson was making herself a sandwich when the doorbell rang.

All that day she'd been consumed with thoughts of Emma, and other than a few brief breaks, she'd spent every moment talking to God. Where was her daughter, and what was happening to her? Was she in danger again? Had she gone back to Charlie? Or had he found her?

But every time fear gathered like storm clouds in her mind, she felt God talk to her.

Be still, daughter. Be still and know that I am God . . . a strong tower, a refuge for Emma.

The words breathed peace into her, calmed her soul, and gave her a strangely curious hope. Something was happening with Emma, something that might lead her back to her faith. Still, Grace had the sense of a battle, and she intensified her prayers, begging God to hold tight to her daughter, to lead her back to Him no matter the struggle.

When the doorbell rang, for a few heartbeats Grace thought maybe it was Emma and the girls. She hurried to the front door, opened it, and felt the thrill of possibility dissipate.

It was Terrence Reid. "Hello, Mrs. Johnson."

"Terrence." Grace smiled and held out her arms. "Come in."

They hugged and Terrence led the way into the living room. He wore jeans and a short-sleeved shirt. "I was coming home from school." He sat on the couch and set his elbows on his knees. "I had to stop."

Grace held her breath. Terrence had been like a son to her, stopping by and holding conversations with her even after Emma left to live with Charlie. Over the years he'd filled out and become a strong young man—strong in stature and faith, conviction and study habits. He was twenty-four now, a medical student. No matter what choices Emma had made, Grace always held out hope that someday—when her daughter came to her senses—she would find her way back to Terrence.

But reality had a thing or two to say about Grace's dreams. The truth was, one of these days Terrence would fall in love, and then that would be that. Now, with him sitting across from her, his face lined with intensity, she wondered if this was that moment.

She exhaled. "What's on your mind?"

He opened his mouth, but for a few seconds he said nothing. His eyes grew damp, and he swallowed hard. "Emma." He shrugged. "I can't stop thinking about her."

A chill passed over Grace's arms. "Me neither. I've been praying all day."

"Something's happening." He sat straighter, his face masked with concern. "Every time I picture her I see a battle, warriors taking up their arms, two sides determined to claim victory."

Grace nodded. "You know what the battle's for, don't you?"

His voice fell a notch. "Emma's soul." He held out his hands. "Pray with me, Mrs. Johnson. I think Emma's life depends on it."

With fingers and hearts and souls joined, Grace and Terrence begged God to bring strength and protection to Emma, wherever she was. They asked for her salvation and her freedom—freedom from a bondage that would kill her otherwise.

When Terrence left half an hour later, there was an understanding between them. They were not merely the two people on earth who loved Emma Johnson the most.

They were warriors.

Chapter 14

Mary never got used to the smell. The masked pungency of urine mixed with the constant scent of disinfectant.

Not that it mattered. This was where Grandma Peggy lived, and three times a week before her meetings on Capitol Hill or her counseling with battered women, before checking on the dozen causes she was politically or financially connected with, Mary Madison came to this place.

Orchard Gardens Senior Living Center.

She came for a precious half an hour with her grandmother. The connection between them was stronger than ever, as if God had given them this season to make up for all the years they'd lost. Sometimes they talked about politics and the bills Mary was testifying for. Other times they drifted back to the past, and Grandma Peggy would tell her how often she'd prayed, how many tears she'd cried waiting for God to bring them back together.

"I always knew the Lord would let us find each other one day," her grandma would tell her. "I just wish it would've happened sooner."

Grandma Peggy understood the current legislation Mary was pulling for, the funding for continuation of the national abstinence program. She also knew about the bills Mary had helped pass in the last year, bills that provided income for battered-women's shelters and teen-recreation centers in low-income areas. Her grandmother had prayed daily for Mary's part in the My Mentor program for disadvantaged and orphaned children, and when it came into being, they'd celebrated quietly together at her bedside.

Her grandma knew about all of it.

Grandma Peggy was sharp and sensitive, splitting her time between lending a sympathetic ear to her friends at Orchard Gardens and seeking God in the quiet of her room on behalf of Mary. The way she'd done all of Mary's life.

Mary's visit this morning would have to be short. She didn't want to keep Emma waiting. She walked quickly down the hall and slowed when she came to room 114. Her grandmother was sleeping, her big brown Bible on her lap. Mary smiled and crossed the room without making a sound. She sat down and studied her grandmother's walls.

She still had Easter cards lined up on the windowsill. One from Esther down the hall and another from a gentleman friend of hers, a man who signed his card *Love you, William B.*

A few feet away were the framed photos that never left the wall. One of her grandma with her mama, when her mama was in third grade. Another of her mama and her, when she was a newborn. Then there was the photo that had hung in her pink bedroom, the one of herself as a three-year-old.

Mary's gaze returned to the photo of her mother. She studied her eyes, the way they looked happy and full of light. There had been no way to tell back then what the future would hold for Jayne Madison—that she'd turn to drugs and living on the street, or that she'd die without hope or love or redemption.

Tears stung Mary's eyes. The hopelessness and loss of her mama drove her on days when she didn't think she could help another person. No one had been there on the streets to show her mama the love of Jesus. There had been no rescue, no forgiveness asked or granted. Her mother's death was the single worst heartache in all Mary's life.

Jesus had healed every other pain, but the pain of knowing that her mama had died without knowing her Lord was almost more than she could bear. Forever it would drive her to meet with the Emmas of the city so that abuse and drugs and prostitution would not lead to senseless, hopeless death—but rather to redemption by the only one with the power to redeem.

Grandma Peggy drew a deep breath and stirred. After a few seconds she blinked twice and smiled at Mary. "Hello, dear." She held out her frail hand.

"Hi, Grandma." Mary worked her fingers around her grandmother's. Her skin was almost translucent now, marked by blue veins and soft bunches of wrinkles. "How are you feeling?"

"Good as ever." Her eyes sparkled. "How are things with Emma?"

Mary thought for a moment. "She's listening to me. I just finished the part about stealing the truck."

Sorrow eased across her grandma's features. She pressed her thumb against the top of Mary's hand. "If only I had known. I never . . . never would've let them take you from me, Mary." There was a pleading in her eyes, as if even now it was crucial that Mary understand.

"I know, Grandma. God worked it all out."

It took a minute for that truth to work its way to the fibers of her grandma's soul. "Yes." She gave the hint of a smile. "I suppose you're right."

"Well, He did work it out. And now He's going to work it out for Emma."

"She has daughters, doesn't she?"

"Two. They're both young."

Grandma Peggy nodded. "No time like now." Her eyes were cloudier than even a year ago, her breathing slower, more labored—proof that her body was signaling the end. She gave Mary's hand a tender squeeze. "Have I told you lately, Mary?"

She stood and pressed the side of her face against her grandmother's. "Told me what?" She drew back and their eyes locked.

"Have I told you . . ." Her grandma's voice cracked. Her chin trembled, and she swallowed twice, searching for the words. "Have I told you how proud I am of you, Mary?"

Mary felt her eyes well up. In that moment, she was not

the powerful Mary Madison, the woman publicly known for her educated voice and painful past. She was a little girl, sitting beside her grandma Peggy in her pink bedroom, feeling more loved than any child in the world.

"Thank you for saying that." She kissed her grandma's feathery soft cheek, and her gaze fell to the Bible. "What are you reading?"

"Joel." Her grandma lifted the Bible and squinted at the words. "Joel 2:25." She lifted it to Mary. "Read it out loud."

Mary picked up the heavy book and found the verse. "'I will repay you for the years the locusts have eaten.'"

Grandma Peggy grinned and gave the Bible a hearty tap. "That's us, Mary dear. God is repaying us for the years the locusts have eaten."

"Yes." Mary's throat was too thick to say much. "I'm worried about Emma. The locusts have had a field day with her."

"What does God say about the locusts?"

Mary nodded, her eyes blurred from fresh tears. What would she do when her grandma was gone? The woman had brought perspective and reason to her life ever since her rescue by Jesus.

It was her grandma who had given her a place to live and encouraged her to go to college. Late into the night, Grandma Peggy would quiz her on upcoming tests and question her about the education process. At her graduation ceremony for her bachelor's degree and again when she'd earned her doctorate in family counseling, her grandma had been there, beaming from the audience, waving and taking pictures, and cheering her on.

Now, with Grandma's steps and abilities slower, she still was a rock of support and encouragement, sharing Scripture like the verse in Joel. She was the quiet support for all of Mary's public accomplishments as well as her private ones.

Her grandma seemed to know what she was thinking. She pulled the Bible close to her chest and hugged it. "God is faithful in all things, dear." She took Mary's hand again. "He will be faithful with Emma."

"I know."

A curious look filled her grandma's features. "You know what the problem is with the world today?"

Mary smiled. She loved it when her grandma was like this, when she was able to sum up all the godly wisdom of a lifetime and put it into a sentence or two. "What's the problem, Grandma?"

"People want to make Jesus into some Gandhi or Rambo figure. A good teacher or a strong leader." She shook her head, and her eyes shone as they hadn't in years. "You know why Jesus had the power to rescue you, Mary Madison?"

Mary grinned. She knew, but she waited for her grandma's answer anyway.

"Because—" Grandma Peggy jabbed her bony finger in the air for emphasis—"Jesus is God Almighty. He is *divine*." Her energy dropped off a bit. "The world can only be rescued by a divine power."

"I'll remember that." Mary put her arms around her grandma's thin shoulders and hugged her. For a few tender moments, the two of them prayed for the political leaders on Capitol Hill and for Emma and for the world—that people might recognize the divinity of Christ.

Afterwards, Mary gave her one last kiss. "Be well, Grandma." She took a step back. "I need you."

"You don't need me." She grinned and waved Mary off. "You need Jesus. Only Jesus."

Mary gave her grandma a teasing look. It was certainly true. She had remained single because of that truth, devoting her life entirely to the work of God, allowing herself to bask in a love that was unconditional and constant. Still . . . she lowered her chin. "Jesus is enough. But I need you too. So be well."

Then her grandma's smile faded, and tears filled her eyes. She touched her fingers to her lips and blew Mary a kiss.

Mary did the same, holding her grandma's gaze for another few moments. As she left the room, her eyes caught a familiar sight on top of her grandma's dresser.

The small red-beaded purse.

It was the single item that best represented to both her and Grandma Peggy the certainty of God's promise, His providence, and His power. Mary smiled at her grandma once more and turned to leave.

All the way to the car she talked to God, begging Him the same thing she asked of Him every time she left Orchard Gardens.

Please, God, don't take her yet.

Mary arrived at her office a few minutes early.

Emma was reaching a breaking point, she could tell. Listening to Mary's story was probably calling to mind the pieces of her own past, and with them two contrasting emotions: great hope and great despair. The last time they were together, Mary had seen the hope. Emma had talked of writing a letter to her mother and regretting her choices.

But as Emma realized the depth of her bondage and the enemy of her soul tried to lure her into thinking change was too difficult, despair was bound to come. When it did, Mary wanted to be on her knees.

There was a knock on the door, and Emma slipped inside. She looked distant, as if her mind were crowded with conflicting thoughts. She sat down and smiled. "I started the letter to my mother."

"Good." Mary studied her. "How are you feeling about yourself?"

"Glad I'm here." Emma thought for a minute. "I should've done a lot of things differently."

Mary drew a slow breath. *Here's the battle, God. Give me the words.* "What about Charlie?"

Emma bristled. A shadow fell across her face, and she slid back in her seat. "A part of me thinks that maybe . . . maybe I could've gotten him help." Her chin trembled, and she bit her lip. "I still love him."

Don't react, Mary told herself. She kept her tone even. "I understand. That's part of the trap, part of the prison of abuse." She leaned over and touched Emma's knee. "Stay with me, okay? Stay with the story. The answers are coming."

"Maybe . . ." Emma's voice cracked. She brought her fingers to her throat and massaged her neck. "Sorry." She struggled for a moment. "Maybe I should have the answers by now."

"They won't make sense to you. Not until you hear the whole story. Please, Emma. Trust me."

"Okay." Emma's voice was small.

"Before I start today, I want to pray." Mary closed her eyes. "Lord, You are the greatest power on earth, more powerful than any situation or addiction or abuse." She felt the arms of Jesus around her. "We ask that Your power reign over us today and in the coming days. Please, God, set Emma free as You—*only* You—can do. Amen."

Mary stood and opened the window. An early fog was burning off, and the fresh air would help to make the dark parts of her story that lay ahead bearable. She sat down and folded her hands. "After my arrest and conviction for grand theft auto, I fell even further from the little girl I'd been, the one who still missed her mama and her grandma. The nightmares and lying were still there, and I felt driven to hurt myself. I'd bite my fingernails and tear at them. Sometimes I'd pull one completely off."

Emma winced. She ran her fingers along the scars on her forearm. "I did that once."

"*Anything* to transfer the pain." Mary paused. "But the years I spent in juvenile detention added more layers to the hurt. I turned my back on God. I told Him I didn't believe in Him and that He wasn't real anymore. Some of the kids introduced me to cocaine, and I became crazy addicted to it, taking it every day, hiding it in my room and in my shoes. Without faith, well, anything was permissible for me. The affair with my math teacher. The way I acted around the boys . . . so they could sneak me drugs. All of it made me feel powerful, like that was the way life was supposed to be lived."

Emma pulled one knee up, held it to her chest, and encouraged Mary to continue with her story.

"By then I had remembered my last name—Madison. And I tried to focus on my studies. As awful as my life had become, I still wanted to learn. I made a lot of poor choices over the next few years, but I could read and write and work my numbers. When I turned eighteen, they set me up in the state's work program and sent me to a place called the New Life Center."

"On 5th Street here in Washington?" Emma looked surprised. "I've eaten there before."

"That's the place. They gave me a job filing papers in the office." Mary was quiet for a minute, thinking back to that time when she'd met the man who changed her life forever. "That's where I met him."

"Who?"

"Nigel." Mary blinked and looked at Emma again. "Nigel Townsend."

Of all the people God used to show her Jesus, Nigel had the greatest impact on her. But she hadn't recognized any of that in the beginning. Because her first feelings for Nigel had nothing to do with Jesus or His power to save her. She wasn't interested in learning from Nigel.

She was in love with him.

Chapter 15

Nigel was the first one to greet Mary the day she was dropped off by a social worker at the front door of the New Life Center in Washington, DC. He was a mountain of a man, maybe thirty years old, burly with tanned skin and a smile that lit the darkest corners of her soul. His green eyes glowed with warmth and kindness and love—a sort of love Mary had never imagined before.

He was the most beautiful man she'd ever seen.

"Hello, Mary." He sat at a desk just inside the front door. "We've been expecting you." He gestured to the hall beyond the desk. "Welcome to the New Life Center, the place where you'll find your freedom." He smiled at her. "You're going to love it here."

There was an accent in his voice, a musical sound to his

words. Mary guessed that he was European. The way he talked made him sound both smart and kind. But that first day the shine in his eyes was too bright for Mary to look at.

She fidgeted with her bag and dropped her gaze to somewhere near her feet. "Hello." Without really looking up, she mumbled, "Where do I sleep?"

Nigel hesitated, as if he wanted to say something else. Instead he stood and walked past her. "Follow me."

Once she'd put away her things, Nigel led her back to the desk just inside the front door and explained her situation once more. Working at the center was one of the conditions of her release from the detention center. She could consider her penalty paid in full so long as she spent a year working at the center.

"You understand what we do here?" He took the chair opposite Mary's new desk.

Mary kept her eyes down. He took her breath away, but it was too soon to let him see that. "It's a mission. Food for street people, that sort of thing." She should know. "Clothes and canned food a few times a week, right?"

"Yes." Nothing about Nigel was rushed. He leaned forward over his knees and folded his hands. "But we're about more than food for the body, Mary. We have classes too."

"Classes?" Mary couldn't help but look up. No one had told her that the New Life Center had classes. "On math or history, you mean?"

"Not exactly. I teach classes on Christianity, on getting to know Jesus Christ."

His words frustrated her. "Oh—" her voice went flat— "church."

"Not that either." He sat back and laced his fingers behind his head; his biceps bulged on either side of his face. "People who come to the center haven't been in a church in years. Maybe never. I teach people how to have a relationship with God, how to find the greatest love they'll ever know."

There it was.

The part that hit her square in the gut and stayed with her every day after that. The part about finding the greatest love ever. Nigel was the first man who had ever talked to her about finding that kind of love. From that moment on she could feel herself falling for him a little more all the time. Nigel Townsend—the man who would rescue her from her ugly past and make her future all sunshine and rainbows.

Mary began a routine, waking early, taking her spot at the desk. Most of the people who came and went from New Life Center were nice to her. "Hi, Mary," they'd say. Sometimes they'd smile. But most of them knew the truth about her.

She was the notorious Mary, the girl who'd been chained to a bed in the basement for five years. The girl who had tried to run and stolen a truck and been convicted of grand theft auto. Her life had been played and replayed for the whole world to stare at in horror.

There was no getting around it, no place where people hadn't heard the awful story. And it *was* awful; she knew that by then. People had one of two reactions when they figured out who she was. Either they would feel sorry for her, or they'd look her up and down and wish they could have a piece of whatever action she might still be providing.

Nigel Townsend wasn't in either group.

Mary figured she'd work a week, then take the first ride she could get to New York City. She wondered if Grandma Peggy was still waiting for her, but just in case she was, she would make her way there eventually. New York was home, so one way or another she'd find her way back.

But all that changed as she got to know Nigel. After fourteen days of working long tiresome hours at the center's front office, having very little money in her pocket, and sleeping on a cot in an oversized closet off the kitchen, the only reason Mary hadn't run was because of him.

Already she had Nigel figured out. *He's one of those poor souls who still believes,* she told herself. That had to be it. Nigel was the pastor in charge of the mission, so that meant he had her grandma's faith and the faith of Ted and Evelyn. It showed in his voice and his eyes and in the gentle way he had about him. Faith was everything to Nigel. But she would change that; she would convince him that he didn't need God nearly as much as he needed her.

She grabbed a folder from a stack on the desk where she worked. It was mindless work—mostly filing papers—and it barely passed the day. But once in a while Nigel would check on her and give her one of his jumbo smiles. For the next hour her heart would sing.

She picked up another folder and filed it in the lower desk drawer. All her life she'd looked for love. Real love. She'd known it once, with her grandma and her mama. But the customers who had visited her in the basement hadn't loved her. Even the nice ones with the sweet words. Love certainly hadn't come her way while she was in juvenile detention.

Even though she no longer believed in God or the idea
that He might have a plan for her life, hearing Nigel talk
about the greatest love made her want to know everything
about him, how he had gotten so tender and how come—
at more than ten years older than she was—he still believed in
love the way she hadn't believed in it since she was a child.

This will be easy, Mary thought. *I'll get him to my room, and we
can show each other about love, and then I'll stay with Nigel Townsend for
the rest of my life.*

Her plan was a simple one, and she tried several times to
get Nigel to go along with it. She would find him alone in his
office. "Nigel, my room's so dark. Could you come sit with me
until I fall asleep?"

"You don't need me, Mary." He would smile but never even
get up from his desk. "God's already in your room. Talk to
Him."

She'd leave, dejected, her cheeks hot from rejection. Then
she'd find another way to try again the next day. But Nigel
was never interested. The only thing he wanted from her was
her attendance at one of his classes. "Jesus wants to show you
real love, Mary. Class starts at seven. I'll be looking for you."

Mary couldn't understand Nigel. No other man had ever
turned down her advances. Back in juvenile detention, whenever she wanted to feel loved, she had only to suggest the idea
to a fellow inmate or a deliveryman or even—two different
times—to an instructor. They were always drawn by her,
unable to say no. "You're a temptress, Mary Madison," one
man told her. "No man could say no to your beauty."

It was a power Mary enjoyed, but it fell flat on Nigel.

And since he wasn't interested in her, she wouldn't consider attending his classes.

Of course that wasn't what she told him. "I'm too tired," she'd say. Or "I'm not feeling good today."

But each time Nigel asked, she was a little more interested. Maybe if she sat in his classroom, making eye contact with him the entire time, he would change his mind about her. Maybe he would be captivated by her the way nearly every other man had always been. Then he would see how good she was at loving, and he would be powerless to do anything but take her as his own. They would marry, and she would become one of those women she saw walking down the streets every now and then. A woman with a clean look and nice clothes and a handsome husband on her arm.

Yes, maybe she would go to one of his classes, and everything would change.

At the end of the day on her third Monday at the center, Mary looked at the clock. Five-twenty. Ten more minutes and she was done. Another folder and another, and then she heard someone outside the front-office door.

It swung open and there was Nigel, filling the doorway, taking her breath. "Mary . . . class starts at seven . . . upstairs."

She gave him a once-over and then found his eyes. "Okay." She angled her head, batting her eyelashes the way her mama used to when she wanted something from a man. "Maybe."

"Maybe, huh?" He crossed his arms and smiled at her. "That's better than no."

She pictured herself sitting in Nigel's classroom, trying to make eyes at him, trying to convince him to come to her room, all while he was talking about God. A sick feeling came over her, and she shrugged. "Or maybe not." She looked away, stood, and pushed her chair in. Nigel would never love her if she interrupted his precious class time.

Normally he would ask her to come to class and then be on his way. This time he stayed. He leaned his shoulder against the doorframe. "You don't need to be afraid."

"I'm not." A smile forced the corners of her mouth a little higher. Afraid? Was that why she couldn't stomach the thought of attending his class? A class on the greatest love of all? She smoothed the wrinkles out of her worn T-shirt. Again she couldn't look at his eyes. "It's just . . . I'm tired." She looked up for a moment. "So maybe, okay?"

"Mary . . ." Nigel's voice felt gentle on the rough edges of her heart. "I already know. A class on God's love scares you to death."

She stuck out her chin. Didn't he see how she felt about him? that her hesitation had nothing to do with God's love? It had to do with her own love—the love she felt for him. She steadied her nerves. "Maybe the idea bores me."

The tough-girl image was an act, but it was one she knew well. It helped cover up whatever she was really feeling inside. She straightened the papers on the desk and stepped out from behind it. Nigel didn't deserve her sarcasm. "I'm sorry." The conversation was making her feel even sicker.

"Love is waiting for you. God's love." This time Nigel's voice was a caress, but not the type of caress she was used to. Not the type she wanted from Nigel. Still it soothed something deep inside her.

"Ah, Nigel." She came to him where he stood in the doorway, and for the first time she let herself get absolutely lost in his eyes, those brilliant eyes so full of light and hope. "Don't you understand?" Her attraction toward him crystallized. What would it be like to meet the needs of a man like Nigel Townsend? "I don't want to love God." She took a step closer, her eyes locked on his. "I want to love you."

"No, Mary." His tone was kind, but it was stronger than cement. "That's not the love I'm talking about."

"Please, Nigel . . ." She lowered her voice, making it breathy, sensual. "Give up on the God part."

"I can't." He looked through the walls that surrounded her heart and into the last remaining tender places inside her. "God won't give up on you. I won't either."

She was only a few feet from him now, and a chill ran down her body. Maybe he did have feelings for her, deeper feelings. A man who wouldn't give up on her? Wasn't that the sort of love she'd been looking for all her life?

She took another step closer—almost touching now. This must be why she'd been brought to the New Life Center. So she could find love with the beautiful man standing before her. "Don't you need anything besides God?" She brushed her knuckles tenderly against his cheek. Forget the class. They could go to her room and she would show him the sort of love she understood. Maybe then he would stop talking about God. The idea danced in the daylight of the moment.

But he remained stone still, with no response to her touch. "Come to class." He drew back. "Then you'll understand real love."

"Teach me about love, and I'll teach you. We don't need a classroom or a Bible." She moved closer again and let her fingers skim lightly over his muscled arm. "I know a better way."

Nigel took her hand gently from his arm and lowered it back to her side. "You're confused." He stepped back, his eyes never leaving hers. "I want to show you. But love isn't what you've known." He smiled, and in his smile there wasn't even a hint of anything weak or compromising, no proof that he was attracted to her the way other men were. Instead he had the look of a father—the way she always imagined a father might look at her.

But she didn't want a father in Nigel.

The rejection stung the same as if he'd reached out and slapped her. She wasn't desirable to him, and in a rush the reasons were obvious. She was trash. Nigel would want a pure woman. In the glow of his light, Mary suddenly felt so dirty she wondered if she had an odor about her. She broke eye contact and stepped around him. "I'm going to my room."

As she walked past him she could feel Nigel turn toward her, hear his voice like a physical touch against her skin. "I'll be expecting you, Mary." He turned then, walked back to his office, and shut the door.

Mary took a step toward his office. What was he doing in there? Was he trembling the way she was? Was he regretting his decision not to follow her to her room? Maybe he was thinking about it, convincing himself that she was right.

She took quiet steps down the hallway until she reached his office. The other residents at the center were serving dinner in the cafeteria, so the hall was empty. She heard his voice, too soft to understand. Maybe he was talking out loud, telling himself he was a fool for turning her down.

"Please, Nigel . . . I'm here waiting for you." She whispered the words to the closed door. Then she pressed her ear against it so she could hear what he was saying.

"Lord . . . she's a lost girl, barely more than a child. . . ."

Something cold and steel-like shot through Mary's heart. He wasn't struggling with whether he should come to her. He was talking to his God. She forced herself to listen.

"She's longing for love the only way she understands it, Father. Through the power of eroticism and seduction."

Shame blew its hot breath on Mary's face. What a fool she'd made of herself. He had seen through her all the while, and the embarrassment almost sent her padding back to her room. But there was something intriguing about a man like Nigel talking to his God about her. It made her feel strangely important.

"She's beautiful, God. . . . I know better than to spend time alone with her. Help her see me in a different light. Help her hear me about true love, Your love, Lord."

Mary wasn't sure how to feel. Nigel thought she was beautiful, and for that she found a moment of private rejoicing. But even so, he had no interest in her. Not the way she'd hoped. She blinked back tears and kept listening.

"I see Mary's soul, the soul that lies gasping for breath so deep inside her." He paused, his voice more anxious than before. "Help me reach her, Lord. Help me know why You've brought her into my life." Another pause. "She is Your daughter, God, and she is so lost. I want to show her the truth.

Please . . . bring her to class tonight. Show me how I can reach her, and help me . . . help me be wise."

Mary's heart sank. No, Nigel was never going to love her the way she loved him. She had been right before. He wanted only her attendance in his precious class. Nothing more. When Nigel fell in love, it would be with an untainted woman, someone who shared his faith. Someone like her was nothing more than a temptation to do evil.

Nigel was still praying. "God?" His voice became more of an anguished cry. "What do You want from me? Why Mary? . . . Why a temptress here at the mission? And how come I keep hearing You tell me that she's the one, the reason I'm here?"

Mary pressed her ear closer to the door. Nigel believed she was the reason he was here at the mission? The possibility gave her a sense of wonder and hope. Maybe something would work out between them after all.

Nigel sighed loud and long. "For now I will keep praying daily, my face to the ground. Until You show me what You're going to do in the life of Mary Madison. Thank You, Father, because You are faithful. All my answers will come to me . . . in Your time. In Jesus' name, amen."

Mary scurried away from the door and darted back down the hallway. She was out of sight when she heard Nigel's office door open, heard him step out and walk the opposite direction toward the room where dinner was being served.

Nigel was wrong about her. God wasn't trying to do something in her life. That wasn't the reason Nigel was drawn to her. He was drawn to her because she loved him. And in some frightening place in his heart, Nigel loved her too. Otherwise he wouldn't spend so much time praying for her.

Now all she had to do was convince him.

Chapter 16

When the burning pain of Nigel's rejection wore off some, Mary sat up in bed and looked at the red numbers glowing from the clock beside her. It was ten after seven. Ten minutes into the two-hour class where Nigel would tell a roomful of street people and drug addicts about the greatest love of all.

What he *thought* was the greatest love.

She gritted her teeth and flipped the covers off. Fine. It was too hot to sleep anyway. She could go and be late, sit in the back of the class, and try to understand Nigel better. Maybe if she heard him talk about Jesus the way she'd heard him pray, she'd get a better take on how to reach him. Because she had to reach him. She thought about him every night and woke up every morning with him on her mind.

There had to be a way.

Her clothing was still limited, but she'd picked up a bag of jeans and shorts and pretty shirts, things donated to the mission. She slipped into a pair of cutoffs and positioned herself in front of the cracked mirror propped up against one wall of her room. She smiled. No question, she was beautiful. More so than ever. Her legs were long and toned, her waist narrow. If these shorts didn't get Nigel's attention, nothing would. Next she found a tight red T-shirt that showed off her figure and made her long blonde curls stand out.

Makeup was something she'd worn daily back in Jimbo's basement, but not much since. Still, she kept a few items in her bag, and now she scrounged around looking for lipstick. She found it and after she'd applied it, she rubbed her fingers into the roots of her hair, making it fuller, more alluring.

She looked in the mirror once more. There. Nigel would be begging for a visit to her room by the time the night was finished. Yes, he had turned her down for the last time. She took nothing with her as she headed through the building to the west end, where the classrooms were.

The sound of Nigel's deep, rich voice filled the hallway, and she felt drawn to him as she followed it. When she reached his classroom, she stopped for a moment in the doorway. It took several seconds for her heart to decide whether it would beat again.

He was walking across the front, his presence filling the place. As much as she wanted him to notice her, she had the strongest desire to be invisible, to watch him and study him.

What was it about the man that drew her so? He turned his back to the class and wrote something on the board.

Mary used that moment to slip in and sit behind a couple of taller men. Maybe Nigel wouldn't see her right away, and she could watch him, listen to him. Learn enough about him so she could find a way into his heart. She watched his back, the way it formed a *V* from his shoulders to his waist, the way his shoulder muscles flexed as he wrote. He finished and stepped aside. Only then did she see what he'd written.

Dead to self . . . alive to Christ.

She frowned. *Dead to self, alive to Christ?* She slumped down in her seat and looked at the words twice more. How could she ever hope to gain the attention of Nigel—not Nigel the teacher, but Nigel the man—if he talked in terms so strange and frightening? She didn't want to die, and Nigel shouldn't want that for her either. All her life had been leading to this point, to knowing Nigel and being loved by him. She was sure of it. Death had no part of what she wanted to share with him.

He faced the class again, and almost at the same time his eyes found hers. He hesitated and smiled, but not the sort of smile she wanted from him. That was okay. She sat a little straighter. One day he'd smile at her that way.

Nigel shifted his gaze to the other side of the classroom and pointed back at the chalkboard. "Jesus Christ wants to be at the center of everything we do. His life *is* life. It's the only life where we will be loved the way we were meant to be loved." He walked to the other end of the room, but he looked at Mary again. "He has the love each one of you has been looking for all your life. The greatest love of all."

Mary shifted in her seat. Was that all this class was? A two-hour talk about why God was so great and how His love was the greatest goal of life? Nigel was asking the people to open their Bibles to John chapter 10. That's when she stopped listening. She'd heard enough. If Nigel didn't have facts, if he didn't have something more interesting than his opinions on God, she wouldn't stay. One day he would listen to her, and then she wouldn't need to come to his class just to hear him talk. Because he'd talk to her whenever she wanted.

In her room . . . on her terms.

She stood and left without looking back. Out in the hallway, down twenty feet or so, was a girl about her age—maybe a few years older. Mary had seen her before, stopping in at the mission for a meal or hanging out with people who took Nigel's class.

There was no way back to her bedroom without walking past her, and as she approached, the girl rolled her eyes. "Like a broken record, huh?"

Rarely did women talk to Mary, so the question took her by surprise. She wanted to look over her shoulder, make sure the girl wasn't talking to someone else. Instead she stopped and leaned against the opposite wall. "Nigel's class?"

"Yep." The girl wore jeans that were a size too small and a low-cut tank top. She was thin and had dark hair. Pretty but hard. She had the look of someone who had spent years on the streets. "Got in there and heard it was about love today." She released a single laugh, but she didn't smile. "I don't need some Holy Roller teacher telling me about love. I already know about love." Another laugh. "In my life, love pays the bills, if you know what I mean."

Mary wasn't sure. She twisted her face, curious.

The girl must've taken her expression as a sign to continue. "You turn tricks, right?"

"Tricks?" Heat filled Mary's cheeks. She must've known about her past. "Prostitution, you mean?"

"Of course." The girl glanced down the hall where they could still hear Nigel's voice. "Let's get out of here. We can talk outside."

"Okay." Mary wasn't tired, and the girl was interesting. Someone she could talk to. She followed her outside the mission and down the street a few doors.

"You're new, right?"

"Sort of. This is my third week."

The girl tossed her hair over her shoulder and propped herself against the wall. "My name's Summer." She gave Mary a once-over. "I know about your past. Of course you turn tricks. I mean, look at you."

Mary wasn't about to acknowledge her past. But she could answer for who she had become. "I'm not a prostitute, no."

Summer laughed. "You will be." She gestured toward the street. "There's a fortune waiting for you out there." She squinted at Mary. "With a face and body like yours, come on."

Strange new feelings tossed around in Mary's heart. A fortune? Why hadn't she ever thought of that before? In juvenile detention she couldn't turn tricks. She could sleep around and almost never get caught. But she couldn't leave the building and get paid for it on the streets.

Now, though, she was an adult, eighteen years old. In a year, when she was finished working at the mission, she could do whatever she wanted. The sun was setting, and the angle hit Mary straight in the face. She shielded her eyes. "I'm still finishing my sentence. A year working at the mission before I can even think about it."

"Nah." Summer swatted at the air above her head. "I had a work program once too. You leave and they put your name on a list. But no one ever comes looking for you." She nodded to the streets again. "How're you ever gonna break free without money?"

It was a good question. The mission work paid something—fifty dollars a week. That and food and a free room. In a year she could have twenty-four hundred dollars if she saved every penny. It sounded like a fortune when she added it up. Plenty of money to find her way back to New York City and see if by some miracle her grandma Peggy was still there.

She leveled her gaze at Summer. "I'll have more than two thousand dollars after a year. That isn't bad."

"Two thousand dollars in a year?" Summer folded her arms and sneered. "You can make that in a *month* on the streets."

For most of her life Mary had known people who serviced men for a price. Her first year in juvenile detention she figured out that prostitution was how her own mother had made a living. A conversation came to mind, something she and her mother had talked about the month before she disappeared.

"How come you dress up some nights, Mama?" Mary had been young and only vaguely aware. She was certain her mother did drugs, because she'd heard her grandma talking about it. But she must've paid for the drugs somehow.

"Mama does her job at night, sweetie."

"What sorta job?"

"Well . . . Mama takes care of men."

It was the same job Mary had done for Jimbo all those years in the basement. Prostitution.

Summer was still talking, something about having a boomer month one year. "I pulled in seven thousand—" she whistled—"but that's when I was young like you. Now I've got twenty-five years on me. Five or ten more and I'll need me a new line of work." She laughed as if it were the funniest thing she'd said all evening.

Mary wondered if she'd feel old when she was twenty-five. She felt sick at the thought. Turning tricks might work for a while. But for a living? She'd sooner starve to death. "Maybe you'd feel better if you found a different job."

"Nothing pays like streetwalking." She shrugged. "You'll figure it out, kid."

"No." Mary's resolve grew stronger. She thought about Nigel. "I'll file papers until I find real love." She made a face. "Not the love Nigel Townsend talks about though."

"Oh . . ." Summer studied her, and then a slow smile filled her face. "You're in love with him." It wasn't a question.

"No." Mary shook her head. "I could never—"

"He'll break your heart. He's gorgeous and strong and good." She whistled again. "No one looks like Nigel Townsend." Her tone changed. "But he isn't your type or mine." Summer narrowed her eyes and looked at the darkening sky. "Almost like he's straight from heaven. The woman who turns Nigel's head will be a God-fearing woman, the kind you and I ain't never gonna be."

The statement made Mary angry. Summer didn't know what Nigel wanted. Besides, all men wanted the same kind of love, right? She could offer that sort like a pro. She was finished talking with Summer. She started walking in the opposite direction of the mission.

"What? Did I scare you off?" Summer called after her, and Mary picked up her pace. Before she was out of earshot, she heard Summer's laughter echoing down the street.

Mary crossed a busy street and headed into a park beyond. Rules at the mission were strict. No leaving without permission from one of the staff members and then only for an express purpose and for a short amount of time. Definitely not after dark, and already it was dusk.

Still . . .

Nigel was in class until after nine, and the other staff would be gone or in class with him. The night had kicked up a warm breeze, something to break the sticky humidity. Mary slowed her steps and stopped. Ahead of her was a couple like the kind she wanted to be a part of. A pretty, well-dressed woman with a nice-looking man on her arm, living in a world of dreams and dates and shared love. That's what she wanted with Nigel. She leaned against a tree. The bark was rough against her back, but she didn't care. The couple stopped at a play area, and the young woman sat in one of the swings.

Mary couldn't quite hear what they were saying, but she could hear the woman's laughter, see the way she tipped her head back as the man pushed her high into the air. Eventually the couple grew tired of the swing and continued down the path through the middle of the park. As they faded from view, Mary thought about what Summer had told her. Nigel would break her heart. He wanted a God-fearing woman, someone clean and pure.

Like the breeze on her face, the truth hit her. Summer was right, of course. Nigel would never want her. He would tell her about God's love and how following Jesus meant being dead to self and alive to Christ. But he could never accept her past— a past he clearly knew about. Every detail was in her file.

She drew a long breath and held it. It was mid-July. The smell of cherry blossoms was gone, and the air was rich with the earthy scent of fresh-cut grass. What if Summer was right about the other stuff too? Two thousand dollars after a year's work? All the while seeing Nigel every day and knowing she couldn't turn his head in any of the usual ways?

It would seem like a decade at least.

Prostitution wasn't something she wanted, but short term . . . a month or two. . . . That was all it would take to have enough money to get back to New York. She bit her lip and pulled away from the tree. The decision didn't have to come tonight. She could work around Nigel for another week or so and see if anything changed. If it didn't, well . . . the tricks would always be there.

She headed back toward the busy intersection. Another block and she'd be at the mission. After a good night's sleep, she'd probably forget she'd ever had thoughts like these. Nigel would see the light eventually. She came to the crosswalk and pushed the button. At that same instant, a shiny black car drove slowly past her. The driver was bald and was wearing a fancy suit. He looked hard at her and then drove on.

But before the light turned, before she could cross the street, he swung his car around and went through the intersection again, his eyes still on her. Once more he passed by and swung his car around. This time he pulled up and rolled down his window. "Hi, beautiful." His eyes were bright. Not like Nigel's, but not mean like Jimbo's either.

Her nerves rattled, it took a moment to find her voice. "Do I know you?" He didn't look familiar. Was it her past? Was that how he knew her?

"Actually . . ." He motioned her down the sidewalk a few feet, away from the busy intersection. Then he turned off his engine. "Here." He patted the seat beside him. "I do business in the area."

Business? The man had a powerful look about him, but he didn't frighten her. She opened his car door and sat inside, one foot still on the curb. "What . . . sort of business?"

The man smiled. "Banking."

"Oh. How do you know me?"

A sadness came across the man's face, but it was a sadness that didn't quite look real. "I don't know." He brushed his fingers against her chin. "You look familiar."

She was about to get out, to walk away so he wouldn't remember where he'd seen her before.

That's when he made a shallow gasp. "Wait, I know." He snapped his fingers a few times. "You're that girl—the one they rescued from the basement." He pointed at her. "Mary, right?"

Her face felt hot, and she stared at her lap. "I should go before—"

"Wait!" He sounded sincere. "It was wrong, what happened to you." He hesitated and brought his lips together tight. "Are you . . . are you by yourself?"

"Yes." She lifted one shoulder. His car smelled rich, like leather and expensive cologne. The man didn't seem quite genuine, but he wasn't going to hurt her. She could tell that much.

The man searched her face. "Do you work down here?"

Mary nodded. She considered telling him about the mission and her filing job, but she changed her mind. "I'm saving money to get back to New York City."

The man ran his tongue along his lower lip. "Are you . . . eighteen yet?"

"Yes."

A smile lifted the man's face. "Mary . . . I think I can help you." He leaned against his door. "How would you like to work for me?"

Mary started to shake her head, but the man held up his hand. "Not *that* sort of work. I mean secretarial tasks—typing, filing, answering the phone." His voice was casual, but the intensity in his eyes doubled. "I'll pay you twice whatever you're making now."

His body language seemed to indicate that he meant her no harm. "That sounds okay."

The man smiled, but it never reached his eyes. "I'd set you up in your own place, get you some nice clothes. You'd start next Monday."

Mary's head was spinning. She hadn't done drugs since she'd been at the mission, but in that moment she was desperate for a hit of something. The man's offer was too fast, too good to be true. "I . . . I don't know."

"The way I see it, Mary—" he reached out and touched her hand briefly—"you deserve a break."

Mary breathed in, but the air refused to fill her lungs. She gripped the door handle of the car. "Come with you? Right now?"

The man squinted through the windshield and looked down the street. "Where do you live?"

Heat filled her cheeks again. Her voice fell some. "At the mission."

Genuine sadness filled his face this time. "That settles it. You'll come with me."

"What about my clothes, my stuff?"

The man shook his head. "We'll get you new things. You have the rest of your life ahead of you."

Mary looked down the street toward the mission. She could play this out, couldn't she? see where it led? She could come back to the New Life Center in a week or so if the job didn't pan out. She felt her confidence swell. Working for a businessman was a respectable job, not like turning tricks on the streets.

Maybe with a job like that, Nigel would see her differently.

"Come on, Mary." The man looked in his rearview mirror. "Everything's going to be okay."

"All right." A rush of fear hit her as she shut the door, as the man pushed a button and the locks slipped into position. "Where are we going first?"

"I have a penthouse where I entertain out-of-town businesspeople." The man pulled the car into traffic. He glanced at her. "You'll be safe there. Tomorrow we can get you some clothes and find you an office in my building."

"You have your own building?" Mary still felt breathless. Everything was happening so fast.

The man chuckled. "I have ten buildings."

Mary had nothing to say in response. The man must've been a millionaire. A billionaire even. But what would he want with her, and how had it all happened so quickly? She sat back in her seat and gripped the armrests. The man hadn't even told her his name or the name of his business. What if he wasn't a businessman at all? A flashback came at her, making her dizzy with fear. The last time she'd climbed into a car and headed off to some unknown destination was with Jimbo and Lou. The place they had taken her had made her a prisoner for the next five years.

Her mouth was dry, and she had to work to push out even a few words. "What's your name?"

The man drove faster than the other cars heading through the city. He didn't look at her. "Clayton Billings." He gave a sideways nod of his head. "You can call me Clayton."

Mary loosened her grip on the armrests. Clayton Billings? As in Billings Savings, the banks set up around the city? She'd seen the name on some of the papers she'd filed. Her emotions fought for position in her mind and heart. One of the richest, most powerful men in the city wanted to give her a job. This was the greatest day of her life, the day when everything would turn around.

Grandma Peggy would be so proud of her.

A quiet gasp slipped from her mouth, and she covered her lips. Her grandma! She looked quickly over her shoulder. The mission was nowhere in sight. Not the mission or her little room or Nigel Townsend, no doubt still talking about the love of Christ. But she needed Clayton to turn around and go back. She'd forgotten the little red purse.

"Wait!" She turned to Clayton. Her face felt cold, and her hands shook. "Go back! Please!"

He slowed, but he didn't stop. "Don't be afraid. Everything will be fine. Better than fine. You'll see."

"No!" She grabbed the door handle and jerked it, but the door was locked. "I forgot something—something special."

Clayton pulled her back into her seat and kept his arm in front of her, blocking her way. "We'll go back for it. Let's get you situated first."

Mary felt herself getting farther from the mission, farther from the strange teaching about death to self that Nigel wanted her to understand. She had no choice but to trust Clayton Billings, trust him that one day soon—as soon as she had the job and a place to live—she could go back and get her little purse.

No matter where life had taken her, regardless of the prison she found herself in, the purse represented hope. A hope that somewhere, somehow, she would find Grandma Peggy again. And if not her grandma, then at least she would find love. All of it was wrapped up in that one small red-beaded purse.

And now—in a matter of minutes, along with everything about her old life—it was gone.

Chapter 17

There was more.

Mary stood up from the sofa and stretched. For a long while she looked out the window at the street. Why had she ever gone with Clayton? She could've gone back and ducked into Nigel's classroom. Even if she wasn't ready to hear about dying to self, she knew one thing: Nigel wanted the best for her.

Behind her, she heard Emma get up and come toward her. She touched Mary's shoulder briefly. "Clayton wasn't a good guy?"

Mary shook her head slowly. She turned and leaned against the windowsill. "He was rich and powerful." She sighed and looked out at the street again. "But he wasn't good."

"I understand."

That much Mary was sure of. Emma had spent the past

four years with a man like Clayton Billings. "Strange how the
lines between pain and love blur when you're with a man who
hurts you."

Emma took a step back. Clearly she didn't want to talk
about that kind of man or how well she could relate. Not in
detail anyway. She motioned toward the door. "I need to check
on my girls." Emma hesitated. "But I'd like to hear more."

Mary looked at her watch. "Ten minutes, okay?"

"Ten minutes."

When Emma was gone, Mary made them each a glass of
iced tea and returned to her place on the sofa. Always at this
part of the story her heart bled for Nigel. He'd been so certain
that she would see the light, but then . . . before he could stop
her, she was gone.

Mary put her thoughts on hold. She needed to save them
for Emma, and in the meantime she would pray. When Emma
heard about Clayton, it was bound to make her think of the
situation she'd just left, her relationship with Charlie.

Then a point would come where Emma would have to
choose.

Not with a hasty decision the way Emma had chosen when
she fled from Charlie. That time she'd run for her life. But
almost all abused women find ways to justify the actions of
the men they love, and most of them at least consider going
back. Emma would be no different. Her next decision would
be a forever one. Go back to Charlie and her old way of life—
or take hold of the rescue Jesus Christ wanted to give her.

Mary heard Emma coming, and in a few seconds her office
door opened and Emma returned to her seat.

"The girls are fine." Emma smiled, but there was anxiety in her eyes. "They like it here."

"Good." Mary nodded to the table. "I made us iced tea."

"Thanks." Emma caught her breath. "Did Nigel . . . did he come after you?"

"He would have." Mary let the memories fill her mind once more. "He was crazy with worry for me, praying for me all the time. But he had no way of finding me—no leads, nothing." She took a sip of her tea. "Truthfully, I wasn't thinking about Nigel at first. Clayton made me feel like I'd stumbled into a fairy tale."

Clayton took Mary to a penthouse with high ceilings, marble countertops and tiled floors, and a bedroom with piles of pillows and sheets that felt like silk. In all her life she'd only dreamed of such a home. It was like something she'd seen on television.

"This is where you'll stay." Clayton showed her around. When they reached the kitchen, he opened a few cupboards. "Eat anything here. I'll have fresh food delivered tomorrow morning."

Mary could hardly believe her good fortune.

When Clayton was finished explaining where everything was, he looked at the clock on the wall. "It's late, Mary."

Was this the part where he was going to take her to the bedroom, same as Jimbo and his friends back in the basement? But instead Clayton took a few steps back and gave her a pleasant smile. "Enjoy yourself. I'll come by tomorrow so we can talk about your job."

"Okay. Thank you." Mary was baffled, breathless. What sort of man would offer her the world on a platter and ask for nothing in return? Even Nigel had wanted something from her—a decision to place her faith in Christ. But not Clayton. The man seemed completely genuine.

Still, that first night, she barely slept, afraid Clayton would sneak back inside the penthouse and chain her to the bed. When she woke the next morning, she found bagels and fruit and coffee in the kitchen—courtesy of Clayton, obviously. Sometime before lunch, a deliveryman came to the door with bags of groceries, and another one followed behind him with a bouquet of roses.

At three o'clock that afternoon, Clayton returned. "Hi, Mary." He grinned at her. "How're you feeling?"

She giggled. "Like I've died and gone to heaven."

"Fitting." He wandered over to the flowers and smelled them. "Someone who looks like an angel should feel like she's in heaven."

She and Clayton sat at the table and shared the most wonderful coffee. After that, he stood to leave. "One of my assistants will be here in the morning. Her name's Betty." He patted her hand, but he withdrew it immediately. "Betty will take you shopping." He winked at her. "By tomorrow at this time you'll have a whole new wardrobe."

Again Clayton left without asking anything of her. He made good on his promise. Betty arrived after breakfast and took Mary to the finest stores in the city. The woman was older and not overly talkative. But she did not seem alarmed by the idea that her boss had taken Mary in. "He likes being around beautiful women," Betty told her. "Clayton usually gets what he wants."

But that was just it. Clayton didn't seem to want anything.

By the end of the week, Mary had new clothes and shoes and perfumes and cosmetics—the very best of everything. Clayton saw that she had wonderful shampoos and soaps and lotions and bubble bath. On Friday, Betty took her to a salon in a high-end part of town.

The woman working on her hair trimmed the ends and then stood back and raised her brow. "Your hair's gorgeous, miss. I wouldn't do much else to it."

Mary didn't.

Now it was Saturday afternoon, and Clayton had told her he was coming over. He'd be here any minute. She wandered around the spacious penthouse and stopped at a bank of windows. She wasn't far from the mission, maybe five miles or so. Looking out toward the setting sun, the view from the fourteenth floor must've included the New Life Center somewhere.

She let her forehead fall against the glass. What was Nigel doing right now? Maybe he'd put aside her things for her, in case she ever returned.

She stood straight, shoulders back, proud and tall. At this point, why would she go back? She thought about Nigel a little less every day, and in the past twenty-four hours she had felt herself falling for Clayton Billings. The man had given no indication that he had feelings for her. Maybe he only wanted to give her a chance in the world, a chance she'd never had before. That's what he told her every time she asked.

But what if someone like Clayton Billings actually had romantic feelings for her? She'd be set for life. He could fall for her and marry her, and she'd have everything she ever imagined. Without ever dying to Christ even a little bit.

If she didn't go back to the New Life Center ever again, then she'd never find her little red purse. So she'd have to go back someday. But maybe the purse didn't matter anyway. Her mama had left her alone with drug dealers, and the drug dealers had used her for five years. Where was her mama all that time? And what about Grandma Peggy? How come neither of them came looking for her? Were they both dead?

Yes, the red-beaded purse represented the sort of love Mary had clung to all her life. But no one had ever loved her the way Clayton was loving her. Even if that love was only platonic so far. If Clayton was willing to take care of her like this, then she didn't need her mama or her grandma or even Nigel Townsend. Because this was love enough. One of these days she'd find her way back to the mission and collect her little purse. But for now, she would ride the wave of good fortune as long as it was rolling.

There was a knock at the door, and Mary jumped. She took a last look in the mirror. She wore black pants and a white fitted blouse, her hair tied up loosely with a black ribbon. In that moment her past didn't matter at all. She had never looked more beautiful. She picked up her pace and opened the door, slightly breathless. "Hello."

Clayton was tall, but not in a way that intimidated her.

Beyond that he wasn't much to look at. Long face, strong jaw, bald. His eyes were every bit as blue as her grandma's. But there was a power about him, a charisma that tightened her throat and made it hard to draw a breath.

He stepped inside. "Hi, Mary." He didn't look below her neck. "I've been thinking about your job."

Mary felt a rush of disappointment. Did he even notice how she looked? Was he another man like Nigel, unwilling or uninterested in seeing her as more than a project? someone to give a hand to? Mary led him to the table, the one where they had shared coffee a few times already. She tried not to sound upset. "I guess we should talk about that."

When Mary had made coffee for both of them, Clayton cleared his throat. "I think maybe it's better to have you work from here, from the penthouse—" he paused—"at least for now."

A curious feeling stirred in Mary's stomach. What sort of work did he have in mind? Was this where the handcuffs would come in? She steadied herself. "Why?"

Sympathy filled Clayton's eyes. "People still remember you, Mary." He pointed to himself. "I recognized you after only a few minutes." He folded his hands around his coffee mug. "I think you'd feel better if you worked from here."

"On the computer, you mean?"

"Yes." He motioned to the den, where a desk and a computer were already set up. "I'll give you files to work on, and you can do the work in there."

Relief soothed the wrinkles in Mary's soul. Clayton was talking about honest work, not the sort of thing Jimbo had

had for her. But still . . . why wasn't he interested in her? even a little interested? "When do I start?"

"Monday. I'll have a stack of work delivered. The files will be easy to figure out." Clayton took a long swig of his coffee. "You mentioned wanting to get to New York. Tell me about what's there."

Mary told him the bare details, how Grandma Peggy had loved her and how she had had a pink room at her grandmother's flat. "I'm not sure exactly where she lives, but if she's still alive, she's looking for me."

"I'm sorry, Mary." His eyes were sympathetic, but even here—relaxing with coffee—the power that came from him was electrifying. "One day I'll take you there, and together we'll find her, okay?"

Was he serious? All this and help finding her grandma too? She felt the sting of tears in her eyes. Whatever happened next, whatever life Clayton Billings had in mind for her, it would be the thing she was born to do. Because no one outside her mama and her grandma had ever cared this much for her.

Not even Nigel Townsend.

Mary began doing the file work Clayton had brought her, and the days blurred. When he visited her later that week he complimented her. "You're a good worker. Maybe we can get you into the office sooner than I thought."

Every compliment he gave her, every hour he spent with her, Mary fell more in love with him. Never mind Nigel and the kindness in his eyes and voice. Clayton had a different sort of kindness and a power that was unmatched by anyone she'd ever known. Spending time with him was like realizing her purpose in life. When he visited she would hang on every word he said and secretly hope he'd never leave.

At the end of the next week, Clayton came earlier than usual. He sat her down at the table and took her hand. Excitement was in his eyes and at the corners of his lips. "I thought of another job for you."

Mary's heart wasn't sure which direction to go. She was happy, of course. If Clayton had thought of another job, then that meant he trusted her. Trust could lead to love, couldn't it? And love might mean she would spend the rest of her life with Clayton Billings.

He touched her cheek, her chin. "I want you to be my friend, Mary." He waved his hand at the rest of the penthouse. "I'll come by more often—maybe every day—and you can have coffee with me and listen to me. Make me feel special." He smiled and wet his lips with his tongue. "How does that sound?"

It sounded wonderful, especially if it meant Clayton would visit her more often. "Would I . . . would I still work on the files?"

"Yes, in the mornings." He let his hand rest on hers. "But the afternoons would be more relaxing. Spending time with me."

"But . . . I need to make money." She looked around her new home. "I can't expect you to keep paying for everything."

"You know what I think?" He brought his hand back to his side. "I think you've worked enough. For now you can be my special girl, someone I can talk to and visit, someone I can take care of." He smiled, and the sincerity in his face lit the room. "The other people in my life don't listen like you do, so that can be your job. What do you think?"

Mary brought her hands together, and her heart jumped

at the possibility. "Really?" How amazing was Clayton Billings? For every horrible turn her life had taken, this was the
break she'd been waiting for. Clayton wasn't talking about
having his physical needs met—though she wouldn't have
minded. In some ways she wanted to meet those needs so she
could show him a sort of love in return for all the love he was
showing her. But at least he wasn't demanding that of her. He
only wanted to take care of her, talk to her, visit her, and
know that she was safe.

The fairy tale was showing no signs of ending.

Then, like the sudden change of music in a scary movie,
Clayton's eyes grew dark. "One thing, though." He leaned forward. "My wife must never, ever know about you. She can't
know, or I could lose everything."

What? Wife? Mary felt the blood leave her face. Clayton was
married? The room tilted wildly to one side, and she gripped
the table to keep from falling. "You're . . . you're married?"

He chuckled. "Of course I'm married. I've been happily
married for almost twenty years."

"But . . . I thought . . . ." She felt like a fool. All this time she
let herself believe that Clayton would fall for her eventually.
Sometime very soon. She tried to catch her breath. "I didn't
know, Clayton."

His eyes grew still darker. "You staying here, this job—it has
to be our secret." He shook his head. "Betty would never say
a word." He stopped, his eyes locked on hers. "And you can't
either." He chuckled. "My wife would divorce me and take half
of everything I've worked for if she found out about you."

Mary felt sick, and she wasn't sure she could stay at the

table. Nothing he was saying made sense. Okay, so he had a wife. He hadn't crossed any lines with her, hadn't shown any interest that could pass as more than helpfulness and generosity. So why would his wife care? "I don't . . . understand."

He slid closer to her. His hand came over hers again. "You're mine now, Mary." He smiled. "If I want you to file, you'll file. If I need a friend, you'll listen." He raised his brow. "You want that, right?"

"Yes." Her answer was quick. "I want everything you've given me."

"Okay, then." He looked calmer. "I need you to promise you'll keep what we have a secret. And that you'll never, ever leave this building without calling me first."

Mary stared at him. "I can't leave without calling you?"

"No." A hint of anger flashed in his eyes. "I'll give you my cell-phone number and—" he took his wallet from his pocket and peeled off a stack of one-hundred-dollar bills and handed them to her—"I'll make sure you have money whenever you need it." He tucked his wallet back in his pants. "If you need anything at all, just call me." A smile tugged at the corners of his mouth. "It's not like you're my prisoner. I just want to know where you are."

Mary counted the cash in her hands. She felt her eyes grow wide. Five hundred dollars? She'd never seen that much money in all her life. *Don't look too excited*, she scolded herself. *Of course he has money. He owns half the city.* Something else . . . he trusted her. Jimbo had never let her out of the house without standing at her side. But Clayton was giving her money and the chance to venture out and spend it as she chose. All she had to do was call him first.

"Here." He took a cell phone from his other pocket and handed it to her. "The penthouse won't have phone service. This is how I'll reach you. My phone number is programmed in the address book." He showed her how to access it. "That way you'll always remember to call me."

She took it and felt her heart rate settle back to normal. Clayton wasn't asking anything strange of her. He merely wanted to keep his friendship with her a secret, and he wanted to know where she was. That was part of being cared for, wasn't it? And maybe one day he would grow tired of his wife—who clearly wasn't very understanding. He'd leave her, and the two of them would get married instead.

The dream still lived. "Thank you, Clayton." She put the cell phone on the counter behind the table. "I understand about this being our secret."

"One more thing." He leaned over and rested his elbows on his knees. His face was more serious than before. "You must only use the phone to call me or to order food or supplies. No personal phone calls. I'll have a record of every number dialed out and every call that comes in. Do you understand?"

She didn't. But maybe this wasn't the time to talk about it. Once he got to know her better, once he realized that he could trust her, he'd let her make phone calls. She needed to find her grandma still, and it wouldn't hurt to call Nigel and tell him she was okay. But for now she dismissed the idea. She nodded. "Whatever you want."

Clayton was looking at her, watching. Waiting. In his eyes

was something Mary was familiar with. He might not want favors from her or a chance to have his needs met. But he wanted her. He was drawn by her beauty the same as any other man. It was the reason he wanted to keep her all to himself. The realization made her love him more than ever. If she had this type of power over him now—when she hadn't shown him what she was capable of—then she could only imagine how he'd fall for her later.

Once she could show him the kind of love she knew about.

"Well . . ." Clayton gave a nervous laugh. "Have I made myself clear? No one can know about this. No one."

She was willing to live by his rules. If her prince only stopped by the palace every now and then, so be it. The love they shared was already better than anything she'd had before. Even if they were only friends. Still, she wanted to know exactly what was at stake. She put her forearms on the table. "Tell me. What'll happen if someone finds out?"

The smile faded, and his laughter died in his throat. "You wanna know?"

"Yes." She was playing with him, teasing.

"If my wife finds out about us . . ." His tone was easy and joking, like hers. But his eyes were stone cold. "I'll have to kill you, Mary."

Her body went cold and she couldn't move, couldn't breathe. When her heart jump-started back into a partial rhythm, she stood. "Clayton! That's an awful thing to say."

He laughed and leaned back, stretching his legs out in front of him. "Don't take everything so seriously." His laughter faded, and this time his eyes sparkled. "I'd never hurt you." He touched her knee with the tips of his finger, sending shivers through her body. "Just don't ever tell anyone." His eyes searched hers. "Okay?"

"Okay." Her breathing wasn't back to normal until he left half an hour later. Only then did she wander to the wall of windows and stare out over the city. He'd been kidding her, right? She was his employee, his friend, someone who could listen to him. A man as kind as Clayton Billings would never kill anyone. Especially not her. His career, his reputation, his freedom would all be lost.

As the night played out, as she washed her face with soft, sweet-smelling creams and tucked herself into a bed thick with luxurious sheets and blankets, she thought about what he'd said: *"I'll have to kill you, Mary . . . kill you, Mary . . . kill you, Mary."* For all the ways her new life felt like a fairy tale, she fell asleep thinking about living by herself and waiting for Clayton, keeping quiet around strangers and avoiding phone calls. In the frightening hours between midnight and six in the morning, she had the strongest, most sickening sense that Clayton's scary words might not be teasing at all.

But a very real, very desperate threat.

Chapter 18

There was a distance in Emma's eyes, and it worried Mary. She set her empty iced-tea glass down and studied the woman across from her. "I found out later that Grandma Peggy caught up with Nigel a week after I'd left."

That got Emma's attention. She frowned. "You mean she left New York and came to Washington?"

"Yes. The police realized the mistake they'd made, and they contacted her. She was on the next flight to DC, and the next morning she met Nigel at the New Life Center. By then Nigel had already notified the police of my disappearance. No one knew where I was." Mary stopped for a moment. It was tragic how close they'd come to finding each other. She would've been spared so much if only she hadn't gone with

Clayton. "My grandma wondered if I was dead, but Nigel didn't think so."

"Why?" Emma looked edgy again, as if her own thoughts had taken a front seat and she couldn't wait to leave the room.

"Nigel's always been a praying man. God gives him a sense, and whenever I came to his mind, that was especially true. He told my grandma not to give up, that I was alive out there somewhere." Mary took a quick breath. "My grandma spent two days combing the streets. She made a poster with my picture on it, the one from my file at the New Life Center."

Again a distance filled Emma's eyes, but this time she said nothing.

"After a few days, Grandma Peggy went back to Nigel and told him what he already knew. Wherever I was, only God could bring me back again." Mary hesitated. "The next day, Summer paid Nigel a visit. She told him that I had been in love with him and that she saw me walking away from the mission. Nigel shared the information with my grandma, and they both became convinced that I was alive."

Emma nodded. "Should we pick up again tomorrow?"

Mary hid her disappointment. "All right." What was it in Emma's eyes? Was she realizing the decision that lay ahead? Was she still considering going back to Charlie? She lowered her voice. "Emma . . . what's wrong?"

"Nothing." She twisted her fingers together and tapped her foot. "I need a fix, I guess."

"You've been without drugs for several days." Mary's statement was intended to show Emma that she trusted her. "Isn't that true?"

"Yes." She looked at the floor and rubbed the back of her neck. "But right now I want some bad."

"This is when the battle is its fiercest. In most cases, the physical addiction is broken after three days. But you used drugs as a way of coping." She paused. "I did too. The nightmares and lying, the pain I caused myself and the faithlessness. The drugs and even my promiscuity. All of it was a way to cope, a way to survive. And that's an addiction no power on earth can break."

"Exactly." Emma tossed up her hands. "So why the meetings? Why the story? I'll never be like you, Mary. You keep my girls, okay?" She pointed toward the window. "My life's out there. With Charlie."

"No, it isn't." There was a cry in Mary's voice this time. "You can't believe that. That's a lie, and it always will be. Jesus wants to rescue you, same as He rescued me. Your girls need you, and they need you whole, free of all this bondage." Mary heard her voice grow still louder, more intense. "Don't start listening to the lies again, believing that Charlie has something you need or that drugs are the answer. Because that's all that garbage is—a pack of lies."

Emma gripped her knees and sat a little straighter. "Maybe you better tell me more of your story."

"Okay." Mary forced herself to look relaxed. *God . . . the battle is fierce. Help me. Give me words to keep her here.* "I have all day. And so do you."

"When you tell me your story . . ." Emma's hands were shaking. She pressed them to her thighs. "I forget about mine for a little while."

"Good." Eventually Mary wanted Emma to connect the two stories, to see Mary's way of escape as her own. But for now it was enough if the story kept Emma's interest, if it kept her in her seat when every fiber of her being wanted to run through the front door, find the nearest dealer, and catch a ride back to Charlie's house. "If that's how you feel, I'll start where I left off."

"Clayton wanted more than friendship, didn't he?"

"Of course. I see that now. Back then I wasn't afraid of his making the next move, taking our friendship to another level. Even if he was married." Shame colored Mary's tone. "I thought I loved him, that he was the only man who loved me without wanting something from me."

❦

Another week passed while Mary filed papers in the morning and held visits with Clayton most afternoons. By that Friday, conversations with him were no longer enough. Mary wanted to work her way deep into the heart of the man, to the place in his soul where she wouldn't be merely a pet in a beautiful cage.

But the woman he would need more than air.

Clayton was running late that day, and Mary wondered if maybe he wasn't going to visit her. But just before dinner he called. "I'm coming over," he told her. "I'll be there in an hour. I have some business to take care of."

Mary smiled to herself. She would be ready for him. Her shower lasted longer than usual, and she was careful to use all

the best-smelling soaps and hair products. She understood
Clayton much better now than the first time they'd met. He
was a good man, a moral man. A man who didn't want to
upset his wife. He had talked to her that week about faith in
the human spirit, that sort of thing. A faith Nigel Townsend
would've scoffed at.

She let thoughts of Nigel linger for a minute; then she
willed them away. He had moved on by now, focused his
efforts on some other lost girl in need of Christ's love. She
turned the shower hotter, and for a long time she let the water
run over her. Hot water had never been so available, and
showers were still one of the best parts of her new life. As the
steady stream washed away the suds, she could picture the
water taking with it all the ugliness and pain of her past.

Fresh from the shower she felt good about herself. The
loss of her mama and her grandma was only a distant memory.
Almost as if the love she felt for the two of them belonged to
someone else entirely.

Mary dressed in her nicest clothes. Something else was
clear now. The reason Clayton had said he'd have to kill her.
He wasn't a crazy madman she needed to fear. His reason for
saying that came from a devotion that was deeper than anything anyone had ever felt for her. He cared about her, and
he'd told her so nearly every time they were together. Sometimes he brought up her past.

"I watched you on television that night, the night they rescued you." He studied her, his face tender. "I couldn't believe
what that . . . that monster had done to you." Clayton was a
calm man whose power and grace made for perfect control.

But when he talked about her past, his teeth came together and his voice sounded different. Full of rage.

"It's okay, Clayton. I'm here. I survived." She touched his face, his hands. Anything to get him to show her the affection she craved.

"It's not okay." He searched her eyes, looking straight to the cold, dark alleys of her soul. "If you were mine . . . if you'd always been mine, that never would've happened."

Yes, his concern for her was almost beyond devotion. He may have been teasing about having to kill her if she talked to anyone about him, but his emotions were so intense it was possible he would kill someone else on her behalf. She could imagine it happening. It was why she wanted the upper hand, so he wouldn't hurt anyone because of her. If she had control, he would do whatever she asked, even if it meant giving her more freedom and loosening his hold on her.

"Mary?" She heard him come through the front door. He sounded breathless, unusual for him.

"Hi." She stepped out into the living room and watched the effect she had on him.

Usually he kept his eyes on hers, refusing to look below her face. But this time his eyes wandered down the length of her. "You look . . . perfect."

"Thanks." She came to him, stopping when they were only a few feet apart. The smell of alcohol rushed at her. This had happened twice that week. Clayton would come to her after he'd been drinking.

His breathing was ragged, fast and uneven. "Mary . . . what you do to me."

It was working. She closed the distance between them and tilted her face to his. "No, Clayton. What you do to me." She lifted her lips to him. "Let me show you."

He brushed his mouth against hers—not a kiss but the closest thing to it. He placed his hands on either side of her face. "What do you want to show me?"

Her answer needed no words. . . .

When it was over, after he promised he'd be back the next day, Mary smiled. The victory was hers. Clayton would fall in love with her for certain now; it was only a matter of time.

But instead of falling in love with her, Clayton grew more agitated and distant with every visit. "Business," he told her. "There's trouble with my business."

Once, a few nights later, when she and Clayton were kissing, she pulled away and asked him the question that was always on her mind. "Do you love me?"

He ran his thumb along her lower lip. "I *own* you." He smiled, but his tone was chilling. "Of course I love you."

His answer made her mad. "I don't like how you said that. People don't own people." She pointed to the entryway. "I could walk out that door tomorrow and go back to the center, and you wouldn't have a thing to say about it."

"Actually—" he shifted and unbuttoned the collar on his dress shirt—"I thought I went over that."

"You told me I couldn't talk to people. I couldn't tell anyone about us." She crossed her arms. "But you didn't tell me I couldn't leave."

"Leaving brings on the same punishment." He gave a weak

laugh, but he didn't sound for a minute like he was kidding. "Okay?"

She moved to the other end of the sofa. "You wouldn't kill me." She stared at him, forced him to look into her eyes, the piercing blue eyes that had cast spells on so many other men. "You wouldn't hurt me." She stood, feeling powerful. "The truth is, Clayton, you need me too much."

"Yes." The corners of his mouth went flat. "Enough to kill for you, Mary. Enough to kill you."

For the first time, she was afraid. "I'm not kidding."

He didn't hesitate. "Me neither." Then, as if nothing were wrong, Clayton stood and joined her at the far end of the sofa. He pulled her down with him, even when she struggled to stay upright.

"Stop it!" She was stiff in his arms, the door to her heart closed shut. "You don't love me." The proud look was back. She could feel it. "Because you have a wife."

"I told you—" he took hold of her shoulders and held her tight, too tight—"I own you. I couldn't love you more because you belong to me." He gave her a quick shake. "Only me."

"No." Mary jerked free from his grip and sprang to her feet. "I don't belong to *anyone*."

Anger colored his features. "How dare you talk to me that way . . . after all I've done for you?" He rose and took a step closer. "I've risked everything for you."

"Stay away." She held her hand out, increasing her distance from him as she backed up. She turned and ran into the bedroom, shouting, "Leave me alone!"

He was only steps behind her. "Don't tell me what to do."

He knocked her hand away from her face. His anger intensified, seething from his eyes, his scowl, his force. "I'll do whatever I want to you." He shoved her roughly onto the bed.

"Get out of here!" Her voice was shrill. She tried to get up, but he had his hand on her shoulder. "You don't own me!"

Like a roaring fire exploding through a tinder-dry forest, rage engulfed him. She watched it happen in a matter of seconds. Clayton climbed onto the bed and gave her another shove, sending her sprawling onto her back. "I told you, Mary, I *own* you."

"No . . . go away!" She scrambled back toward the headboard. Her voice was loud and frantic, her face hot. "You can't—"

He crawled after her and grabbed her arm. Then he pressed his hand to her throat and pushed her down onto the pillow. She made a gurgling sound and shook her head, her eyes wide. She couldn't breathe, couldn't inhale even a precious bit of air. He could kill her—he really could. Fear swallowed her whole, and when his hand eased up, she shook as if she were having a seizure.

"I do own you, Mary Madison." Clayton forced his lips onto hers. After a minute he pulled back. "Watch me prove it."

When it was over—after he'd taken her body and spirit, her dignity and determination—she lay in a heap, weeping for what he'd done.

Clayton stood over her. He touched her forehead with the strangest tenderness. "Shhh . . ." His voice was calm again, his anger spent. He wiped his thumb over her damp cheeks. "Stop crying, little one."

She whimpered in response and turned her face from him.

"I love you, Mary." He leaned down and kissed her forehead. "Don't forget that."

And in that moment, Mary had yet further proof that Nigel hadn't known what he was talking about. Love wasn't good and right and true. It was horrific and painful.

The way it had been as far back as she could remember.

Chapter 19

The worst of it was this: even after he attacked her, Mary couldn't stop her fascination for Clayton. If love was what he felt for her, then she loved him too. Loved him the way she hadn't loved anyone in all her life. After he had raged at her and taken her against her will, after he had scowled at her and screamed at her and told her he owned her, she still loved him. She loved his strength and his power and the way he took care of her.

He had demonstrated love to her—what she knew of love—the way no other man had.

A week passed, and Clayton came to see her three times. Always he was gentle. He felt bad, clearly. She looked outside at the sunny Monday morning, the way the leaves were full and green on the streets below her penthouse. Ever since his attack on her, she had felt driven to go against Clayton's orders. Not just on principle. But because she had someone she needed to see.

Nigel Townsend.

She had enough money to easily pay for a cab, and maybe if she spent time with Nigel she could make sense of her feelings for Clayton. That, and she could get her little red purse. Once she had the idea in her mind, it wouldn't let go. Clayton wouldn't be by until that afternoon. What would a morning visit to the mission hurt? She wouldn't mention Clayton after all.

Finally, before lunch, she slipped her bag over her shoulder, locked the door behind her, and headed downstairs.

"Beautiful day, miss." The doorman grinned at her and tipped his hat. He was good-looking, twenty-five years old or so. In another life she might've been interested. But she lived for just one man now. Clayton Billings.

"Yes." She smiled at him. "I need a cab." She waited while a yellow cab pulled up. This was her first time in a taxi. She gave the doorman two dollars as she climbed inside, the way she'd seen it done in the movies.

"Where to?" The driver looked at her in the rearview mirror.

For a moment she considered telling him New York City. She could take the cab all the way to some place familiar, find a phone book or someone who could help her locate her grandmother.

But two things stopped her. First, she couldn't do that to Clayton, not after all he'd done to set her up in the penthouse and give her the best clothes and makeup and jewelry, the best of his time every afternoon.

Second, she didn't think he'd kill her, but Clayton was a powerful man. If she left, he would find her. And she didn't want to think about what would happen then. Besides, she needed to see Nigel Townsend almost more than she needed to see her grandmother. At least for now.

Mary gave the driver the cross streets of the New Life Center and settled back into her seat.

Ever since Clayton attacked her, she'd had the strangest feeling. Morning, night—it didn't matter. She would remember his rage and the way he'd hurt her; then she would remind herself how much she needed him, how terribly she loved him. And then with amazing force came a new thought. The certainty that she should kill herself.

Which was why she needed to see Nigel.

The cabdriver pulled off to the side of the road and looked over his shoulder. "Eight dollars, twenty cents."

Mary pulled a ten from her purse and gave it to the man. "Keep the change." She climbed out and stared down the street at the mission a block ahead. This was almost the exact place where she had first spotted Clayton's car, first agreed to climb inside and head off with him to some dream life.

She took quick steps toward the mission. Her look was different now—low-heeled pumps, tailored pants, silk blouse conservatively buttoned to the hollow of her neck. Her navy cardigan vest was the highest quality, and her long blonde curls were pinned back. As she reached the front door, she hesitated. What if Nigel didn't recognize her or remember her? What if he called the authorities and reported that she was back? They could probably put her in jail.

Worse, what if Clayton found out she'd come? Doubts hit her like so many hailstones.

Calm, Mary. Be calm. Nigel wouldn't turn her in. She walked the rest of the way and went inside.

The receptionist—the one who sat where she should've been sitting—was someone new, a teenage girl with eyes far too old for her face. She gave Mary a look. "Can I help you?"

"Yes." Mary clutched her purse to her middle. "Nigel Townsend, please."

Another look and the girl nodded. "All right." She stood and moved toward a door behind her desk. "I'll get him."

Mary exhaled in short bursts, trying to slow her heart rate. She took a seat opposite the desk and waited.

After a minute or so, the girl returned with Nigel behind her. He looked at Mary, and it took only a moment for him to make the connection. As soon as his eyes locked with hers, it was obvious that he knew. Everything about his expression softened, and his steps slowed. "Mary . . ."

Her heart filled with warmth. "Nigel." She had missed him so much, missed the look of something pure and real and true in his eyes. He glowed with goodness, and she didn't hesitate another moment. She stood and went to him, put her arms around his neck, and hugged him. "I missed you."

Nigel didn't allow the hug to linger. He pulled back and nodded over his shoulder. "Let's go to my office."

The receptionist eyed them, obviously suspicious. But

Nigel only smiled at her. "The door will be open, but I need you to hold my calls."

"Okay." The girl cast Mary another look of dislike . . . or maybe jealousy.

Poor girl, Mary thought. *She's probably in love with him the same way I was.* She followed Nigel, and when they reached his office, he lowered himself into the chair behind his desk and motioned for her to sit in a chair on the opposite side of the desk.

For a long time he said nothing, only looked at her. She wasn't sure, but his eyes seemed to grow damp as he searched hers. "You look . . . different."

Mary folded her hands. "I am." Her voice trembled. Now that she was here she felt suddenly terrified, as if Clayton could walk through the door any minute. She pushed the fear down and took a deep breath. Clayton couldn't intimidate her this way. She had a right to visit an old friend, and she had a right to talk about her feelings.

"I've spoken to your grandmother."

Nigel had spoken to Grandma Peggy? Tears poked at her eyes and filled them with a veil that made Nigel's image blur. "When . . . when did she call?"

"Right after you left. She came here." He paused, letting the words sink in.

"You *saw* her?" Mary couldn't take a breath. "You know how to reach her?"

"Yes. She spent two days looking for you. Putting up flyers, asking people on the street. After that, she gave up and went home." Pain colored his voice. "She loves you very much, Mary. She wants you to come home."

Mary hung her head and covered her face with her hands. She could feel her heart ripping in half. Her grandma was alive and still looking for her? It was more than she had dared to hope for. She wiped her eyes and looked at Nigel. "She never gave up on me."

"No, she didn't." Nigel pursed his lips. "Like I said, she misses you very much."

"I miss her too." *Don't cry, Mary . . . not now.* There wasn't time. She had to get back before Clayton came home and . . . "Tell her I can't . . . I can't come see her just yet. But tell her I'm okay." Mary's throat hurt. She blinked back the tears that kept filling her eyes. "Tell her I'm fine and that I love her." She sniffed. The wall holding back a flood of sorrow was crumbling. "Tell her I love her very much."

Nigel pulled what looked like an address book from his desk; then he scribbled something on a slip of paper. "This is her number." A sad smile touched his eyes. "She'd love to hear from you."

Mary looked at it. After all those years of wondering how she could find her grandma, here it was—the number that would connect the two of them in seconds. Her voice fell to a whisper. "Thank you, Nigel."

"You're welcome." Nigel sat back and planted his elbows on the arms of his chair. "So . . . where have you been?"

Mary considered him, the light in his green eyes, the sincerity in his voice. He was so different from Clayton, his kindness so much more authentic. So why were her feelings for Clayton stronger than any she'd known before?

She opened her mouth to answer him, but her words died

before they reached her lips. Clayton had warned her against this. She couldn't tell anyone where she was living or who was keeping her there. It was one thing to disobey his orders about leaving home. But to tell Nigel the truth? She cleared her throat. "I found a man who . . . takes care of me."

Something sharp like pain crossed Nigel's expression. "Is this man married?"

Mary couldn't contain her reaction. Her eyes grew wide, and she sat up straight and folded her arms tight across her middle. Nigel hadn't changed. He still seemed to know exactly what she was thinking, what she was feeling. She lifted her chin, doing her best to look proud and sure of herself. "It doesn't matter."

"It does." His words were a caress against Mary's soul. He clearly had no intentions of judging her. Even if she was living a life he didn't approve of, he cared. But he was also honest. He crossed one leg over the other and gave a slight nod. "Of course it matters."

"He loves me."

"No one will ever love you the way Jesus does." Nigel looked deeply at her. "He died to make you His own. Only He doesn't expect anything in return."

"Anyway . . ." Mary's knees were shaking. She pressed them together and leaned closer to his desk. "I can't stay long. I . . . I have to get back."

"Why'd you come?" Nigel's words were slow, thoughtful. "I could report you."

"I know." She shrugged. "I'd only run again."

He narrowed his eyes. "You're scared."

"Yes." She looked at her hands, the way her fingernails were bitten so far down that the tips of her fingers showed. She was having nightmares again, and nothing seemed to make sense. Maybe she would find a crack dealer and load up before she went back home. Her eyes found Nigel's again. "I have a question."

"Ask it."

"If I kill myself . . . if I took my own life . . . would I go to hell?"

Nigel looked like he'd been punched in the gut. He sat back against his chair and sank down a few inches. "Is it that bad, Mary?"

She wanted to say no, it wasn't that bad. Not really. She had a man who loved her, even if he had gotten out of control once. But her throat was too tight with emotion, and no words would come. Her heart pounded, and though sunshine streamed through the window, she felt chilled to the bone. The cold moved to the center of her soul. She wrapped her arms around herself. Then she stood and took a step back. "I need to leave."

"Hold on." He reached into one of his desk drawers, and when he stood, his fingers were wrapped around something. He came around the desk and put his other hand on her shoulder. "You're asking the wrong question, Mary. Don't ask me about going to hell for killing yourself." He waited. "Ask me how to find life."

Life? Mary shook from the cold. Yes, maybe that's what she was looking for. Because it wasn't what she was going through with Clayton, locked up, there for him to treat her as he wished. "I c-c-can't ask you, Nigel. I have to g-g-go."

He gave her shoulder a light squeeze. "I want to pray for you, Mary."

A picture came to mind. Clayton standing over her, slapping her and shouting at her and . . . She squeezed her eyes shut and shook her head. Then she looked at Nigel and tried to focus. She had to go. "Quick, all right?"

Nigel held her gaze for a few seconds, then he bowed his head. "Dear Jesus—" his voice was low and calm, filled with peace—"You are the great Savior, our mighty God, our Lord and our Friend. Mary has questions and she has great fear. I don't know who she's running from, but You do. Please grant her safety and a very deep hunger. That she might find true love, the kind she's always wanted, by coming here again and again and asking questions. Because You hold all the answers, Jesus. In Your name, amen."

"Nigel . . . thanks." She went to hug him, but he stopped her.

Instead he held out his hand, the one still clutching something. "Here."

She opened her palm, and he pressed something familiar against it. Mary didn't look at it—she couldn't. There was no time to break down, no time to do anything but get out. "I'm glad I came."

A siren sounded in the distance, and it made her jump. With her empty hand she touched Nigel's arm. "Tell my grandma I'm okay." She turned away, then looked back over her shoulder at him. "I have to go."

"Give me your address, your phone number." Nigel reached for a pad of paper. "In case I need to reach you."

Terror clawed its fingernails down her back. "I can't." She backed up to the office door. "I'm sorry, Nigel. Good-bye."

Mary left the office and began to run. She had no time for discussion, no time to do anything but get back outside and hail a cab before it was too late. If Clayton found out she'd gone to the New Life Center and that she'd talked to Nigel . . . she wasn't sure what he'd do.

She felt alone and cold and scared. Her breathing came in shallow gulps, and no amount of air satisfied the urgency in her lungs. Not until she was in the cab did she unfold her fingers and look at the item in her hand that Nigel had given her. She had known what it was from the beginning, because the feel of it was as familiar as her own name. Nigel must've found it in her room when she'd left and saved it for her.

The tiny red-beaded purse.

A sick feeling settled like wet cement in her stomach. Her grandma was looking for her, so how could she go back to Clayton? back to a man who would beat her and control her and threaten her? She stayed on the edge of the seat, her heart slamming against her chest. The answer was easy. She loved Clayton because he took care of her. No matter what he did or how he treated her, he didn't mean to hurt her, didn't want to frighten her.

She took the folded piece of paper with her grandma's phone number scrawled across it. Then she opened the clasp at the top of the purse and slipped the paper inside with the other one, the one with the words her grandma had written for her years ago. She wanted to read it, but she was scared to touch it, scared to take it out. It was almost one o'clock. She needed all her energy to think of a story for Clayton—in case he was waiting for her when she got back.

Not until she had the cabdriver drop her off a block from her penthouse, not until she ran home and scrambled into the elevator and tore down the hallway to her unit, not until she was certain she was alone and Clayton hadn't come yet did she drop to the sofa and bury her head in her hands. She had come too close. Going to see Nigel had been a crazy idea, especially so late in the morning.

Next time she would have to be more careful.

Chapter 20

Regardless of the dangers of disobeying Clayton, nothing could've stopped Mary from going back to Nigel. She had questions, and he had answers. It was that simple, that profound.

Weeks passed, and twice more Clayton had beaten her. The last time he spat at her and called her trash. Now it was September, and Mary could feel her life crumbling like a sand castle at high tide. She had nowhere to run, no way to escape.

Sometimes in the shower she would grab the bar of soap and scrub it hard along her arms and her stomach. Hard enough to leave red marks on her body. But no amount of soap could take away the dirt, the filthiness she felt inside. Trash? That's all she was to Clayton? She still loved him— what she thought was love. But now she had to admit the obvious: Clayton was using her like every other man in her life had used her.

Every man except Nigel Townsend.

Sometimes as the hours passed with Clayton she would count down the minutes until she could see Nigel again. She didn't have feelings for him like before. This time she had questions. More questions than she could hold in her head. Questions about God and the love Nigel talked about so often during her visits. If Clayton didn't love her, if no man had ever really loved her, then maybe she needed to know more about Nigel's Jesus. Maybe all these years she really had been missing the greatest love of all. The love that had put the warmth in her grandma's smile and the oceans of peace in the eyes of Evelyn and Ted and Nigel. It was possible, wasn't it?

One Thursday, when Clayton left her at four o'clock, Mary didn't hesitate. He wouldn't come back until the next day after lunch, which meant she had the whole night to herself. This time she dressed in jeans and a green blouse. She had nothing to prove, no reason to make Nigel think she was doing better than she was. Her goal was simple now. She wanted as many answers as Nigel could give her.

That evening as the driver sped through the streets of Washington, DC, for the first time Mary thought of Clayton as he really was. Like a week-old bandage being ripped off an old wound, she felt her heart pull away from him. If only she could break free from him completely, convince herself that she didn't need him. Then she would never again think of killing herself. She could bid him good-bye and leave for good.

If she could do that, she could call her grandma and go to her without fear. Until then, she didn't dare involve the one family member she had left—or Nigel, for that matter. That's why all her visits had to take place at night. For everyone's safety.

She arrived at the center just as dinner was being served. Quietly, she took a seat at one of the tables in the back of the room. It really was a wonderful thing Nigel was doing here, the way he helped the people of DC. She looked around the room. Some of the faces were familiar, people who had come for a meal back when she worked here.

A tableful of people caught her eye, especially an older woman and two younger women. A mother and her daughters, maybe. Mary squinted, trying to remember. Yes, that was it. A mother and her daughters, and the two toddlers sitting at the table were the little girls of one of the young women. The five of them made up a family, one who lived on the streets. Mary studied them—their easy way of laughing, the light in their eyes. Something was different about them, something Mary couldn't quite figure out.

Mary kept watching them, the way the young mother helped her children butter their bread. The details were coming back. The week before Mary left, Nigel had just found them housing. An apartment a few blocks away. And the women had started attending Nigel's classes. Her thoughts stalled and she blinked. Was that it? Had this family found the love Nigel talked so intensely about?

She narrowed her eyes, studying their faces, their expressions. That's when she saw it. They weren't only familiar because they'd been coming to the mission back when Mary was here. They were familiar because of the look in their eyes. The same look her grandma and Nigel and Evelyn and Ted had.

Goose bumps rose on Mary's arms, and at the same time she felt a hand on her shoulder. She jumped and turned, and there he was. Nigel. Standing behind her, grinning at her as if he were seeing a long-lost daughter for the first time in a decade.

Mary stood and put her hand on his arm. Hugging him here in front of a cafeteria full of people would be awkward. Some of them would remember how she had once felt about the man, how shamelessly she'd tried to gain his affection. She dropped her hand back to her side and looked deep into his heart. But she kept her distance. "What is it about the eyes?" She glanced back at the table of women and then at Nigel again. "Those women . . . Grandma Peggy." Her voice fell. "You. There's something different about the eyes."

Nigel didn't hesitate. "The eyes are the window to the soul." He leaned his hand on the closest table. "People who love the Lord, who receive His love, His rescue . . . their eyes change." He had never looked more handsome, his own eyes never so full of light. "Jesus eyes. That's what I call them."

She didn't really understand, but she nodded anyway. Peace filled her because even as beautiful as Nigel was—inside and out—she didn't want to go to him. Not in the physical way she'd wanted to in the past. Rather she wanted only to learn from him. So she could have the life that Nigel so clearly had. True life. She lowered her chin, humbled. "I have more questions."

He smiled, and a low rumble of laughter sounded in his throat. "I prayed you would."

"Can you . . . can you talk?"

"How long do you have?" The noise of more than a hundred people made their conversation private, even in the middle of the cafeteria.

"All night. Clayton won't be back until—" The moment she said his name, she stopped. Her hand came to her mouth, and she shook her head. "What I mean is, the man I'm with . . . he doesn't come until the afternoon and . . . he's not really anyone who—" Her words scrambled in her head and came out all wrong.

"Mary." Nigel said her name with a calm and peace that were otherworldly. "Your secrets are safe with me. Whatever they are."

She gulped, and his eyes told her she could trust him. "Okay."

"You have time." Nigel's smile was the kind look of a father. "That's what you're trying to say."

"Yes."

"Come to class. We're talking about God's desire to rescue us."

"*Rescue?*" The word played across her wounded heart like a soothing balm. *Rescue?* That's what she'd always needed, always wanted. Back in Jimbo's basement, later at the Lakes' home, even now with Clayton controlling and abusing her. All her life she'd needed rescuing. The word made her eyes damp, and she could only nod in response.

"Good." Nigel looked past her to the food line. "I need to

help finish up dinner." He found her eyes again. "We'll meet after class."

"Okay." Mary watched him go. She was about to sit back down when she spotted the family again, the older woman and her daughters and her grandchildren. The three adults were clearing plates. Not just theirs, but plates from other tables also. As they worked, they'd stop and smile at the street people at each table, putting a hand on someone's shoulder or chatting for a few minutes.

Mary pulled up her sleeves and took a few steps to the nearest table. Two older men and a few empty-eyed teenage girls sat there. They were finished eating, but no one was talking or making a move to clean the table. She leaned in and smiled at them. "All finished here?"

Two of the girls met her eyes, and one of them nodded. Mary's heart ached for them. Was this how she'd looked when she first came here? Was it how she appeared now beneath the carefully kept hair and face and the new clothes? She cleared that table and three others, following the lead of a few volunteers as she made her way to the dirty-dish bin at the back of the room.

"Time for class!" a woman announced.

Nigel was nowhere around, probably already at the front of his classroom, asking God for direction about what to say and how to say it. The concept was still foreign to Mary, but it had her attention. Who had she ever asked for direction or guidance? She'd spent the last few years making her own decisions, justifying them along the way.

The auditorium-style classroom was full that night. The

walls were dusty cement block, and the carpet was worn through in patches, but the hundred or so people who sat in the rows of old desks had an energy, a warmth that was undeniable.

Mary found a seat in the back row and bowed her head when Nigel opened the night by praying for God's leading. "There are walls in this room, in these hearts." He paused, his tone rich. "Let this be the night that they fall. For everyone here. In Jesus' name . . ."

In unison the crowd said, "Amen."

Nigel opened his eyes and grinned big at the faces that filled the room. "Tonight we talk about the martyr Stephen."

A hand shot up in the first row. "Nigel, man, you know we ain't got that Bible talk down yet." It was a skinny white guy with a scraggly goatee. He gestured with his hands as he spoke. One entire arm was covered with dragon tattoos. "Break it down, brother."

Nigel chuckled and gave a few understanding nods. A three-legged stool stood near the blackboard, and he pulled it up and sat on it. The corners of his mouth eased back to a serious straight line. "A martyr is someone who dies for his faith."

The skinny guy slid down in his seat and turned his backwards baseball cap around so the bill shaded his eyes. "That's deep, man."

"Yes." Nigel looked at a man in one of the middle rows and then at a woman a few seats from him. The way he shifted his attention around the room, they all must've felt the same. Like Nigel would've stood up there and given that lesson even if they were the only one in the room.

"I mean, really deep." The skinny guy sat up again and made a sound with his lips, sort of like a leaking tire. "Dying for your beliefs, man? Crazy deep."

"Giving your life to Christ, trusting Him to make you into something new *is* deep." Nigel was on his feet again, pacing to the other side of the room. "That's how it was for Stephen."

Nigel went into the story, how this Stephen became a believer in Jesus and how his new faith was everything to him. "Stephen was a man full of God's grace and power."

A Hispanic woman in the back pointed her finger in the air. "That's what I like about God." She did a rhythmic head bob and smiled at the people around her. "He's got the *power!*"

A few random *amens* broke out across the room. Nigel was amazing. He had street people and alcoholics and drug addicts hanging on every word. Every word of a Bible story, of all things. Mary hushed her thoughts. She didn't want to miss what came next.

Nigel grinned. "Yes, God's definitely got the power." He walked slowly to the other side of the room, taking in the eyes of several people along the way. Nigel told them that Stephen, through God's power, did great wonders and miraculous signs among the people. So miraculous that some of the people were upset by all he was doing.

"They tried to stand up against Stephen's wisdom." Nigel's voice was clear, passionate. "But they could not. Because it was not his own wisdom, but the wisdom of God."

"I thought he gets killed." The skinny guy was sitting straighter now, massaging his goatee, his face a twist of confusion.

Sadness washed over Nigel's eyes. "He does." He brought his lips together and puffed his cheeks, exhaling slowly. Clearly this part of the story was harder to tell. "The people couldn't argue with Stephen's wisdom, but they could lie about him."

"Man—" the Hispanic woman shook her head—"people always lying."

"That's right. The people made up a story about Stephen, and he was brought before the head court." Nigel shrugged one shoulder. "Stephen didn't stand a chance. There were plenty of false witnesses, and a crowd of people accused Stephen, pointing fingers at him."

"I know that feeling, man." A black teenager two seats down from the skinny white guy raised his hand and nodded. He crossed his fingers and waved them in the air. "Me and my homeboy, Stephen . . . we're like this, man. Tight."

Nigel nodded. "A lot of people are accused of things." He stood right in front of the black teen. "But not everyone handles accusation the way Stephen did." He held up his hand. "Listen to the rest of the story."

There were nods from the class, and Nigel continued, pacing to the other end of the room. "As they were accusing Stephen and shouting lies about him, Stephen didn't yell back or cry for help. He just sat there. And everyone in the room who watched Stephen said the same thing." Nigel's steps slowed and he stopped again. "Stephen had the face of an angel."

The face of an angel? That was it, wasn't it? The face Mary had seen on the few people in her life who seemed truly content. Not always, of course, but most of the time when she would look at her grandma or Ted and Evelyn or Nigel, even the truck driver Big Dave and the police officer who had rescued her from Jimbo's basement. On all of those faces she had seen that very same thing: the face of an angel.

Mary squirmed in her seat. Stephen had been doing good, miraculous deeds in God's name. A group of people started telling lies about him, and he ended up in court being accused and threatened. And he had the face of an angel? Poor Stephen. Tears nipped at her eyes, and she blinked them back.

"Finally the court asked Stephen to speak for himself, give an answer about whether the charges against him were true." Nigel shook his head and anchored his hands on his hips. "Stephen opened his mouth to speak, but he didn't say a word about the lies or the false accusations. Instead he went on for half an hour about the faithfulness of God through time and how people throughout the ages had ignored their heavenly Father.

"Then—" Nigel narrowed his eyes—"Stephen told it like it was. He accused his listeners of being stiff-necked."

"Nigel?" The skinny white guy tossed his hands up.

"Sorry." Nigel looked at him and smiled. "He accused them of being stubborn. Stubborn and disobedient."

"I bet that didn't go over too good." The black teen had needle tracks along the inside of both arms, but here, now, his eyes were wide and alert.

"The people grew furious with Stephen." Nigel's voice fell again. "They began threatening him, but Stephen was full of God's Holy Spirit. He looked up and saw Jesus *standing* at the right hand of God. When he told the people what he saw, his words pushed them over the edge. They rushed at him, angry and shouting, and dragged him out of the city. There, they began to stone him."

Nigel must've observed a dozen confused faces, because he moved to a table and picked up a rock the size of an orange. He turned it over in his hand for a few seconds; then he gave it a few light upward tosses.

Mary looked around the room. Every set of eyes was on the rock.

"You hear the word *stoned*—" Nigel stared at the rock in his hands—"and you think of drugs. The street life." His eyes lifted to theirs. "Back in Stephen's day, getting stoned meant people threw rocks like this one." He stopped and faced the cement block wall at the far end of the room. Then with a sudden windup he reeled back, and with all his might he threw the rock at the wall.

It tore through the air and smashed into the cement block. The crash brought the room to a complete and breathless silence.

Seconds passed. Nigel turned to them. Agony was written across his face, his voice thick with passionate concern when he spoke. "That was getting stoned in Stephen's day. One after another after another . . . they threw rocks at him, and the whole time—the whole entire time—Stephen never took his eyes off Jesus. *Standing* there at the right hand of the Father."

"So . . . he died?" The skinny white guy tugged on the bill of his hat again.

Around the room a few people were sniffing and wiping fingers beneath their eyes.

"He did." Peace filled Nigel's features once more. "But he didn't die screaming for help. In fact . . . he died asking Jesus to forgive his enemies. And that . . ." There was a catch in Nigel's voice. He pierced his pointer finger through the air above him. "That is what it looks like to be rescued by Jesus."

Silence settled around them like late-night fog on the Potomac.

Finally the black teen folded his arms. "I thought he'd get a *real* rescue." He jutted his chin out. "You said we were talking about God's way of rescuing us, man." He set his forearms on the desk. "Stephen didn't get no rescue."

Nigel's eyes shone so brightly that they warmed something deep inside Mary all the way in the back row. Nigel walked up to the teen and put his hand on the boy's shoulder. "Oh, son, but Jesus *did* rescue him."

Nigel looked around the room, and his voice began to build. "Everywhere else in Scripture—when Jesus is pictured in heaven—He's *seated* at the right hand of the Father. Seated in the position of authority. But this time, with Stephen in big trouble—deadly trouble—Jesus was *standing*." Nigel held his arms up high as if he were embracing an invisible God. "One of His kids was in need, and Jesus took the position of action."

Mary sat up straighter. Something was happening inside her, like sunshine breaking through, sending rays of light into the darkest places of her heart. When Stephen was being attacked, Jesus stood up for him. Rescued him. Emotion built inside her. How wonderful for Stephen, knowing that God was on his side. What would it feel like to know God loved you that much?

The sunny feeling dimmed. Mary wasn't good like Stephen. How sad that she would never know that sort of love or protection from God. How could she, when her insides were as dark as night, when nothing—absolutely nothing—could clean the stench her life made.

"I don't get it." The Hispanic woman had tears in her eyes. "But Stephen died anyway."

Nigel turned toward her. "His work here on earth was done, and Jesus was on His feet, the first to welcome Stephen into heaven. That, my friends—" he spread his hands out before them—"is the rescue of our mighty Savior."

A cross hung at the front of the room above the blackboard. Nigel pointed to it. "Jesus died on a cross so that He could rescue us—me and you—from everything in this world. From loneliness, hunger, homelessness, and the pain of being stoned. Even the pain of death."

The skinny white guy crooked his hand, gang style, and slashed it through the air. "Man, why'd He go do a crazy thing like that?" Confusion sounded like anger in his voice.

"One reason."

Mary held her breath. She needed the answer more than she needed to breathe.

Nigel sat back on a stool and clasped his hands. "Because Jesus loves you." He leaned forward, intensely serious. "That's what love is; it's what love looks like." He directed his hand toward the ceiling again. "Jesus *standing* at the right hand of the Father, holding out a hand to us. Rescuing us. Freeing us.

"Even when it doesn't look that way to anyone else."

Chapter 21

The story was supposed to make Emma feel better about Jesus. But it didn't.

Of course Stephen saw Jesus standing at his rescue when he died. Stephen was a good guy. He was a follower of Christ, and in the power of God he worked miracles and signs and wonders for the people.

But she, Emma Johnson, was not a good person. She'd rebelled against her mother. She'd violated moral codes by sleeping with boys throughout her high school years, and she'd aborted two babies. She'd left home to live with Charlie and stayed with him after she knew the truth—that he was plagued by dangerous fits of rage. And she felt crazy most of the time because of the evil voices in her head.

On top of all that she was a drug addict, who sometimes

could convince herself briefly that she was not a user, that she was a normal mother like the ones she saw at the park with their children. But really, she was nothing but a lowlife. Trash, just like the voices in her head always reminded her.

The only way things were going to get better was by making up with Charlie. He was the father of her girls after all, and if he got the help he needed, everything about their life would turn out all right. At least with Charlie she had a home. He could learn to be patient and protective, and the girls would blossom under the care of two happy parents. Then Emma could get treatment for her drug problems.

Mary Madison's story was gripping, no doubt. But how was it going to make Charlie change? How would it help her and her girls find a normal life? Mary had talked some about the love of Jesus, the power of Jesus. But Jesus couldn't ward off the cold in the middle of the night, could He?

Emma didn't think so.

Because of that, Emma lay in bed early the next morning and came up with a plan. After breakfast she dropped the girls off in day care like she'd done the last several days; then, without catching the attention of Leah in the office or anyone else at the shelter, she slipped out the front door and caught a cab.

Fifteen minutes later she stood in front of the door of the apartment she'd shared with Charlie for the past four years. She raised her hand and knocked.

After nearly a minute, the door opened and there he was. "Emma . . ." Emotions played across his face: shock, joy, and finally the one she expected most—anger. "Where have you been for the last week?"

Sobs built in Emma's chest. She worked hard to find the words. "We need help, Charlie." She held her hand out to him. "Please . . . tell me we can get help."

The anger grew and darkened his features. He grabbed her hand, jerked her inside, and shut the door. "What'd you do, Emma?" His voice was loud, panicked. "Did you tell the cops what happened?" He let go of her hand and paced across the living room and back again. He pointed at her, his finger inches from her face. "Did you? Did you tell the cops?"

She shook her head and shrank back, pressing herself against the door. This wasn't happening . . . it couldn't be happening. She didn't come back to fight with him. "I promise, Charlie." Her mouth was dry, her heart pounding. "I didn't tell the cops. No one knows anything about us."

He stopped and raised his fist. His lips trembled, and rage turned his eyes into squinty slits. Emma could already feel the blow, already sense his knuckles crashing into her cheekbone. But at the last second, he put his hand through the wall instead. The force of the hit left a gaping hole in the plaster.

Charlie grunted as he pulled his hand from the mess. "You're lying to me, Emma. Tell me now!" He took a step closer and shook his fist at her. His fingers were bleeding, but he didn't seem to notice. "Where have you been, and where are the girls?"

"At some friends'. Then I went to a shelter!" Emma grabbed at her hair and covered her ears. "Stop screaming at me. We need to talk!"

That was all Charlie needed to hear. "A shelter?" He yelled louder now. "Where you sit down and tell your troubles to some do-gooder?" He took a few steps and knocked a lamp to the floor. It shattered in a pile of glass and wires. The whole time he never took his eyes from Emma. "Of course the cops know." He turned and started toward her. "You tell someone at a shelter and you might as well have called the cops yourself!"

Emma tried to duck, but his fist came hard and fast against her face before she could move. She fell to the floor; after that there was no escaping him. He attacked her, dragging her into the bedroom and throwing her onto the bed in a heap.

"No, Charlie!" she shouted. "Please . . . stop!"

Her cries grew faint as the attack continued. Then—as quickly as it had started—Charlie drew back and wiped his brow. He looked at her for a long time, breathing hard. Without speaking, he turned and went to the bathroom. She could hear him washing his hands, his face. Then he came back.

This is it, she told herself. *He's going to finish me off. Why'd I come back, anyway? Mary was right, but I wouldn't listen. I never listen.*

But when Charlie reached the bed, his shoulders slumped forward and he was contrite. "I'm sorry, Emma. I guess I was . . . I don't know, crazy for you." He sat on the edge of the bed and studied her. "I don't mean to hurt you."

She was shaking, every bone in her body bruised, and her right shoulder throbbed with an intensity that made her feel faint from the pain. Her face was bleeding, and her head hurt. She pulled away when he tried to touch her.

"Look—" he sighed—"you're right, okay? I need help. I wouldn't have gotten so mad, but I don't want you and the girls leaving again." He touched her knee. "Understand?"

She wanted to spit at him, run from him, and never come

back. But the things he was saying made sense. Maybe if she hadn't left they could've gotten help sooner. Of course he was mad at her for leaving. Either way she couldn't answer him. She was shaking too hard from the silent sobs racking her body.

"I'm going to take a shower." He gave her a slow look down the length of her body. "When I come out, I'll show you how sorry I am. I don't want to hurt you." He pinched the bridge of his nose and closed his eyes for a moment. When he opened them, he gave her another long look. "I want to love you, Emma. Fifteen minutes. You'll see."

He turned and went back to the bathroom. She heard the shower turn on.

Panic squeezed the air from her. She couldn't wait around for him to return. He had tried to kill her too many times. She would die if he came back and forced himself on her.

She struggled to a sitting position and grabbed the phone from the nearby table. With a whispered voice, she called for a cab. "Hurry, please. I don't have a lot of time."

The dispatch promised a car in five minutes. Emma stumbled out of bed and went to the other bathroom, the one off the living room. Her face was bruised and scraped, swollen around both eyes. She dabbed at the bloody areas and started to cry again. The cabdriver would know she'd been beaten up. Not only that, but she couldn't use her right arm. Her shoulder hurt too badly, and her arm hung at a strange angle.

Help me, God. . . . I need to get out of here. . . .

If Charlie came out of the shower and found her trying to escape, he'd kill her. She had no doubt. She reached into the coat closet and found a lightweight scarf. It was enough to cover the obvious injuries. She tied it around her neck and face, grabbed her wallet, and checked first one drawer then another. Where were the joints? Didn't Charlie keep them here somewhere? They were his stash, forbidden goods. But where she was going it wouldn't matter if she took a few. After looking in three drawers, she gave up. Every second mattered.

As quietly as she could, she slipped outside and strained to see down the street. Where was the cab? It should be here by now.

Hurry. . . . Please, hurry. . . .

Suddenly from inside she heard Charlie's voice. "Emma?" He was out of the shower, earlier than expected. "Where are you?"

She walked to the curb and searched down the street. A car was coming. *Please, God . . . let it be the cab . . . please!*

"Emma!" Charlie was at the door now, his hair wet, a robe wrapped around his thick frame. The rage was back, worse than before. "What are you doing?" He opened the door and started down the walk. "Get back here!"

Emma started to run. The approaching car was yellow; it was the cab, for sure. She hurried toward it, waving at the driver. She could still hear Charlie, hear him yelling and running toward her.

The cab pulled over, and she flung the door open. "Hurry!" she shouted at the driver. She closed the door just as Charlie reached them.

The driver looked in his rearview mirror and scowled. "That guy bothering you, lady?"

Emma fell against the backseat, her chest heaving. If he

only knew. "Yes . . . he was." Three hard breaths. "Thank you
. . . for hurrying." She didn't catch her breath until the end of
the block.

"No problem." The guy was smacking a piece of gum. He
glanced at her and raised a single eyebrow. "Where to, lady?"

The voices kicked in then. *Look at you, Emma Johnson. You're
pathetic. You crawl back to Charlie every time, no matter what he does to
you. One of these days he'll kill you, and he'll kill the girls too.*

Emma put her hands over her ears. Then she realized how
she must look, and she released them. "Uh . . . S Street, please.
I want to go to S Street."

But that wasn't where she really wanted to go. She wanted
a tall bridge with nowhere to go but down. *Do it, Emma. It's the
only way out. Your girls will thank you for it later. Charlie can't hurt
you if you end it all. Think about it. Go on, Emma. Go to the bridge. You
know the one.*

Yes. The 14th Street Bridge. She could go to East Potomac
Park and look for the best way onto the bridge. The bike
path, probably. She'd walk halfway across, then hunker down
and think about her life—all it never was, all it never would
be. The cars flowed faster than the river on the 14th Street
Bridge—so many lanes of traffic that no one would notice her
crouched on the walkway. When she was ready she would
simply rise and vault herself over the edge.

Death might not be instantaneous, but it would come soon
enough. And then—finally—she would have the freedom
Mary Madison talked about. Emma gripped her knees and
leaned forward. "Take me to the 14th Street Bridge, near East
Potomac Park on the DC side, please."

The man nodded absently. He made a turn at the next light and picked up speed.

Her plan was a good one, a right one. Charlie would come after her now, especially since she'd told him about the shelter. It would only be a matter of time before he figured out which one and found her. If she ended it all today, none of them would ever have to worry again.

But there was one problem.

She needed to tell Mary. Not the details, not where she was going, but that she wasn't coming back. She would give Mary her mother's phone number, and that way the girls could live with her. Her mother would know how to handle Charlie. She'd see that he was put in jail where he belonged.

Charlie would already be out of their lives if Emma had a strong bone in her body. But she didn't. That's why she needed to get to the bridge. She leaned forward and tapped the driver on the shoulder. "Sir . . . could I use your phone?" She tried to sound sweet and helpless. "It's sort of an emergency."

The man shrugged. "Sure." He handed her a cell phone and turned the radio down. "Just sweeten the tip."

Emma called information and got the number for the shelter. A minute later the call was going through.

"S Street shelter—" the voice belonged to Leah Hamilton— "may I help you?"

"Yes . . ." Emma closed her eyes. If she had life to do over again, she would've wanted to be just like Leah, volunteering her time and talents to help women find hope. She dismissed the thought and found her focus. "This is Emma Johnson."

Tears crowded her throat, and her voice grew pinched. "May I speak to Mary, please?"

"Certainly."

Emma was waiting for Mary to pick up when the driver glanced at her in the mirror. "What bridge you want, lady?"

"The 14th Street Bridge. You can drop me off at East Potomac Park . . . on the DC side. And please hurry."

There was a sound on the other end of the line, and Emma covered her mouth with her fingers. What if Mary had heard her? "Mary? Are you there?"

But there was only silence.

Emma felt relief work through her battered bones. If Mary had heard her, everything would be ruined. She closed her eyes and waited.

She could already feel the water closing in around her.

Chapter 22

Mary had called the police the moment she learned Emma was gone.

A pair of officers had come to the shelter and taken a report, but by the time they checked the apartment where Emma had lived with Charlie, no one was home. With no search warrant or proof of a crime in progress, the officers could do nothing. Still, they had searched the streets around the shelter, but they had no leads so far.

It had been nearly two hours since Emma left.

Mary was in her office, pacing from the window to her desk and back again. *God, this can't be happening. She doesn't understand Your power . . . Your ability to save her.* When the police called with no leads, Mary even placed a quick call to her grandmother, who promised to pray without ceasing until they heard news.

When the phone rang, Mary spun toward it and picked up the receiver on the first ring. It was a woman's voice talking on the other end. But at first it sounded like a wrong number, a misplaced call.

"The 14th Street Bridge. You can drop me off at East Potomac Park . . . on the DC side. And please hurry." There was a short, slight gasp. "Mary? Are you there?"

What was this? The voice sounded like Emma's.

Mary opened her mouth to say something, to respond to the question, but something stopped her. Instead she waited a few beats. Maybe she wasn't supposed to hear that first part. She breathed a silent prayer; then she acted as if she'd just answered the phone. "Hello, this is Mary."

"Oh, Mary . . . I'm sorry. . . ." The voice on the other end was definitely Emma's. She started to cry.

"Emma, where are you?" Mary worked to keep her panic in check. "Let me come get you."

"No!" Emma's tone was adamant. "I'm done with it; I can't do this anymore." Her sobs fell off some, and her words came faster than before. "Here . . . write this down. It's my mother's phone number. When I'm gone, I want her to have my girls, okay? Can you do that for me?"

"Emma, don't talk like that." Mary sat at her desk and raked her fingers through her hair. *No, God . . . please, no. Stop her right now.* "You told me you'd come every day until the story was finished."

"I know. I'm sorry." Emma cried harder. "I can't break away from Charlie. I can't do it." She coughed a few times, and her voice grew frantic. "Tell the girls . . . tell them I love them."

The call ended.

Mary checked her phone, but the caller ID showed a restricted number. Adrenaline shot through her. The first part of the call was the most crucial of all. Whoever was driving, Emma had asked them to take her to East Potomac Park, across from the 14th Street Bridge.

Mary grabbed her purse, her car keys, and her cell phone and paused at Leah's desk. "I'm going to get Emma."

"She told you where she is?" Leah was on her feet, her face twisted with concern.

"No. God told me."

Mary didn't have to take a moment to ask Leah to pray. She could tell by the look on the girl's face that prayer was a given. They'd run into conflicts and crises with the women at the shelter before.

Once she was in the car, Mary thought about calling the police. But she was bound to beat them to the scene. Besides, officers would frighten Emma, maybe push her to make the jump sooner rather than later.

God . . . I don't know what to do!

Daughter . . . A calm soothed the desperate turmoil in Mary's soul. *I am with you . . . go in My strength.*

Mary tightened her grip on the steering wheel. Five minutes later she pulled into East Potomac Park and found a spot for her car. The bridge was a hundred yards away on the other side of the street. Mary began to run, moving as fast as she could. As she drew closer she saw a woman cross the street and head for the bike path, the one that crossed the bridge.

"Emma!" She screamed her name, but the sound of it was

lost in the noise of the 14th Street traffic. *Please, God, stop her. Hold her back. Don't let her jump. Please . . .*

The woman was definitely Emma. She looked over her shoulder, but she didn't see Mary reaching the street and stepping into the crosswalk.

Mary picked up her pace. She darted across the road, not waiting for traffic and ignoring the drivers who honked at her. "Emma!"

Again Emma must not have heard her, because she didn't turn around. But she started jogging toward the middle of the bridge.

Mary kept running.

Emma was fifty yards ahead of her now . . . forty . . . thirty.

The traffic blocked out the sound of Mary's feet and allowed her to close in on Emma without Emma's noticing her.

Twenty yards . . . ten . . .

At the bridge's railing Emma stopped and turned around, her eyes wide. "Mary!" She shook her head and faced the water. Then she grabbed the railing and put one leg over the edge.

"Stop!" Mary was five yards away when she came to a halt. She forced herself not to react, but she was horrified. Emma had been badly beaten. Her face was barely recognizable. "Emma . . . you can't do this!"

"How'd you know?" Emma was shaking. She stared at the water and made a surge as if she might throw herself over. But something seemed to stop her. She looked at Mary, and her fear turned to sorrow. "I can't live another day. I'm a wreck. A worthless wreck."

"But—" Mary had to shout to be heard above the traffic—

"I was a wreck first. Way before you. Worthless, faithless, trapped by sin."

"No!" Emma looked at the water, then over her shoulder at Mary. "You're strong and smart. You broke free from—" she waved her hand—"from all this."

Mary came a few steps closer. "I didn't break free." Another step. "I was *set* free." She held out her hand. "You can be too."

"Don't come closer!" Emma hung her head, and another wave of sobs shook her body. "I'm not . . . strong enough."

Mary held her breath. Six lanes of traffic whizzed by, but not one person seemed to notice the drama playing out. Just one more desperate life, one more person at the end of her rope. Mary caught a glimpse of the water below, swirling as it rushed past. If Emma jumped, there would be nothing Mary could do.

"Emma . . . please." She had to get closer, had to get a hand on Emma if she was going to stop her. "No one's strong enough." She took another step and another. "Don't you see? That's the point of the story. No one on earth has that sort of power except for one."

Emma squeezed her eyes shut. She gripped the railing and leaned toward the water.

At the same time, Mary took a final step and grabbed hold of Emma's shoulder from behind. In a blur of motion she put her arms around Emma.

When Emma cried out in pain and turned around, Mary was shocked at the extent of Emma's injuries. "This isn't the answer." She spoke the words inches from Emma's face. "Let me tell you about Jesus!"

The moment Mary said the Lord's name, she felt the fight leave Emma's body. Her tears came harder, but she let Mary ease her back onto the bike path. Then, with eyes as scared and desperate as a child's, Emma looked at Mary. "Show me the way. . . . I don't want to die."

Mary had been holding her breath, and at Emma's admission, she exhaled. She drew Emma gently into her arms, and for a long moment they stayed that way—clinging to each other, to hope, to the possibility that there was some other way out. After a full minute, Mary pulled back, her arm still around Emma's shoulders. They walked back to 14th Street, back across the busy roadway and through the park to Mary's car.

Emma pressed herself into the seat back and huddled there, terrified. She looked at Mary. "I'm so scared." Her teeth chattered, and she was shivering hard. "What if . . . you hadn't saved me?"

Mary was scared too. They still had a long way to go, and today Mary had almost lost her. But she said the words that filled her heart instead. "I didn't save you, Emma. Jesus did. In fact . . . He's only just getting started."

Mary drove her straight to the hospital. The emergency-room doctor examined Emma and then called the police and reported Charlie.

Fifteen minutes later they got the news from one of the nurses. Emma's boyfriend had been picked up at his apartment and arrested, charged with battery and attempted murder. An officer came by the hospital and told Emma she didn't have to worry. Hopefully, it would be more than a decade before Charlie saw the outside of a prison cell. Emma was questioned and photographed. Her arm was broken just below the shoulder. Doctors fitted her with a cast and released her to Mary's care.

The day had been exhausting, but it was the turning point Mary knew had to come. When they reached the shelter, they ate dinner in Mary's office, and for the next hour Mary talked with Emma about her decisions. Mary's training had given her tools to evaluate a suicidal person. If Emma was far enough gone, Mary would have called a lockdown facility, where Emma could be admitted and restrained until the danger of suicide passed.

But Emma didn't qualify.

A number of times during that hour Emma told Mary that she didn't want to die, not really. And now that Charlie was in custody, she wasn't nearly as fearful. Still, Mary made a decision. She set up a cot in her office for Emma and laid a blanket on the sofa for herself. "Leah's staying overnight with your girls. I checked on them; they're fine." She started the coffeepot in the corner of her office, never taking her eyes from Emma. "We're staying here all night. We'll talk about whatever's on your mind."

"Thank you." The lines at the corners of Emma's eyes relaxed a little. "Actually . . ." She wasn't shaking anymore, but she held her casted arm in her lap and winced whenever she moved. "I want to hear the rest of your story—" she hesitated— "if you don't mind."

Mary took her place on the sofa. As wild as the day had been, as tragic as things might've turned out, peace reigned in her heart. God was in control, even now. "I told you about being at the New Life Center and hearing about Stephen, right?"

"Yes. You were talking about how God can rescue a person." A realization filled Emma's eyes. "Sort of like how He rescued me earlier today. A few times, really."

Mary felt joy surge through her. If Emma could recognize God's role in saving her first from Charlie and then from herself, there was no question about it.

Emma was ready for the next part of the story.

Chapter 23

M ary had no trouble finding her way back to this
part of her past.

She could still see dear Nigel finishing his lesson on Stephen, still hear the way his voice rang with passion in the
silent classroom, touching the empty places in her soul. This
was Mary's favorite leg of the journey back to yesterday—this
part where the love of Christ finally and completely came
alive to her.

It was the scene of her rescue, and Mary went to it willingly.

⁓ ⁕ ⁓

The lesson on Stephen was over, the street people and drug
addicts silently awed. A hush fell over the classroom, and
Nigel began to pray. A few seconds later, a heavyset man who

worked evenings washing dishes for the center brought a gui-
tar up front and began to play. He sang about amazing grace
and what a wretch he'd been before the love of God came and
rescued him.

Halfway through the song, Mary felt something damp on
her cheeks. She was crying. From her place at the back of the
room she was weeping, a bit of crusty ice from the frozen
edges of her heart melting without her even knowing it.

Mary stole a look at the others near her. Several of them
were crying too.

When the song ended, the man kept strumming, sending
soothing, gentle sounds throughout the room.

Nigel began talking again. "Anyone here who wants to
know that love, feel that love in your own heart, now's the
time. Jesus doesn't ask for much." He came as close as he
could to the first row, taking in the faces one at a time. "He
wants us to trust Him, believe in Him. Then He wants us to
turn away from our past—however ugly—and start a new life
His way." Nigel held his hand out—palm down—toward the
roomful of students. "Bow your heads and close your eyes."

When they had done so, he continued. "Anyone here
tonight who wants to be rescued by God, raise your hand."

Mary had to watch, had to know if people around her
were really able to believe what Nigel was saying. Then it
began to happen. One at a time, hands went up around the
room, including the hands belonging to the skinny white guy
and the black teenager. Mary wanted to raise her hand,
wanted to believe in a God who would rescue her and love
her no matter what.

And in that moment she realized something had changed. She *did* believe. Regardless of every night she had spent chained to a bed in Jimbo's basement and the way she'd found peace through seducing a married man, despite her fears and faithlessness, and the life she'd lived every day since then, she actually *believed* in God.

But that didn't mean she could be loved by Him.

Tomorrow she'd be with Clayton again, dirtier than ever. She made fists and crossed her arms tight against herself, just in case her hand had a mind of its own and somehow wound up in the air. She couldn't raise her hand—wouldn't raise it. Not even for Nigel's mighty God.

That night before she left, she went to Nigel's office and sat across from him. She spent most of an hour asking Nigel about the face-of-an-angel thing. "There's something different in the eyes of people with faith. I can see it, but I can't figure out what it is. You called it Jesus eyes."

Nigel smiled. "It's the Holy Spirit. When people give their lives to Christ, He gives them His Spirit. It breathes from the center of the soul, giving life to the heart and shining bright through the eyes of believers."

"Sometimes I think it's only my imagination." Mary's words were slow, thoughtful. Even though it meant going home alone in the dark, she didn't care. Clayton wouldn't be back until the next afternoon, and at least she didn't have to race through her visit. She rested her chin in her hands. "Like it's all in my mind."

"Definitely not." Church music played in the background, coming from some room in the mission. It gave their conversation a depth that shone in Nigel's expression. "What you see in the eyes of believers isn't your imagination. It's real. As real as God's Spirit, as real as His love."

There it was. The thing Mary *really* wanted to know about. The reason she had come. She bit the inside of her cheek and looked at her knees. Fear towered over her, daring her to believe that she was good enough to ask about love. Anyone's love. When her entire past was riddled with filth.

"Mary . . . you have something to say?"

Nigel's voice gave her strength and sent fear just far enough away that she felt brave enough to answer. "God's love . . ." She winced and looked at Nigel without lifting her head. "What would I have to do . . . you know . . . for Him to love me?"

Nigel stood, his eyes never leaving hers. "Stand up, Mary."

She had no idea what he was going to do or how standing would give her the answer she was looking for. Maybe he was going to tell her that he was tired of her questions and send her home. Maybe there was no hope for her, no way God would ever love her. Rather than tell her that, perhaps he would just call it a night. Slowly, with fear laughing at her from a few feet away, she did as he asked.

When she was standing across from him, Nigel motioned for her to step into the center of the office. He stood a few feet from her. "Pretend I'm Jesus."

Mary swallowed. "Okay." Her pulse was zipping along much faster than before. Was this where he would shout at her and condemn her for the choices she'd made, for sleeping with a married man day after day after day? Her knees and hands trembled, but she remained standing. Whatever was coming, she deserved it.

"All right." Nigel placed his hands at his sides. He was a teacher again, his tone the same sincere one he'd used in the classroom earlier. "Let's say I know everything you've ever done. I know about your time with Jimbo, and I know about the foster families—especially the man in the second family. I know about the truck you stole, and I know about your intentions once you came to the mission. I know what was your fault, and I know the things you had no control over." He paused. "I know about the man who's taking care of you . . . and the ways you're taking care of him." Nigel's voice was somber now. "I know that you're still a victim, but you're also choosing the way of darkness. You know it too."

Mary hung her head. The light in Nigel's eyes was so bright it hurt.

"Look at me, Mary." It wasn't a sharp command but rather a request. A gentle request.

Inches at a time, she let her eyes find his again. She squinted, and she could feel the way her deep pain must've colored her features.

"If Jesus were here, knowing everything He knows, imagine what He would do."

She wanted to cover her face, her body. Her heart. Protect herself from the barrage of accusations that was bound to follow. What would Jesus do? "It would be . . . terrible." It was all she could do to keep her eyes on Nigel. "I would . . . have to look away."

"No, Mary." Nigel's chin trembled. With slow, measured steps he came to her until their feet were so close they were almost touching.

Mary wanted to turn and run. Why couldn't he leave space between them? She could take whatever he might say as long as he was across the room. That way she could say a few polite words and be on her way.

But this close?

So close she could see the pain and disappointment when it came into his expression, the way it would come any second now? It was more than she could take. She looked away, turned her cheek the way she had when Clayton had hit her. Then there was nothing to do but wait. Whatever he was about to say, she deserved it.

"Mary—" Nigel's voice dropped to a whisper—"look at me."

At first she didn't respond, but gradually it dawned on her. This—this looking into Nigel's eyes and seeing his disapproval—was part of her punishment. Wincing so she could see only through the narrow slits in her eyelids, she turned her eyes to him once more. "Tell me, Nigel." She set her jaw. "I'm ready."

There was something different in his expression, but it wasn't disappointment or anger or even disapproval. He held out his hands. "This is what Jesus would do." Slowly, Nigel folded his arms around her shoulders, her back, and he pulled her into an embrace.

Mary sucked in a slow breath, but she couldn't breathe out. She was lost in the feeling, a sensation unlike anything she'd ever experienced.

Where was the condemnation? the judgment and reprimand? The barrage of anger never came, nor did the pointing finger. His wasn't the hug of a lover or a brother, nor was it the hug of any other man she'd ever been with. It was the embrace of a father, the sort of embrace she'd never known, and it spoke things she'd never imagined straight to her heart. Acceptance and protection and concern and, most of all, the emotion she hadn't known since she was a little girl.

Love.

Seconds passed, and Mary felt herself relax. Layers of bitterness and shame crumbled, and she fell against his chest. Was Nigel right? Would Jesus see her and know her and still take her in His arms like a lost daughter? Would He really love away the pain? Was it possible?

All her life she'd wanted to believe in a God like that, but He never seemed to be around. Not in the basement of Jimbo's house, not when she had to leave Ted and Evelyn's, and not when she came just short of finding her grandmother. He certainly hadn't been around when she gave her heart and soul to Clayton Billings.

But now?

Nigel's arms still held her. He stroked her back, and ever so slightly he rocked her. Never in all her life had she felt so safe, so treasured.

After a long while, Nigel pulled back. He kept his hands on her shoulders, his eyes locked on hers. "That is the love of Christ, Mary. Full and whole, without judgment or reservation. Unconditional. When you fall, Jesus holds out a hand. When you turn away, He stands at the door of your heart, waiting, always waiting."

Mary's heart swelled, and tears flooded her eyes. Full and whole? Without judgment or reservation? A love that would pick her up when she stumbled and hug her when she . . . when she deserved hell? "I thought—" she searched his eyes— "I thought Jesus would be mad at me, punish me."

Nigel's eyes were deeper than the ocean. "Punishment, discipline—they come because of our choices. Jesus makes sure of that, for one reason."

Confusion dropped a pebble into the calm waters of Mary's soul. "So . . . He *will* punish me?"

A patient smile played at the corners of Nigel's lips. "Only to make you turn around, Mary. To make you stop running away and start running to Him. You're experiencing that punishment every day, trapped in a life with this man who keeps you so afraid. Jesus wants to set you free."

"Free?" It was something she'd never known. Freedom. Not when she was dragged around the city streets by her mother, not in the basement handcuffed to the bedpost, and not now, with Clayton. "Jesus wants me to be free?"

"More than that." Nigel wiped his thumb beneath her eyes. "He bought your freedom . . . with His life. His death."

The intensity in Nigel's eyes told her clearly that this was the most important part of his message that night: Jesus died to free her. But freedom wouldn't happen until she stopped the life she was living and turned to Him. Wholly. Completely. The idea sent shock waves through her. "And once I'm free . . ."

"Once you're free . . ." He pulled her close once more, hugged the life and joy and hope into all the places of her heart that had never known them. "Then this is the way Jesus will hold you, Mary."

The feeling of Nigel's embrace stayed with her long after

she took a cab home and found her way to bed. She felt dreamy and light and new. Was it possible? Did God long to set her free? Free from the life she was living so that He could hold her that way? so He could wrap His divine arms around her and shelter her with a love that would carry her through the rest of her days?

Giddiness came over her at the thought. Maybe she wouldn't have to be a slave or a victim or a mistress. Maybe she could be a daughter of Jesus, a child. For the first time. Tears came, the way they often did since she'd started seeing Nigel again. But this time they weren't tears of despair or fear. They were tears of joy. Because Jesus was closer than she'd ever dreamed, His very tangible love warming her even now, when she wasn't quite sure how to walk away, how to accept the freedom He offered her.

Even if He had died to give it to her.

<hr />

The next afternoon Mary told Clayton some of what she was feeling.

She sat across from him at the small kitchen table. He had brought her a new nightgown, silky and short and see-through, and he'd ordered her to put it on. She wore it now, hating the way it made her feel like trash. Her heart pounded in her throat so loudly she was certain he could hear it. "Clayton," she said. *Help me, God . . . give me the words.* "I want to leave this place."

His surprise couldn't have been greater if she'd said she

wanted to fly to the moon. His brow lifted and forged a series of deep creases on his forehead. He set his forearms on the table and chuckled, disbelieving.

Mary felt sick to her stomach. "I'm serious. I want to find my grandmother in New York City and start life over."

The lines on his face faded, and his jaw went slack. Anger stirred the shallow surfaces of his eyes. "Don't tell me what you want to do." He leaned over the table so his face was closer, his words angry darts. "Don't you see?" His mouth curved upward, but his look was hardly a smile. "You can't go now. You know too much."

Her body trembled, and something inside her told her to run as far as she could, because at least then she might have a chance at getting away. She slid her chair back and shook her head. "I know nothing, Clayton. I won't say a word."

He was on his feet, coming around the table and grabbing a handful of her hair. "Don't flash those blue eyes at me, Mary." He gave her head a solid jerk and pinched his lips together, each word a hiss. "You could destroy me, woman. It'll be years before you leave this place." He straightened and stared at her, the anger in his eyes building like a sudden storm.

Still she had to try. "I promise I won't say a—"

He raised his hand high over her head and brought it hard against the side of her face.

She screamed as she fell to her knees and began scrambling toward the door. She could run, and if he caught her and killed her, then she might be facing the open arms of Jesus when she died. But she might not. She hadn't really given her life to Jesus yet, had she? The possibilities chilled her with terror. She couldn't stay here, not another minute. Not without knowing what would happen to her if she died.

Her knees burned as she shuffled fast along the carpet. She was halfway to the door when he grabbed her hair once more and yanked her up and onto her back. He reeled back and struck her face, her arms, again and again. Only then did she realize the restraint he'd shown before. Because this beating was too horrific to believe, sending shock waves of pain and nausea through every inch of her body. Something warm dripped down her face and into her eyes, and as she felt herself losing consciousness, her senses no longer registered the damage being done to her.

Because in every way that mattered, she could feel herself turning away, running to Jesus, her arms open wide. And there He was . . . standing at the door of her heart, waiting for her, longing for her. The picture sent her soul soaring on the winds of a joy that knew no bounds. *Jesus . . . faithful Jesus . . . I'm sorry I didn't see You there before.*

Nigel had showed her the unfathomable love of Christ, and now she believed in it with everything she was. Nigel had told her dozens of stories about Jesus and—in a blur of wonder—each of them came back to her now. One image stood out from the others, something that happened at the Lord's last supper with His disciples. It was the picture of Jesus washing the feet of His disciples—including the one who had already betrayed Him.

That was the sort of love Jesus had for her, even while she struggled for every breath under Clayton's heavy hand. The love of Jesus was warm and safe and wonderful, different from anything the world knew of love. It was a caring and a devotion that in an instant gave her a new and wonderful strength. Now, no matter what Clayton did to her, she was existing in a different sort of reality.

Something else became clear. Jesus was fully God and fully man. That's what Nigel had said, and it was why people feared getting to know Jesus. An amazing thought flashed in her mind. She—Mary Madison, daughter of the streets, child of a prostitute, former slave, and mistress to one of the most powerful businessmen in the city—had the power to share the truth about Jesus with anyone who would listen. The way Nigel did. She had the power to defend history.

His story—the story of Christ.

The beating continued, blow after blow, but none of them mattered. Mary could feel the arms of Jesus around her, protecting her, sheltering her to a safe place in her mind. Finally, after every awful deed she'd done, after every unspeakable horror that had been done to her—even while she was still being beaten—the impossible had happened. She had turned completely away from Clayton Billings.

I see You, Lord. . . . I feel You with me.

Beloved daughter, you belong to Me . . . only Me. I will be your shelter.

Her shelter? Who had said that? Was it Jesus, calling to her, talking to her the way Nigel had the night before? A certainty rushed through her. Indeed, God was speaking straight to her heart. His words breathed life into her and released her from the great pain of the moment. *I love You, Lord Jesus. I'm sorry for missing You every time before, sorry for every wrong thing I've ever done. Hold me. Don't let me go.*

I will never leave you, never forsake you, precious child.

The newness of love changed everything. The pain faded. Now all she could feel were the gentlest arms in all the world, embracing her, stroking her back, and cradling her like a beloved, precious daughter. All she could hear was the wonderful truth being whispered to her. She was free. No matter what Clayton did to her after this, it didn't matter. For the rest of her days she would revel in the great and awesome splendor of God Almighty, basking in His all-consuming love. Because she didn't belong to Clayton anymore.

She belonged to Jesus Christ.

Chapter 24

Mary took a long breath and looked at Emma. The young woman's eyes were teary, and Mary felt for her. "Are you okay?"

"I don't know." Emma pulled the blanket off the cot and tucked it in around her lap with her left hand. "I'm cold."

"It's a hard story."

Emma nodded. "I can feel every blow, Mary." She ran her fingers over her cast. "In a moment like that, all I can think about is dying, how Charlie's going to kill me, and what my girls will think when they find me."

"I thought that the first few times. What Grandma Peggy would think when she found out how I died." Mary looked up, and in that moment she saw Jesus, arms outstretched, the same way she'd seen Him in those horrible moments of abuse.

"That's why I know my rescue was a miracle." She touched her fingers to the place above her heart. "He rescued me here, on the inside, even when I had no idea how I was going to survive the next few minutes."

Emma blinked, and a trail of tears slid down her cheeks. "All because Nigel showed you the love of Jesus."

"Yes." Mary's heart stirred at the mention of Nigel's name. "Nigel loved me enough to tell me the truth." Talking about him made her miss him, more than she had in years. "No man ever loved me the way Nigel did."

Emma tilted her head. She looked at Mary for a long time. "Then . . . you're still in love with him?"

"No." A sweet sadness stung at Mary's heart, the way it always would when she thought of Nigel. "It was never meant that I feel that way for him. Not then . . . and not now." Mary adjusted a pillow beneath her elbow and leaned onto the arm of the sofa. She pictured Nigel's eyes, remembered the tenderness in his voice. She missed him as much now as she had the day they said good-bye.

"But you love him." Emma sat unmoving, trying to understand.

"Yes, I love him." Mary felt the sting of tears. "Just not the way you're talking about. Not the way the world understands." She sat a little straighter. "I'm almost done. At the end I'll tell you about Nigel, the two of us."

When Mary closed her eyes, she could see it all again, the front door of the center as she climbed out of the cab and ran toward it, an hour after Clayton left her that night. . . .

Mary looked like death—the mirror told her that much. But she didn't care. She had escaped with her life, and she wasn't ever going back. She had a shopping bag full of her things— a few clothes, some essentials, and her little red-beaded purse.

When she found Nigel in the kitchen she fell into his arms.

"Who did this to you?" He looked angrier than ever. Angry and protective and full of his Jesus kind of love all at the same time. "What's his name?" Nigel could barely contain himself, but he kept his voice even.

Mary looked away. "I left him. I won't go back."

His fingers made contact with her swollen eye, and she jerked. "Mary . . . you mentioned the name Clayton when we talked once." He steadied himself. "Is it Clayton Billings?"

She opened her mouth to deny it, to lie the way she'd done so much of her life. But the lie wouldn't come. She looked away, ashamed and terrified. "I can't talk about it."

"I know who he is."

"He does a lot of business in the city." She felt her head start to spin. If Clayton knew about this conversation . . .

Nigel frowned. "Clayton Billings is one of the most power-ful men in DC. His name's been linked with organized crime for a decade." Righteous anger filled Nigel's tone. "He's on the board of the largest church in town."

Organized crime? And he was on the board of a church? The news hit Mary like another one of Clayton's blows. No wonder he'd told her she couldn't leave, that she knew too much. If people found out about her, his image would be shattered. "He'll kill me, Nigel. I'm not supposed to say anything." She bit her lip. "He'll kill me."

"He already tried." Nigel brought his fingers to her cheek. His eyes were damp, filled with horror at the damage Clayton had already wrought. "Mary . . . I can't stand that he did this to you." He clenched his jaw and took a deep breath through his nose. Then he took a step back and turned toward the phone. "I'll call the police right now and set this whole thing straight before—"

"No!" Mary came after him. She grabbed his arm, shrieking. "No, Nigel, please! I'll be okay."

"Mary." He turned, broken. His hand soothed the worry lines on her forehead, her battered cheeks. "The police need to know about this."

"Not now. I'll report him after I get to New York."

Nigel waited a long time before he answered. His eyes told her what she already knew—he loved her. Not the way she had wanted to be loved by him, but with a love that was straight from heaven. A love that would fight for her, even die for her. But gradually his shoulders settled and resignation showed in his eyes. "Are you sure?"

"Yes." Her mind raced faster than her heart. "I need to hurry; I know that. When he finds out I'm gone he'll come for me. But we can't . . . can't call the police now."

A long sigh left Nigel's lips, and he held out his arms.

She went to him, the way she'd done the other night. With an understanding that Christ's love could sometimes best be felt in human arms. "Thank you." She pulled back and marveled at the emotions building in her heart, her soul.

Boundless joy at finding freedom, great victory in knowing
she would soon see Grandma Peggy again. But sorrow
because her time with Nigel was short.

He studied her for a long time, and a smile tugged at his
lips. "You're glowing. Despite everything."

She took his hands. "That's what I wanted to tell you. Can
you believe it, Nigel? I've done it." Her smile bunched up the
swollen skin beneath her puffy eyes and made it hard for her
to see. "I stopped running and gave my life to Jesus!"

Tears filled her eyes and glistened in the glow of the over-
head kitchen lights. "Jesus has done so much for me. He's . . .
He's changed me. And He used you to do it." A few sobs
sounded from deep inside her, from a place that had never felt
so loved.

She sniffed, searching for control. "Jesus loves me. He
loves me like I've never been loved in all my life." She placed
her hand over her heart. "He talked to me and held me, and I
know I'll never be alone again. Never."

"God is faithful." Nigel was quieter than usual. "He
answered all of my prayers, but . . ." He brought his finger to
her face and touched the swollen areas near her eyes. "How
could this happen to you? How could he do this?"

"Shhh." Mary took hold of his wrists and brought his
hands down to his sides. "We can talk about that later.
The important thing is I understand now. Jesus really,
truly set me free. Now I have just one thing I can do for
Him." The tears became tiny rivers, like so much melted ice
streaming from her eyes. "I'll give Him my life. Every day
I have left."

Nigel sighed. "Clayton Billings needs to pay for what he's done."

"He will one day. For now . . . I can't have him finding out about you. He'd kill you, Nigel. I know he would."

Nigel didn't blink. "I'm not afraid of him."

"I know." Mary hugged him again. For all the ways she'd fallen for Nigel, for the days when she would've given anything to be in his arms this way, the feelings now were different. She was still attracted to him, and a part of her wanted to dream that somehow . . . someday they might find their way together.

But overriding all of that was a very real, very basic truth: Nigel didn't love her like that. He loved her because she was a broken child of God. He loved her soul. And even now—with him so close she could smell his shampoo, his cologne—God's love was enough.

Far more than enough.

Nigel released her and leaned against the kitchen counter. His eyes held hers. "You'll stay here tonight."

She nodded. "In my old room, if that's okay."

"It is." He looked pale, sick about her. "I'll take you to the doctor first, get you checked out." He touched her chin. "Then we'll call your grandma."

She was about to say something about her grandma, how much she'd missed her, when the phone rang. They both stared at the receiver.

The look on Nigel's face must have mirrored her own. Was it someone calling about service times or information about a meal? It was almost midnight, too late for those kinds of calls. Or had Clayton found her?

Nigel waited two more rings; then he picked up the receiver. "Hello?"

Mary could hear the caller's voice at the other end of the line—a man's voice. "Yes, I'm sorry," he said. "I'm looking for a woman named Mary Madison. It's an emergency." The caller hesitated. "I believe she used to live at your center." Another pause. "Would you know where I can reach her?"

"No." Nigel's voice left no room for discussion. He stared straight at Mary and held his finger to his lips. "There's no one here by that name."

Fear took deep swipes at Mary. She leaned in to hear better.

"Okay." The caller didn't sound convinced, but the way he said the word left no doubt. It was Clayton Billings. He had left Mary in a hurry, mumbling something about a date with his wife. But he must've come back to check on her, to make sure she'd survived his attack. He cleared his throat. "If you see her, tell her . . . uh . . . tell her people are looking for her."

Then, without giving a name or further explanation, the man hung up.

Nigel returned the receiver and searched Mary's eyes. "I think it's him."

"It is." She looked down at her hands. "I'd know his voice anywhere."

"We need a new plan." He grabbed his keys from the top of the refrigerator. "I'll take you to the airport tonight. You can catch the next flight to New York and see a doctor once you meet up with your grandma."

Mary hesitated. What if Clayton came after her? What if he was on his way right now? "Let me take a cab." She couldn't tolerate the idea of putting Nigel in danger. Not for a minute. "You need to be here."

"They won't miss me, not for a few hours." He still had his keys in his hand.

She took hold of his wrist. "I'd rather have you here." She could feel the sincerity in her expression. "Please, Nigel. I don't want to involve you in this."

"I'm already involved." Nigel gritted his teeth. "I go with you. No debate."

"I don't like it." Mary's mind raced. She couldn't put him in danger, no matter what.

"You don't have to like it. I'm not letting you leave here alone."

Mary exhaled slowly. "Okay." She didn't want to involve him, but he was too much a gentleman, too much a friend to give in to her. Maybe if she changed the subject. She glanced at the phone and then back at Nigel. "Would it be okay . . . if I call my grandma first?"

Nigel's expression changed instantly. His eyes danced as he motioned for her to follow. "Let's go to my office."

Every minute counted; Mary knew that. But now that she was free she couldn't wait to make the call. She took the chair behind Nigel's desk and found her grandma's number. It took a few seconds, but eventually a woman answered the phone.

"Hello?" Even glazed with the effects of sleep the voice sounded familiar.

It worked its way into Mary's heart and soul and made her feel like dancing. "Grandma?" The depth of her emotions caught her off guard. She put her hand to her throat and smoothed away the tightness. "Grandma . . . it's me, Mary."

"Mary?" Her voice made only the slightest sound. "My Mary?" She inhaled loud and sharp, and tears filled her words. "Mary . . . I can't believe it's you! Are you okay?"

She thought about the phone call from Clayton. He was coming for her, no question. "I'm fine." Her eyes filled, and she brushed at them. Now that she knew the love of God, she was always crying. "I'm flying home today. Maybe you could meet me at the airport."

"Of course. Oh, Mary . . . I've prayed for this moment every day since I saw you last." Her voice snagged on a wave of sadness. "I'm so sorry . . . everything that's happened to you. I wanted to save you, but I didn't know how . . . didn't know where you were."

"I know, Grandma. I couldn't find you, and then I couldn't call. But I'm okay." She ran her hand over her swollen cheek. Her injuries would heal, and one day the other scars would fade too. A smile lifted her mouth. "I've found Jesus. You were right." She dug around her bag, pulled the little red purse from inside, and stared at the familiar words on the paper from inside the purse. "God does have great plans for me. I'll tell you all about it when we're together."

Her grandma sniffed. "Nigel was everything I couldn't be."

"Yes. He was." Mary closed her eyes, allowing herself to be filled with the warmth of all she'd learned about the Lord that past month. She looked at Nigel. "I can feel the arms of Jesus around me all the time now."

"I'm so glad." Her grandma muffled a few sobs. "We'll be together soon."

"Yes." A light laugh made its way up from her heart. For the first time in days, Mary could envision a time in the not-too-distant future when laughter would be a regular part of her life. "Isn't that wonderful?"

On the other end of the phone, her grandma was getting over the shock of hearing from her. The tears were gone from her voice. "Mary . . . I can't wait." She exhaled, a sigh of relief that spanned the years. "I've missed you so much, darling. So much."

"Me too." She looked at the clock on the wall. She couldn't waste another moment. "I have to run, Grandma. I'll call you from the airport."

"Be careful, honey. I love you."

"I love you too."

The call ended, and Mary imagined her grandmother, the sweet weathered face, the warm hands, the eyes that had always held hope and promise and God's love. It wouldn't be long now.

The sound of shattering glass interrupted her thoughts, and a piercing scream filled the hallways.

"Nigel, it's him!" Mary's voice was a panicked whisper. She took a step backward, away from the office door.

"You're safe here. I'll stay with you." Nigel held out his arm, protecting her.

But at that moment they heard the noise of running foot-steps, and the cook huffed up to Nigel's door. "It's one of the girls, the heroin addict—she was sleepwalking or dreaming—

something." His eyes were startled, frightened. "She broke through the window. Please, Nigel, come. She's out of control."

Mary felt herself relax. It wasn't Clayton. Of course not. He had only just called. It would take him another fifteen minutes to get in his car and reach the center. Fifteen at least. Her heartbeat found a normal rhythm.

Nigel looked from the cook to Mary and back. "Is she hurt?"

"Not bad, a few scratches. But she's calling for you." The cook shook his head. "No one can calm her down."

Mary touched Nigel's elbow. "Go on. Make sure she's okay."

He took a step toward the door and let his eyes find hers once more. "Stay here. I'll be right back."

She nodded and watched him leave. Already her heart was breaking. Because good-bye was only minutes away. She smiled, even as tears stung her eyes. "Be careful."

When Nigel was gone, Mary slipped her red purse back into the shopping bag with her other belongings. Then she looped the handle around her arm and realized something. She could spare herself a sad good-bye with Nigel, couldn't she? She could slip through the back door and call him from the airport. That way she wouldn't put him in any danger whatsoever.

A lump formed in her throat. She was going to miss Nigel, miss the way he prayed for her and looked out for her. The way he had shown her the love of Jesus. But it was time to go.

She went quietly to the kitchen door and scurried across the parking lot. She was a few yards from the alleyway, her heart pounding, when she saw the figures of two people ahead. Homeless people probably, spending the night near the center so they'd be first in line for a morning meal. But she couldn't be too careful. She didn't want to take any chances, not when she was this close to getting out of the city.

The night air was cool against her face as she turned around and slipped back into the building. No one would be out front. Nigel was still nowhere in sight, so she hurried down the hall and eased her way out the main door. The street was empty, except for a few cars at the other end of the block. In the far distance, a siren wailed and then grew faint.

She shivered and held her bag close. *Hurry,* she told herself. *Get a cab and get out of here.* She started to run, and then she slowed down. *Don't be ridiculous. Your imagination's scaring you to death. Clayton isn't here. Just stay calm and find a cab. Jesus, help me find a cab.*

She squinted and tried to make out the cars a hundred yards down the street. Cabs were usually everywhere, but it was past midnight. She might have to walk two blocks to Jefferson before she found one at this hour. She picked up her pace and turned a corner.

A block from the main street a hand suddenly shot out from the darkness of an alleyway and grabbed her from behind. He had his hand over her mouth before she could scream.

"Thought you'd run, did you?" The man wasn't someone she recognized. He was small and wiry.

No, this isn't happening. Mary tried to scream, but the man's fingers were pressed hard against her lips.

The man laughed low and menacing. "Billings told me you were a knockout." The man gave her a slow once-over in the dim lamplight. "He didn't tell me you were this pretty, though."

She tried to jerk free, but he held her tighter. This couldn't be happening, not when she was so close to getting away. The man's fingers felt grimy against her face. They smelled of tobacco and dirty money. *God . . . please help me.*

"I owe Billings a favor." He yanked her close against himself and sneered at her. "But I should have a little fun with you first."

From a few blocks away someone shouted. It wasn't loud enough to make out, but it startled the man. "Too bad." He chuckled. His ice-cold eyes drilled into her. "We're out of time."

Mary tried to buckle her knees, make herself fall to the ground. If she was loud enough, someone was bound to hear her. She squirmed, fighting against him with everything she had, and then—

The man grabbed a handful of her hair and put his face inches from hers. "Walk." He squeezed the word through clenched teeth. "Walk or I'll kill you right here."

As he dragged her along the empty sidewalk, all Mary could think was that she'd waited too long. Her grandmother was up by now, getting dressed and celebrating her phone call. She tried to pull herself from her captor, but every time he held on tighter.

"You don't mess with Billings, lady," he hissed near her ear. "You must've made him crazy mad. He wanted to finish you off himself."

At the next alley, the man pulled her into the deep darkness. "But he asked me to do it instead. Billings likes to keep his hands clean." He swore at her. "Did you really think you could get away from him?" He grabbed her by the throat and slammed her against a brick wall.

Dark spots danced before her eyes. *No, God, this isn't happen-*

ing. She had to catch a flight, had to get to her grandma's flat. *God . . . please!* She struggled to keep her eyelids from closing.

"Too bad." He spat at the ground and grabbed a handful of her hair again. "I could've had a lot of fun with you." He held her hair tight. "Besides . . . Billings told me to make it quick."

Even half conscious, Mary felt something change inside her. An overwhelming sense of victory. Whatever happened from here on, she had Jesus and she had her freedom. And something else. She'd spared Nigel this nightmare. She lifted her chin. He was going to kill her, wasn't he? *God . . . what about my grandma?*

I know the plans I have for you, precious daughter.

Peace washed over her. *Thank You, Jesus.* No matter what happened she believed the words: God had plans for her, and they were good plans. Here or in heaven. Whatever took place in this dark alley, it would all end well because God was good. She met the eyes of her assailant, forcing herself to stay conscious another moment longer. "It doesn't matter . . . what you do to—"

Before she could finish her sentence, the man aimed a gun at her middle and fired. The shot made almost no sound. Before she could move or scream or fully register what had happened, the bullet sliced through her. She could feel it ripping its way through her body, tearing into her flesh and bones and leaving a trail of fiery heat in its wake. The man was gone, and she felt herself slipping, melting down the side of the wall. With all her being she found the strength for one last word . . .

"God!"

The sound of His name echoed loudly in the alley, and suddenly Mary could see something taking shape just above her.

The scene was brilliant and bright and warm and welcoming. As the lines came into focus, she realized what she was seeing. Jesus . . . at the right hand of the Father. He was smiling at her, holding out His arms. Welcoming her. The most wonderful feeling washed over her, filling her with a peace and love that made everything she'd ever felt pale in comparison.

And in that moment, she knew that her grandma would be okay and that one day very soon they'd be together again. In the greatest place of all.

Mary drew a final breath and then smiled back at Jesus. He was beckoning her, and she could feel herself moving toward Him. That's when she noticed the most wonderful part. Jesus wasn't sitting at the right hand of the Father. In this, her most dire hour, her most glorious hour, He was doing what He'd done for Stephen.

Jesus was standing.

Chapter 25

Emma looked like she might jump to her feet. "But . . . you lived."

Mary felt exhilarated, the way she always felt at this part of the story. She shouldn't have lived; the doctors and nurses—everyone—told her that. She was alive because of God's miraculous power to save—from the horrors of abuse and lifelong sin and even the piercing of a bullet. Mary smiled. "God wasn't finished with me yet."

"Did . . . did someone find you in the alley?" Emma was breathless, completely wrapped up in the story.

"A husband and wife found me and took me to the hospital. I never got their names. They came at just the right time."

Emma gasped. Fresh understanding seemed to brighten her eyes. "The way . . . you did for me. This morning."

"Exactly like that." Mary was touched deep inside. The awe of it all, the way the Lord continued to show Himself to be all-knowing, all-powerful. Every day she found a new reason to marvel at His power in her life.

Emma pulled the blanket up to her chin. Mary's office had cooled, and it was nearly nine o'clock. "What happened at the hospital? When they took you there?"

"The police contacted Nigel. They figured I might've come from the New Life Center since I was only half a block away." Mary settled back against the sofa. It was never easy, picturing Nigel getting the news. He had cared so much for her. "He was the first person I saw when I woke up at the hospital."

Mary closed her eyes for a moment, and as she began telling this final part of her story, the memory came back in vivid color.

She had been dead, right? Jesus had been beckoning her home. But somehow—without explanation—Mary came to in a strange bed. Tubes were in her nose and arms, and the room was filled with unfamiliar noises—soft whooshings and clicks and beeps. She struggled to open her eyes, and there, surrounding her, were half a dozen machines. And close to her bed, sitting in a chair, was Nigel.

As soon as she opened her eyes, he slid closer. "Mary . . ."

"You're here." She searched his face. "I thought . . . I was dead."

His expression was tense, serious. "It was close." He reached out and covered her hand with his. "We almost lost you."

"What about . . . Grandma Peggy?"

"I called her." Nigel held her gaze, worry tugging at the corners of his eyes. "She's praying for you. Every minute."

Mary found a weak smile. Of course she was praying. Her grandma was always praying for her. She put her fingers to her neck. Her throat was dry, and her words didn't come easily. "The shooter . . . he was one of Clayton's men. . . ." She still couldn't believe she was having this conversation. How could she be alive? And how kind Nigel was to be here sitting with her. Showing her that same strange and amazing love he'd shown her since the first day she walked through the doors of the New Life Center.

"The police have a lead." Nigel clenched his jaw. "Clayton Billings will go to prison for this." He touched her cheek where it was still swollen from the attack she'd gone through the day before. "He'll go to prison for everything he's done to you."

Mary tried to move, but the pain in her middle was too strong. "I saw Jesus . . . standing, coming to take me . . . to heaven."

"No, Mary." His eyes shone. "He was coming to save you."

Nigel stayed with her most of that day and into the night. With every passing hour, he grew more animated, his expression lighter. He talked to Mary about new people at the mission and how God had been showing him more of what he was supposed to spend his life doing. Where he was supposed to go.

Mary listened and secretly hoped that maybe—now that she believed in Jesus the way Nigel did—his future plans might somehow include her. She could go to New York for a little while, but then maybe Nigel could take her with him. Whatever he did next, wherever he went.

As he talked she felt dreamy inside. What would it be like to spend every day with someone so wonderfully unique, someone who glowed with goodness and loved God more than life?

Night came, and finally Nigel left. But the next morning he was back, full of more talk about God.

Mary drank in every word, full of joy despite the pain in her body. She could've spent forever this way, near Nigel, listening to him talk about God's ways and His plans, His wisdom.

Finally, just before lunch, she propped an extra pillow beneath her head and smiled at him. "Nigel . . . I'm keeping you. They need you back at the center, so go. I'll be fine."

He opened his mouth, but before he could protest, there was a knock at the door. Nigel looked at her, and his eyes danced. He went to the door and opened it. Standing in the hallway just outside her door, with tears in her eyes, was the kind woman Mary had searched for and thought of and dreamed about for almost a decade.

"Grandma!" Mary tried to sit up, but she couldn't. Instead she held out a trembling hand. She had come! After all the years of not knowing and not talking, not seeing each other, after all the times when her grandma's last words to her in the small red purse were all that kept her going, she was here. She was actually here.

Nigel was beaming. He stepped aside, and her grandmother came through the door. She was older, certainly. Her hair had more gray and her body was thinner. But she walked easily to Mary's bed, with the mobility and energy of a woman half her age. "Mary . . ." Her voice was a whisper. "Thank God you're alive."

In that moment, Mary saw that something else hadn't changed. Her grandmother still had the same eyes, the eyes full of gentle love and undying faith. Eyes that had been different enough from her mama's that Mary remembered them every day since the last time they'd been together.

Jesus eyes.

Her grandma reached her and took her hand. "I've missed you so much." She leaned close and gently hugged her. Her expression changed as she studied Mary's face—the bruises and swelling. "I'm so sorry." Her voice broke. "If I could've, I would've kept you safe from all of this."

Dampness clouded Mary's eyes. She tried to find her voice, but she couldn't. Instead, with Nigel watching them from several feet away, Mary let her emotions go, let the tears come. There were no words for how much she'd missed her grandmother. She squeezed her eyes shut and brought her grandma's hand to her cheek. "Don't ever leave me." She held on tighter. "Please, Grandma."

"I never will, child." Her grandma came closer, and their cheeks brushed against each other. "As soon as you're well, you're coming home with me."

Tears blurred Mary's eyes as she looked at Emma. "Since the day I moved in with my grandma, I haven't gone a day without talking to her, seeing her." She sniffed. "Sorry. It's just . . . she's very frail now. I don't have much time left with her."

Emma sat cross-legged on the cot and let the blanket fall to her waist. "So . . . you went back to New York with her?"

"When I was discharged from the hospital, I spent a day with Nigel at the center. Then, yes, I flew to New York. I enrolled in college that fall, majoring in psychology. And with my grandma's help and encouragement I went on to earn my masters and then my doctorate in family counseling." She took a long breath. "After that, Nigel put me in touch with one of the senators here, and, because of my background, I was invited to speak at a hearing about the importance of women's shelters."

"God really did have plans for you." Emma's voice held a note of awe.

"Yes. It was all His design." Mary hesitated, remembering. "After I testified for the Senate, the media got ahold of my story—all of it—and ran it on the front page of the *New York Times*." She made an invisible headline in the air. "'Former Victim Takes Education to the White House.' That sort of thing." Mary smiled. "The outpouring from people was amazing. My grandma and I started a charity, and the donations poured in. At the end of that year I opened my first shelter here in DC." Her voice dropped a notch. "The next winter we found out about Grandma's heart."

"She's sick?"

"Congestive heart failure." Mary raised one shoulder. "There's nothing we can do for her. She's tired, out of energy."

Emma touched her casted arm and frowned. "Mary?"

"Hmmm?" She was tired, drained from the events of the day and the telling of her story.

"Whatever happened with Nigel?" Emma bit her lip. "You said you'd tell me when you reached the end."

Mary felt a gentle whisper of sadness against the edges of her heart. "On the last day we spent together he told me what God had been pressing on his heart."

After so much reminiscing, the memories of that day came vividly to life one last time. . . .

It was clothing day at the center, the day needy people from the streets of DC could line up and take a bag of shirts and jeans and sweaters from the donation room.

Mary arrived early to spend her last day in DC at the center. She worked alongside Nigel until well after lunch.

Then he motioned her toward his office down the hall. "I need to talk to you."

Suddenly her shoulders felt like someone had flung a load of bricks across them. Her flight to New York was set to leave that night. There was no way around the inevitable. For her and Nigel, this would most likely be good-bye.

When they reached the privacy of his office, he nodded for her to take the chair near the door. He sat on the edge of his desk. For a long time he only stared at her. Then he rested his hands on his knees, and for a moment his gaze dropped. When he looked up again, she knew whatever his plans were, they didn't include her.

"Go ahead." She refused to cry. God had brought her to Nigel; He would show her a way to live without him.

"I'll be leaving the mission at the end of the month. Some-one from Chicago is coming to run it after I'm gone."

For a few beats, Mary held her breath. Maybe he was tak-ing over at a mission in New York City. She waited for him to explain.

"My parents are older; my brothers are married and have children." He rubbed the back of his neck. "They are all in Portugal." His tone became the passionate one she was famil-iar with when he talked about mission work. "So many people there in my hometown need to know about Jesus. And now—" his eyes lit up some—"there is a position for a mission director there. Five miles from my parents' house."

The pain was sure and swift, slicing into Mary's heart and making her grip the edge of the chair. He was leaving the country. For an instant she still wanted to cry out to him, beg him to take her with him. But clearly that wasn't part of his plan, and she wouldn't make the moment awkward. Her heart dropped. Almost certainly this would be the last time she'd see him this side of heaven.

She found the saddest hint of a smile. "Good, Nigel." She would be happy for him, no matter how much the news hurt. "That's perfect for you."

Nigel studied her. Twice he opened his mouth and both times he seemed to change his mind about speaking. Then he exhaled hard and shook his head. "If I were a different man . . ." His eyes held a longing she hadn't seen before. "I decided years ago that my life would be God's completely.

That He would be enough for me. But you . . ." He stood and
held his hand out to her.

She went to him, but with measured steps, the realization
of what he was saying dawning slowly like morning in her
soul. "You love me, don't you, Nigel?"

He took both her hands in his, and his eyes shone light on
the darkest places in her heart. "I do." He worked the muscles
in his jaw, clearly battling a struggle she knew nothing of. "But
not the way I sometimes want to." He rubbed his thumbs over
the tops of her hands. "I love you the way Jesus loves you . . .
and I always will." His voice grew thick. "When I move back
to Portugal, I will think of you every day, Mary Madison."

Her eyes grew teary, but she didn't blink, didn't dare move.
This was the good-bye she'd been dreading and then some.
Because he cared for her more than even he knew. She swal-
lowed hard. "And I . . . will think of you, Nigel."

"Still—" he clenched his teeth, struggling more than
before—"I cling to the promises of Christ. That He alone is
enough, that He is all I need." He squeezed her hands. "All
you need too. That serving Him is all the life, all the love
I could ever want, all by itself."

Mary nodded, and a resolve built inside her. This was
why Jesus had saved her, so she could live a life like Nigel's—
wholly devoted to Christ in ministry. So she could show Jesus
to battered and hurting women, giving them the chance at
freedom her mama never knew.

She reached up and brushed her fingers against Nigel's
cheek. "I understand."

"I won't write often. It would be too easy to become

confused, distracted. To start thinking my love for you is something . . . something more than the love Jesus has for you."

She nodded.

Then Nigel pulled her close, wrapped his arms around her, and held her for a long time. He held her the way he'd held her that first night, when he had explained the love of Jesus better than anyone ever had before.

She stayed at the center through dinner, working with Nigel and his staff. That evening she sat in on Nigel's class. This time it was about the apostle Peter and his determination to follow Jesus—even when his faith was shaky.

"The problem," Nigel told the class, "was that once in a while Peter had a tendency to take his eyes off Jesus. For Peter, that was when he'd start to sink." He looked at Mary in the back of the room. "We must . . . must keep our eyes on Jesus. No matter what our flesh tells us."

Mary nodded, and even with the ache in her heart, she smiled and mouthed the words *I will.*

Their good-bye was a quick hug after class, with a cab waiting a few feet outside the center's front door to take Mary to the airport.

Nigel took her hand. "When I first prayed for you, I could hear God telling me that you—Mary Madison—were the reason I came to Washington, DC." He took a step back and released her hand. "Go change the world for Christ, Mary."

Her heart soared and broke through the clouds of sorrow. He believed in her! It was his final gift to her. Before she stepped into the cab, she took a final look at him. "I won't forget you."

"Nor I, you."

Mary hugged herself. Their good-bye hurt still, the way it always would. She let the memory fade as she looked at Emma. "That's how things ended with Nigel." She sat a little straighter, ordering her heart to get back in line. "Once a year he writes to me, tells me about the lives of people changed by Christ at his mission in Portugal. I do the same, telling him about the abuse shelters and how many women—" she smiled at Emma—"like you God keeps bringing into my life."

Emma looked at the dark window for a long time. Her chin trembled. "Your story is amazing."

"Jesus rescued me from everything that trapped me. My fear and deception, my pain and my addiction. My faithlessness and promiscuity." She took a breath. "Even my desire to end my life. It's all in the past now."

"Nothing on earth could save a person from that." Emma's words were pinched by emotion, almost too soft to hear. "So what about me? How do I find that love, Mary? that love of Jesus that's so big He's all I could ever need?"

Mary felt elation race through her veins. Telling her story was draining. It took her back to unspeakable darkness and horror, back to the doubts and uncertainties and loneliness that had driven her into a life that should've killed her. But she would tell it over and over again until she died, for the privilege of having a woman like Emma ask her about Jesus.

Mary explained to Emma about the forgiveness of Christ and His power to break strongholds. "Is that what you want, Emma? To give your life to Jesus and let His power set you free?"

"Yes." Emma set the blanket aside and slid to the edge of the cot. "But the way I treated my mother, the danger I put my girls in . . ." She hung her head. "I've been so far from God." Her voice fell as she looked at Mary again. "If He could only forgive me."

"He already has." Mary smiled, and somewhere in a thriving mission in Portugal, she could see Nigel smiling too.

Mary stood and held out her hands. When Emma came to her, Mary could see that she understood. She was indeed forgiven. Set free by the only one with the power to do so. Mary met her eyes. "Let's pray, okay?"

"Okay." Emma smiled through her tears.

Mary prayed, and then she did for Emma what Nigel had done for her so long ago.

For a long time, with the arms of Jesus, Mary hugged Emma.

Chapter 26

*E*mma could hardly wait to make things right.
When she woke the next morning, she hurried to
her room to wake the girls. She found that they had spent a
peaceful night with Leah.

Kami ran to Emma, smoothed the hair from her face, and
said, "Hi, Mommy . . . your face isn't so purple."

There was no time for sorrow, not anymore. She took
Kami's hand and kissed it. "That's right, honey. No more purple for Mommy."

Kaitlyn spilled out of bed, her favorite tattered blanket
tucked between her thumb and forefinger and pressed to her
face. "Mommy . . . eat?"

"Yes. Let's get dressed and go down to eat." Emma's heart
sang with a giddiness that filled her to overflowing. It was

hard to imagine that just twenty-four hours ago she'd considered ending it all, giving up on life and her children and everything good God still had for her. She kissed Kaitlyn on the cheek. "Mommy has a lot to do today."

Every minute of the morning routine was like a celebration for Emma. The sweet high sounds of her little girls' voices, the way their hair felt in her fingers as she combed it and fashioned a ponytail for each of them. The sensation of their small hands in hers as they walked to breakfast. The stream of sunshine through the windows in the cafeteria.

All of it she would've missed if it weren't for Mary Madison. Mary introducing her to Jesus Christ.

After breakfast she noticed Leah at the front desk of the shelter. She was talking to a thirtysomething mother with two small boys at her side. Leah had her hand on the woman's shoulder.

"That's right, yes," Leah was saying, "you can stay here at no cost."

"And no one will know?"

"We believe in very strict confidentiality." Leah's tone held compassion and sympathy. She was a beautiful girl, self-possessed and articulate. "We ask you not to tell your husband where you're at. If you decide on a time for counseling with him, you'll meet at a neutral site." She handed the woman a clipboard. "I'll need you to read this and fill it out."

The woman's hand shook as she took the board. Her boys were silent, empty-eyed.

I know what you're going through, Emma wanted to say. And in that moment something struck her. Maybe one day she would have the chance to do for someone else what Mary had done for her. What Nigel had done for Mary. The thought made the day even brighter, her heart even more filled with joy.

When the woman and her two sons had gone into another room, Leah smiled at her. "Emma, I hear this is a big day for you!"

"It is." Happy tears stung at her eyes. The voices in her head had been silent since she prayed with Mary last night. Completely silent. "I never finished writing the letter to my mom. So I'm going to see her instead, to tell her I'm sorry."

Leah touched Emma's hand. "I'm so glad. I was hoping this would happen before I left."

"You're leaving?" Emma put her arms around her daughters. The feel of them against her legs was as right as her own heartbeat. "But you're . . . you're so good for this place."

Leah blushed. "Thanks. It might be something I come back to." She grabbed a bright blue folder from her desk and held it up, her eyes shining. "I've been accepted to Juilliard, the art school in New York City! I prayed that if God wanted me going to school here and working at the shelter, they would turn my application down cold." She made a cutting motion with her hand. "But if it was His will . . . I'd love to celebrate Him through the arts—any way I possibly can." She squealed. "I guess it was His will!"

Now it was Emma's turn to rejoice. "Leah, that's wonderful!"

"Mary's going to take a day off and show me around Manhattan." She paused. "It's where she used to live, you know."

"Yes." Emma smiled as Mary's story—all of it—came together in a moment's time. "She told me about New York."

She looked at Kami on her right and Kaitlyn on her left and then at Leah. "When my girls are grown, Leah . . . I want them to be just like you."

The two of them hugged.

Five minutes later Emma and her girls were in a cab heading toward forgiveness and reconciliation and home—the place that had always been home to her no matter what choices she'd made.

And if that wasn't proof that God's power was real, nothing was.

<hr />

Grace Johnson was working in her garden when the cab pulled up. She set her spade down and slowly peeled off her yellow rubber gloves. All the while her eyes never left the backseat.

Was it Emma? She hadn't called, hadn't said anything since the phone call she'd made several days ago saying that she and the girls were fine. Every day since then Grace had spent hours searching the city for Emma and then hurrying home, praying constantly, willing the phone to ring so she'd know where they were. Grace hadn't been by Charlie's again—if Emma said she wasn't going back there, then there was no point.

The passenger was paying the cabdriver. Grace stood, and the gloves fell to the ground. It looked like there were children in the backseat also. She was halfway down the sidewalk when Emma opened the taxi door. Their eyes met and held, and in an instant's time Grace knew something had changed.

Not just the fact that Emma and the girls had come, but something in Emma's face.

In her eyes.

Emma climbed out and waited for her girls to follow. That's when Grace saw the cast on her daughter's arm, the bruises on her cheek. New bruises. When they were all standing on the sidewalk, Emma shut the door with her good hand, and the driver pulled away from the curb. Emma turned, and the three of them walked the rest of the way up the sidewalk together.

"Mom . . ." Emma was smiling, but tears glistened on her swollen face. Her words were broken, colored with a lifetime of regret. "I'm so, so sorry."

Grace's knees felt weak, her world spinning from the impossibility of what was happening. She took her daughter into her arms, held her close, and rocked her. "Emma, you came home!"

"Yes." Emma's hand came up along one side of her mother's face. "I was so awful to you, Mom. The whole time . . ." A single sob slipped from her throat. She put one hand to her mouth and waited until she had control again. "The whole time I only wanted you to grab me and hold me and make me stop. But I was so . . . so rude and rebellious." She shook her head, clearly desperate to be understood. "Please, Mom, forgive me."

"Honey . . . you're here. That's all that matters." However Emma had gotten the bruises, she was home now. And she had been right! There had indeed been a change. No, not a change—a miracle! She cradled Emma's head against her own, and the tears came for both of them.

"Gamma." Kaitlyn tugged on Grace's sleeve.

Grace drew away long enough to sweep the child into her arms. She pulled Kami close also, and the four of them stayed huddled that way. "Dear God . . . thank You," she whispered. Then she spoke close to Emma's ear. "What happened to you? How come you're here?"

"It's a long story, Mom." Emma laughed through her tears. Then she looked toward heaven and laughed harder. "But it has the happiest ending of all."

Grace started to lead them toward the house when she stopped. "Are you here for good?" She had to ask. The fresh bruises told her that Emma had been to see Charlie not long ago. "Or is Charlie waiting?"

"Charlie's in jail. I'm free from him and from so much more." Emma's expression grew serious. "I still need counseling, and I want to go to church with you. Church and a Bible study maybe." Her whole face was taken up with a smile. "But it's a beginning. The beginning of the rest of my life—" she looked at her girls—"the rest of all of our lives."

The sidewalk might as well have been made of clouds, because Grace had the feeling they were floating into the house. How long had she waited for this moment, prayed for it? And here she was—her daughter home and willing to try life God's way for the first time.

She hugged Emma and the girls again once they were inside, and then she remembered something. "Terrence is coming by today." She looked at the old grandfather clock against the wall. "In less than an hour."

"Terrence?" Emma absently touched her cast. Her eyes

were suddenly wide and anxious. "I thought . . . he was in medical school."

"He is. He transferred so he's closer now."

Emma stood there, her jaw slack.

Grace ushered the girls into the kitchen and sat them at the small round table. She took a pitcher of juice from the fridge and poured them each a cup. She grabbed four cookies from a jar on her counter and spread them on two napkins. When they were settled, she led Emma into the living room. "Terrence . . . he came by the other day."

Emma sat down slowly on the sofa. "He did?" She shrugged. "Why?"

God, please, let her hear this right. "To pray for you, Emma. The two of us have committed to pray for you." Alarm rang through Grace's body. What if the idea of the two of them praying for her was enough to send Emma running again? What if it was more than she could handle this soon? Grace took the spot next to Emma and met her eyes. "I can call him and tell him not to come. Whatever you want, honey."

Emma stood and walked to the window. She held on to the sill and stared out for a long while. Then, perhaps when she had digested the information, she turned and the hint of a smile on her face answered all Grace's fears. "I haven't seen him in so long."

Grace's heart thudded against her chest. "He still cares for you very much, Emma. He loves you."

Genuine shock played on her daughter's face. "He does?" She walked back to the sofa with measured steps, almost trancelike. "I never allowed myself to see him that way. He was my friend, nothing more."

"I think—" Grace's voice was tentative—"he always had a bit of a crush on you."

Emma blinked. "Really?"

"Yes, I think so."

The grin still played at the corners of Emma's mouth. But her tone was serious. "Mary told me all I need is Jesus now. It's true; I know because I've seen it to be true in Mary's life." She hesitated and sat down again. "But I think I would like it very much—" her smile grew—"if Terrence came over today." Her eyes sparkled, even against the backdrop of regret that was still there. "Maybe the three of us can pray together. Mary would like that."

"Mary?" Grace forced herself to be patient. There was so much she didn't know about this new Emma, the changes she'd been through.

"Mary Madison." Emma gave her a quick, tight hug. "I'll tell you all about her."

"You mean . . . *the* Mary Madison? the woman they feature on the news, the one with the shelters in the city?"

"Yes." Emma's expression deepened. "That Mary."

"Well, honey . . . everyone knows the story of Mary Madison."

"No, Mom." A sadness crossed Emma's face. "Not the way I know it."

Grace couldn't believe it. The famous Mary Madison had counseled Emma? No wonder her change was so dramatic. She touched her daughter's shoulder. "I want to hear every detail."

"Later, okay?" Emma took a long breath and stood. "Right now I want to clean up." Something soft and tender filled her eyes. "Terrence will be here soon."

<hr />

The shower felt wonderful. Emma had wrapped her casted arm in a plastic bag and now she let the hot water run over her, taking with it the pain and regret of every yesterday, every missed opportunity and bad decision since she first rebelled against her mother as a teenager.

She was home! Joy filled her and made her feel like a child again. She replayed in her mind the reunion with her mother, the look on her beautiful brown face as she and the girls climbed out of the cab and walked up the sidewalk. The warm and wonderful way it had felt to be in her arms, making peace with the mother she had never stopped loving.

The years with Charlie had left their mark. The broken bones would heal and the bruises would fade, but she would keep her promise to Mary. Counseling was a must. Otherwise she would never learn how to function in a healthy relationship.

Terrence's face came to mind. Kind and conscientious Terrence, devoted to God all the while, even now praying for her. It was another part of the miracle. She remembered her mother's words: *"He always had a bit of a crush on you."* She closed her eyes and let the shampoo run down her face. Why hadn't she seen the good in Terrence before? How could she have walked away from a man like him and run to someone like

Charlie? Seconds passed, and like a sudden storm the guilt and doubt and regret nearly suffocated her.

But then she remembered what Mary had told her the day before. Jesus died to take all the pain from *yesterday*, to offer people a new life, a new start *today*. A start that would build one tomorrow on top of another until change in that life became obvious to everyone. It was true. The power of Christ wasn't a one-time fix. It would keep working in her life today and tomorrow and every day that she woke up believing the truth.

As she dressed, applied makeup to the bruises on her cheeks and around her eyes, and straightened her hair, she reveled in that very truth.

And when the doorbell rang, she could feel God whispering to her. *Today, precious daughter, is only the beginning. . . .*

Chapter 27

Three Months Later

ary Madison took the call on the way to the cemetery.

"Mary, it's Joe." The caller didn't need to say more than that. He was Joe Keane, Senate Majority Leader, and he contacted Mary often. "I'm sorry; this isn't the best time to be calling."

"That's okay." She tightened her fingers around the steering wheel and braced herself. The abstinence bill had been up for debate that morning. "Give me the news."

"We took the vote." Subdued victory rang in his tone. Joe Keane was a moderate by all standards, but he believed in every cause Mary supported. By Joe's thinking, faith-based or faith-inspired teen centers and shelters and abstinence programs had a beneficial place in the landscape of government funding.

"Well . . . ?" Mary held her breath.

"It passed! The margin wasn't big, but it passed." He exhaled, relieved. "You were the one, Mary. Your statistics, your testimony. They bought it all."

Mary allowed a smile, one of the few that week. "I had a feeling."

"This is huge. I set up a press conference for you and the supporters for four o'clock on the Capitol steps." He paused. "Will that work?"

"Definitely." Mary pursed her lips. The day would be a roller coaster for sure. "Good work, Joe. We'll catch up later."

"Okay." He sighed. "I'm sorry about your grandma."

"Thanks." Tears stung her eyes. "Me too."

The call ended, and Mary inhaled as deeply as she could. She blinked back tears so she could see the road. *Jesus . . . how am I supposed to do this without her? Please let me feel Your arms today. I miss her so much already.*

The reality was still sinking in. Grandma Peggy was gone. She had died in her sleep three days ago, hours after Mary's morning visit. The traffic light ahead turned red, and Mary could envision clearly every moment of their last morning together. . . .

⌘

She and her grandma had held hands and talked about how well Emma was doing, how close the vote on the abstinence bill could be, and how much they needed to pray for a victory.

Before their visit ended, Grandma Peggy had looked at
Mary with tender eyes. "I'm tired. Very tired."

Mary stood and hugged her. "I'll leave then . . . let you take
a nap."

"No . . ." Her grandma didn't sound anxious or afraid.
More like she must've somehow known what was coming.
"Not that kind of tired. The kind that has me longing for
Jesus." She smiled, and the twinkle in her eyes was bright even
through the milky haze of the years. "I'm ready, Mary."

"Grandma, don't talk like that." She reached for her frail
fingers. "I still need you."

"You need Jesus, only Jesus." Her tone held a kindhearted
scold.

Panic breathed down her neck. "But Jesus gave me you."
Mary leaned in and kissed her grandma's brow. "Now get
some sleep and I'll see you tomorrow."

Not for one minute had it felt like a final good-bye, like
her grandma would be gone in a few hours.

Mary took a tissue from the console next to the front seat.
She didn't know it was possible to cry so much, but she had
no closure, no way to have that last conversation with her
grandma—the one where she would tell her how, if not for
her, Mary might not have survived.

She would've hugged Grandma Peggy longer and stayed
until her heart stopped beating. She would've begged her—if
it were possible—to hold on, to not give up. To stay another

week or another day. Another hour. It was wrong that she hadn't been there in her grandma's final moments, not there to hold her hand or pray with her or bid her good-bye.

There was still so much to say.

Mary dried her eyes and turned her car into the parking lot of the cemetery.

That's when she saw him.

Her heart skipped a beat, and without meaning to she lifted her foot from the gas pedal. He had come, he really had.

Nigel was here, and now she wouldn't have to get through this saddest day alone.

She squinted in the glare of the sun. Nigel was leaning against the hood of his rental car, his back to her as he stared at the sea of tombstones. Mary took the first parking spot. Her eyes never left him.

Nigel.

She had called him the hour after she got the news. It had been early evening in Portugal, and his response had been immediate. He would be there for her, no questions. His flight had landed at Dulles Airport a few hours ago.

She studied him, and her heart hurt for all the years of missing him. More than a decade had passed, but he had the same broad shoulders, the same proud stance.

She cut the engine, and he turned around. Their eyes met and held while she stepped out of her car and as she closed the distance between them. He took her hands in his, and they came together in a hug that bridged the years in a handful of heartbeats.

His embrace told her what his words did not, what they

could not. He had never stopped caring for her—not for a week or a day or even an hour. But it also told her that the decision they'd made had been the right one, that devoting their lives to Jesus was more than enough. The love they shared was God's love, a deeper love than anything they might've found otherwise. Even if time hadn't dimmed their feelings for each other.

Nigel drew back and searched her eyes. "How are you?"

Mary tilted her head, holding his gaze. When her emotions gave her permission to speak, she managed the slightest whisper. "Sad, Nigel. So sad."

"I know." He brought his hand to the back of her head and stroked her hair. "I'm so sorry."

She nodded. "Walk with me." She led the way through the small Virginia cemetery. The sun shone brightly that day, warm against her face, and Mary found it strangely fitting. No matter how many tears she'd cried or how much she'd grieved for Grandma Peggy, the despair she expected to feel never came. Sadness, yes. Longing and a desire to have one more day, one more conversation. One more hug.

But not despair.

The greatest tragedy wasn't her grandma's death. It was the years they had missed together. Years when Mary had suffered horrors no little girl could ever overcome without Jesus.

Mary looked over her shoulder at Nigel, the way his broad shoulders filled out his suit coat. She pointed toward a clump of trees. "It's this way."

Nigel nodded. He'd put on his sunglasses, so it was impossible to see his eyes now. But the muscles in his jaw flexed often, and Mary figured he was fighting tears. Tears on a lot of levels maybe. Her grandmother had been special to both of them.

They moved past various-sized tombstones beyond a small hedge. On the other side, Mary stopped. Two rows of chairs were set up, and her grandmother's pastor stood in hushed conversation with the cemetery caretaker.

Mary felt her heart sink. It was really happening. She was going to bury Grandma Peggy, even if all she wanted to do was turn and run back to Orchard Gardens, back to her grandma's cozy room and big bed and Grandma Peggy there waiting for her.

She stopped, and Nigel did the same. "Here it is."

The casket sat above a hole in the ground. The freshly turned dirt to the side was covered with dozens of flower arrangements—gifts sent from people across Washington, DC—both on Capitol Hill and from the shelters. One bouquet was even from the group of older kids who hung out on the street and came to the teen center for the weekly Bible study Mary led there.

A few blades of grass poked through the brown dirt, proof that life would always have the last word—at least for people who chose to accept Christ's offer.

Side by side, she and Nigel looked down and read the words on the temporary grave marker, the one propped up near the front of the casket: *Peggy Madison, beloved grandmother.* Then it gave the dates that showed she'd been just sixty-seven. Too young. The last line read simply this: *She loved Jesus.*

"That says it." Nigel knelt and brushed the dirt and grass clippings off the marker.

Mary folded her arms and clutched her sides. She hated being here, hated saying good-bye. A dozen times since she'd gotten the news she had reached for the phone, anxious to share details of a political battle or another victim with her grandma. There would always be more to say. The loss cut her to the core, made her wonder if she'd walk the rest of her life with a limp.

Nigel seemed to sense her struggle. He reached out and took her hand. He said nothing, but no words were needed. His touch, his comfort were the same as they had been so many years earlier. As if Jesus Himself were standing beside her, helping her through, reminding her that somehow . . . some way she would survive this loss.

She didn't want to think about the obvious—that soon she would have to say good-bye to Nigel too.

"I miss her so much." Mary squeezed Nigel's hand. Sobs overtook her, and for a long time she couldn't speak.

She had missed so many years with Grandma Peggy, and now . . . what family did she have? Who would be there to know the truth—that Mary Madison—strong and successful, educated and powerful—was really just a girl who sometimes got lonely and tired, a girl who would go to sleep crying on the nights when there would be no one to talk to and when missing her grandma was a physical ache?

Finally she blinked back the tears and looked at Nigel. "You know what I realized today?"

"What?" He searched her face, waiting.

"Heaven . . . never felt so far away."

"Hmmm." Nigel leaned closer to her, supporting her. He

looked at the casket and nodded. "I never thought of it that way."

Mary had a tissue in her other hand. She dabbed her eyes before the fresh tears could reach her cheeks. "I mean, I believe, of course. I know she's free now. No more pain, no more exhaustion. She's happy and healthy and home. I know all that in here." She spread her fingers across her chest. "But all I want is to go to her and hug her. Talk to her one more time."

Nigel put his arm around her and held her close, stroking her hair. "I know."

In some ways this was a good-bye on many levels. A final good-bye to that chapter in their lives when the three of them had been drawn together by circumstances and prayer and God Himself.

Mary turned at the sound of voices behind them. She released Nigel's hand and faced the group of people coming toward them. A smile lifted her lips. "Emma . . ."

Emma Johnson was surrounded by her girls and a woman Mary guessed was Emma's mother. And someone else . . . a handsome young man who stayed close to Emma's side.

Mary held out her hand. "Hello . . ." Even in her sorrow, seeing the group of them made her heart sing. They came together in a hug. Mary studied Emma. The cast and the bruises were gone. A softness filled Emma's face, and her eyes glowed. Mary smiled. "You have Jesus eyes."

"Really?" Emma's voice was soft, humble. The hint of a smile played on her lips.

"Really." The young woman before Mary was nothing like

the one who had hung on the guardrail, threatening to jump into the Potomac. Emma was changed, a new person entirely.

She touched Mary's shoulder. "I'm sorry about your grandma. I know . . . how much she meant to you."

"Thanks." Mary felt a lump in her throat. She looked at the woman standing a few feet away, and she went to her. "I'm Mary. You must be Emma's mother."

"Yes." The woman's smile was subdued but warm. "I'm Grace." She brought her fingers to her mouth and hesitated. "How can I ever thank you? I have my daughter back."

Mary understood. She let go of the formalities and hugged Grace. "I'm so glad." She spoke softly, the undertone of tears still in her voice. "Now—" she looked at Emma—"it's her turn to tell others."

Emma's eyes glowed with sincerity. "Yes."

Mary dabbed at her eyes. "Thanks for coming. It'll be a very small ceremony. The way my grandma would've wanted it."

Emma linked hands with the young man beside her. "This is Terrence Reid." Emma gave him an adoring smile.

"Terrence—" Mary held out her hand—"nice to meet you."

He said the same, and then he turned his attention back to Emma.

Mary watched them, and something strange stirred in her heart. Emma had mentioned Terrence. The boy who had always been there, the friend. Mary thought of Nigel, and she understood the strange stirrings. They were more of a longing really. She was content in her life, deeply satisfied. But how wonderful that God had allowed these two to find each other, that out of the ashes of Emma's shattered past might come this new sprig of life.

Emma nodded toward Nigel. He was facing her grandma's casket, his head bowed, his back to them, giving them their space. She looked at him and then back at Mary. "Is that . . . ?"

"Nigel," Mary whispered and let her eyes find him again. "Yes."

Emma raised an eyebrow. She gave Mary's arm a gentle tug. "Introduce me."

They walked to him, and he turned and removed his sunglasses as he heard them coming. Mary looked to the eyes of the man. "Nigel, I'd like you to meet Emma Johnson. The young woman I told you about in my last letter."

Nigel smiled and politely took Emma's hand. But nothing more—no questions about her faith or curiosities about how she was doing. Mary saw the difference. Nigel was kind and warm to everyone he met. But he had always felt differently about her.

It was part of the struggle, the reason he wrote only once a year. His feelings for her were deep and complicated, the way hers were for him. That was why they had to hold on to the truth. God brought them together, yes, but only so Nigel could introduce Mary to Jesus. She had to remind herself of that fact often. Christ and His undying love, His work, His ministry would always consume their days.

Still . . . times like this Mary wondered.

Emma returned to her young man, and the group helped the children to seats in the second row. A few more people—nurses from Orchard Gardens, two volunteers from one of the shelters—filed in and quietly took seats.

Mary and Nigel were last to sit down in the front row, closest to the casket.

The minister said only a few words, making it a brief service in keeping with what Grandma Peggy had wanted. Mary closed her eyes, and she could hear her grandma's words, something she'd said in one of their last conversations:

"When I'm gone . . . remember me in a sunset or in the smile of a friend. Remember me when you think of my favorite Bible verses. But don't spend a lot of time and money on me after I die. I'll be celebrating with Jesus by then, and I want you to celebrate too."

Mary opened her eyes and focused on the minister, his words.

"'As the sufferings of Christ flow over into our lives, so also through Christ our comfort overflows.'"

The Scripture was a familiar one, a verse Mary could relate to deeply. She could picture her grandma smiling at her, giving her that knowing look that told her the Bible was true, that the comfort would be there. Even now.

When the service was over, the others said their good-byes until finally it was only Mary and Nigel. They remained in their seats near the casket, silent for a long while. It was still hard to believe. Every year for more than a decade Mary hadn't gone a day without talking to her grandma Peggy. Even when she was going through the nightmare of their years apart, she always had the comfort of believing her grandmother was out there, praying for her, looking for her.

Nigel must've known what she was thinking. He folded his hands in front of him and looked at her. "God's plans aren't always our plans."

"No." Mary's arms ached, the way they did sometimes. As a prisoner in Jimbo's basement and all the years before her rescue, she had longed for the chance to be in her grandma's arms, safe and protected. She could picture herself and her grandma sitting in the pink bedroom, reading together. Sometimes—when the sadness was its greatest, as it was now—the loss was a physical hurt. She ran her fingers over the scars on her wrist. "Life can be very hard."

Nigel looked up. His eyes seemed to take in all of the heavens above. "I don't know why, but this loss is hard for me." He squinted against the sunlight. For a moment he didn't speak, probably couldn't speak. Finally he coughed and tried again. "I wanted God to reward you." His eyes met hers, and she saw more than his goodness. She saw his humanity. "All those years without her . . . I guess I wanted God to give you three more decades with Peggy. Something to make up for the ugliness of all those years when you were apart."

Nigel was a strong man, a missionary known for his spiritual strength and wisdom. The admission he was making now couldn't have been easy. Not any easier than the time in his office, twelve years earlier, when he had admitted his feelings for her.

Mary gave his arm a gentle squeeze. It felt so good having him beside her. So safe and warm and right. She exhaled slowly. "We *will* have those years together. And a whole lot more than that." She looked deep into his eyes. "It's the waiting that's so difficult."

Nigel nodded and looked at the tombstone again. "Peggy's

whole life was about loving God. It was . . . the most beautiful picture."

"And it will be for all eternity." Mary released Nigel's arm. She stood and touched the casket. "Her final years might not be remembered by anyone else." She closed her eyes. When she opened them she looked at Nigel through her tears. "But I'll remember. My grandma prayed for me all the time. She prayed about women like Emma and the political challenges and the responsibilities I face."

"Hers will be a very great loss."

She returned to her seat beside him. For ten minutes they sat there in silence, lost in their own memories. Then Nigel turned to her. "I have to go, Mary. My flight leaves soon."

"I know." Their eyes held.

Then, tenderly, she fell into his arms.

He whispered into her hair, "I will pray, Mary. Every day. I will be there in Portugal lifting you and your work here in this nation's capital to God." He drew back and searched her face. "I promise you."

"Nigel . . . you haven't changed. You still love me." She rested her head on his chest for another few beats. Then she forced herself to draw away from him, to distance herself from him. If she stayed in his arms another minute, she would question her ability to ever let him go.

"Yes, Mary." He took her hands in his. "I still love you." He hesitated. "The way Jesus loves you. The only way I can love you and still return to the place God has called me." His voice fell, and in his exhale, his struggle was clear. "Still . . . I don't want to say good-bye."

"I know." Mary understood everything he said, everything he felt. Because she felt the same way. "Let me pray for you, Nigel."

He nodded. The hold he had on her fingers doubled in intensity.

"Jesus, be with my friend Nigel." She sniffed, finding more of the strength she hadn't known she had until he came into her life. "This chapter—the one with Grandma Peggy—is closed. But You have so much ahead for both of us . . . in the separate places where You've called us. I feel it in my soul, Lord. Keep Nigel safe, keep his eyes open, so that the next time a Mary Madison walks through his doors, he'll be ready—once again—to show her Your love." She smiled even as tears fell onto her cheeks. "Because that sort of love changes everything."

They hugged, and Nigel's voice was strained by emotion. "I'll miss you."

Mary couldn't believe he was already leaving. She felt her throat grow tighter, and she nodded. "Me too." For a second, she wanted to shout at him. Didn't he see? He could do his mission work here, in Washington, DC, and they could be together every day. Best friends at least.

But Nigel was already drawing back, studying her eyes, her face, as if he wanted to memorize her. "Mary . . . walk me to my car."

She did, and when they reached the parking lot, Nigel hugged her one last time. With a final look first in the direction of Grandma Peggy's grave and then at her, he climbed into his car and drove away.

Mary watched him leave; then she turned and slowly made her way back to her grandmother's grave.

Only then did Mary take the small red-beaded purse from her sweater pocket. All those years, through the horrible things Mary had been through, she'd kept the purse. The message Peggy had written to her granddaughter was still tucked inside.

She opened the yellowed piece of paper carefully and read the words out loud:

> "'I know the plans I have for you,' declares the Lord, 'plans to prosper you and not to harm you, plans to give you hope and a future.' — Jeremiah 29:11

> "Mary, I will always be here for you. I love you.
> Grandma"

The message was as true now as it had been then. They were words that had been a lifeline to Mary during her years in the wasteland. Now they would be a lifeline to her until she drew her final breath. Until heaven, when she and Grandma Peggy could again sit for hours talking.

She had thought of placing the little red purse in the casket with her grandma. But she had changed her mind. She would keep it in her office, a tangible reminder of her grandmother's concern for her. But more than that, a reminder of the love of Christ.

Mary lifted her face toward the sun and closed her eyes. Jesus hadn't only loved her. He had sought her, pursued her, called out to her day after day, year after year. All along He had known the plans He had for her, and when she stopped running long enough to listen, those plans had unfolded like a miracle.

The red purse would always be proof of that.

She thought about Nigel again. Something about letting him go, watching him drive away—maybe for the last time—was causing a gradual dawning in her heart. She reached the casket and sat near it once more. The sunshine felt warm on her shoulders, and slowly the dawning became a realization. As if the darkest cloud in all her life was finally being lifted away.

There was something she had almost forgotten in the past week, through the shock of losing her grandmother to the pain of bidding Nigel good-bye.

Jesus was all she needed. He really was enough.

She couldn't begrudge God for taking her grandmother now. It was her grandma's time to celebrate in heaven with Jesus. And it was Nigel's time to show Jesus to other people—new people who would come through his mission door in Portugal every day of the week.

Women like Emma. Women like Mary.

She would have to walk the journey without her grandma and even without Nigel. But she would not walk it alone. Never alone. The arms of Jesus would surround her, and she would feel them every time she hugged a new believer, every time she visited a teen center or a shelter that existed because of her tireless fight for government-supported ministries. Every time the next Emma walked through the door of her office.

Mary looked at her grandma's grave marker, and the words ran over and over in her mind: *She loved Jesus.* They were the words she hoped someone would write on her tombstone one day.

No matter how difficult her life or her losses, peace was finding its reign in her heart once more, certainty taking control of her soul. The love of Jesus was great and vast and wide and high. Greater than anything mankind would ever know. But it wasn't only Christ's love that made the difference. It was His power, His innate power because of who He is. Who He really is.

Fully God, fully man.

Divine.

Discussion Questions

Use these questions for individual reflection or for discussion with a book club or other small group. They will help you not only understand some of the issues in *Divine* but also integrate the book's messages into your own life.

1. We know very little about the real Mary Magdalene. What we know for certain is that Jesus rescued her from seven demons—Scripture tells us that twice. Mary Madison was delivered from seven strongholds also: fear, lying, self-inflicted pain, addiction, faithlessness, promiscuity, and thoughts of taking her life. How could any one of these ruin a person's life? Explain how these troubles were too strong for Mary to work out by herself.

2. What strongholds have you seen in your life or the lives of people you know? Give an example of how Jesus has rescued you or one of those people.

3. Do you think the real Mary Magdalene understood that Jesus was divine—fully man and fully God? Why or why not?

4. We also know that Mary Magdalene had a major impact on the spread of Christianity, the ministry of Christ. She loved Jesus with all her life and resources. How did you see that part of Mary Magdalene's real story played out in *Divine*, through the life of Mary Madison?

5. Why did Mary Madison believe so completely in the divinity of Christ? What proof have you seen in your life of the power and divinity of Christ?

6. Jesus was the original storyteller. Look through one or more parables from the Bible. Retell one or two.

7. Why do you think Jesus told stories? How has your life been changed by the power of a story?

8. Mary Madison was a victim through most of her life. Explain how you felt about Mary's childhood.

9. What are your thoughts on the pain in this world? Why do you think God allows it, and what can be gained from it?

10. How did Mary's past shape her into the adult she became?

11. Oftentimes being a victim can lead to a life of poor choices. How did this happen in Mary's life? in Emma's life?

12. Addiction is often a consequence of poor choices. Give an example of how worldly answers to addiction fall short. Why is freedom from addiction proof that a divine power intervened?

13. Explain how Nigel Townsend was finally able to convince

Mary of Christ's love. What was the illustration he acted out for her, and why was it so powerful? What emotional impact did you experience while reading that scene?

14. How were you personally convinced of Christ's love? What led to that moment, and how did it affect your life?

15. Many times Mary and Nigel would pray and hear a response from God. Have you ever prayed and heard or felt a response? Describe how that happened and how it made you feel.

16. Was there a time in your life when you prayed fervently for something and then felt that your prayers were not answered? How did you react? Did that change your relationship with Christ?

17. Read the Bible passages about Mary Magdalene (see author's note at the beginning of this book). If Mary were alive today, what do you think she would say about heretical teachings that she and Jesus were married?

18. Do you think Mary would have wanted to play a part in defending the divinity of Christ? Why or why not?

— BREAK THE SILENCE —
MAKE THE CALL

If you are in an abusive situation, don't wait to ask for help. Call the toll-free number below—or visit www.ndvh.org—for information or to be connected to domestic violence resources in your area. All calls are free, anonymous, and confidential.

National Domestic Violence HOTLINE

1-800-799-SAFE (7233)
1-800-787-3224 TTY For the Deaf

The **Best-Selling**
Firstborn Series
by Karen Kingsbury

Catch up with your favorite Baxter characters from the best-selling Redemption series. Dayne Matthews is an A-list Hollywood actor with a bright future. But his heart is pulling him toward a woman and a family who have no idea how their lives are tied to his. Katy Hart, the director of Christian Kids Theater, finally feels content and at home in Bloomington, Indiana. But that changes when she meets Dayne Matthews and he promises a future she left in her past. Meanwhile, John Baxter struggles to fulfill a promise he made to his dying wife—a promise to reconnect the entire family, including the one child they never spoke of.

Fame
A story of hope, healing, and God's divine leading—even in the face of impossible circumstances

Forgiven
A story of God's divine leading and the realization that peace comes only after forgiveness

Found
A story of God's divine leading and the truth that God rewards those who seek Him with all their heart

Family
A story of the search for renewed hope and the desperate need to be loved and to belong

Forever
A story about surviving tough times and drawing strength and hope from family and deep faith

Other Life-Changing Fiction by

KAREN KINGSBURY

To see what readers are saying about Karen Kingsbury's fiction, go to www.KarenKingsbury.com and click the guest-book link.

REDEMPTION SERIES
Redemption
Remember
Return
Rejoice
Reunion

FIRSTBORN SERIES
Fame
Forgiven
Found
Family
Forever

SUNRISE SERIES
Sunrise
Summer (Fall 2007)
Someday (Spring 2008)
Sunset (Spring 2008)

RED GLOVE SERIES
Gideon's Gift
Maggie's Miracle
Sarah's Song
Hannah's Hope

SEPTEMBER 11 SERIES
One Tuesday Morning
Beyond Tuesday Morning

FOREVER FAITHFUL SERIES
Waiting for Morning
A Moment of Weakness
Halfway to Forever

WOMEN OF FAITH FICTION SERIES
A Time to Dance
A Time to Embrace

STAND-ALONE TITLES
A Thousand Tomorrows
Oceans Apart
Where Yesterday Lives
When Joy Came to Stay
On Every Side
Even Now
Ever After
Divine
Like Dandelion Dust

CHILDREN'S TITLE
Let Me Hold You Longer

MIRACLE COLLECTIONS
A Treasury of Christmas Miracles
A Treasury of Miracles for Women
A Treasury of Miracles for Teens
A Treasury of Miracles for Friends
A Treasury of Adoption Miracles

GIFT BOOKS
Stay Close Little Girl
Be Safe Little Boy

www.KarenKingsbury.com

CP0038